# JOURNEY

BY KATHRYN MATTINGLY

This publication is a work of fiction. Names, characters, places, and incidents either are products of the author's imagination or are used fictitiously. This work is protected in full by all applicable copyright laws, as well as by misappropriation, trade secret, unfair competition, and other applicable laws. No part of this book may be reproduced or transmitted in any manner without written permission from Winter Goose Publishing, except in the case of brief quotations embodied in critical articles or reviews. All rights reserved.

Winter Goose Publishing
2701 Del Paso Road, 130-92
Sacramento, CA 95835

www.wintergoosepublishing.com
Contact Information: info@wintergoosepublishing.com

Journey

COPYRIGHT © 2015 by Kathryn Mattingly

Library of Congress Control Number: 2015950436

First Edition, September 2015

Cover Art by Ladd Woodland
Typesetting by Odyssey Books

ISBN: 978-1-941058-29-9

Published in the United States of America

*For my daughter, Sasha
who more than anyone else makes me want to be
the best writer I can possibly be*

# CHAPTER ONE

I had not seen a death certificate before, let alone one that states the cause of death to be undetermined. It would be fitting for my little sister to have an undetermined cause of death. I had just turned nine when she was born, and seeing no evidence of a father, I briefly thought her cause of life to be undetermined.

The deliveryman informed me that a teak wood chest accompanied the death certificate. I nodded as he returned to his truck for it. All I could think about was how her name, Journey, had been a premonition. My half Hawaiian sister never set down roots in the shifting sands of her short life. I walked out onto the porch and saw the chest, peeking out the back of a delivery truck. Open-ended questions surrounded this teak wood chest just as they had Journey Luvay Tyner all her life.

Luvay was our mama's maiden name, Tyner her married name. Journey was not a Tyner, her father being a Hawaiian doctor that moved his practice to the mainland before my mama even realized what he'd left behind, growing in her belly. But that didn't stop Mama from putting Daddy's name on the birth certificate. I will never forget looking into Mama's tired, worried eyes while she held the curly-haired newborn, telling me we would call her Journey. "What do you think, Kylie? This isn't the journey I'd hoped for when moving to the Big Island, but it will be a trip all right."

This recollection caused a suffocating heaviness in me, as I stood on the porch staring at the chest on the truck bed. Memories were flooding back of my parents' divorce, Mama bringing me to this island, and her brief affair on the rebound of a broken marriage. I felt unspeakable grief as the deliveryman lifted the chest onto a dolly. What had happened to the vibrant young woman who ran away in the dead of night and was never seen or heard from again until this moment?

I tried to recall a time before my baby sister was born, long ago in Illinois, when I'd lived in a sprawling two-story home with blue shutters. I'd spent my free time cartwheeling across an endless expanse of mowed lawn. Now my lawn was a barren beachfront edged against a sea of blue. I had lost all communication with my daddy, and for a while it seemed as if I had lost my mama, too. The Hawaiian doctor filled her late evenings and early mornings more days of the week than not. And then one day he was gone.

My mama was a gifted trauma nurse, or so a doctor told me once. He'd patted me on the head and exclaimed, "I don't know what we'd do without your mother. She's simply brilliant. Think you'll follow in her footsteps?" I don't recall my reply, but I am guessing it was no. For as long as I can remember I had wanted to teach communication studies. Communication was something my family was not good at. Maybe that's what drove me to get a doctorate in it.

All these memories came flooding back as the short muscular man wheeled the chest into this house on a bluff above the sea, where Journey's journey had begun. Mama and I had barely finished unpacking when she'd quit coming home from the hospital in time to walk the beach with me at sunset. Just when I thought I would mail a letter to my daddy on the mainland to come and rescue me from a life of isolation among sand crabs and sea urchins, Mama started coming home before dusk again.

After that when we walked the shoreline she would rub her ever-swelling belly as if it were a magic lamp. Once Journey had been born Mama was never present long enough to appreciate having given birth. She began working double shifts at the hospital to put food in our mouths. When my fatherless little sister came into the world, I knew that for all practical purposes, I didn't have a daddy either. We had been separated by an ocean he never planned to cross.

How I ached for him and everything else familiar to me at home in Illinois. I had sorely missed the big oak tree beside my bedroom window, with sprawling limbs strong enough to shimmy down. Our two-story house was often filled with aunts and uncles, grandparents and cousins for birthday and holiday gatherings. In those carefree days of my younger years I would dream of frivolous things in my rose-colored room, while snuggled beneath a white taffeta comforter.

My life was irrevocably upended when brought to this tropical island, which has been more of a paradox to me than a paradise, especially now that Mama's love child was gone forever. This death certificate and teak wood chest told me it was too late for making peace with Journey. She and Mama were both gone before I'd had my fill of either. Despite the twist of fate that changed my course in life, I had loved them both beyond measure.

The balding man removed the straps from the box. I stood in stunned silence as he waited for me to sign paperwork. My neighbor, Chenlei, peeked shyly around the kitchen door at the sweaty man. She quietly entered the house after he'd left, and stood beside me as I stared at the chest. My little friend watched as I pushed it into position under the window. A shiver ran down my spine as I set the key inside the lock, but I couldn't bring myself to lift the lid. My guilt and remorse for the years that Journey and I had spent apart came crashing down upon me in that moment. I wished that I could crawl into the chest and have it take me back to that fateful day, let me change the events that unfolded and caused her to leave.

Chenlei ventured closer to take a better look.

"The finest teak wood in the world comes from the rainforests of Thailand," I told Chenlei, who dropped by at this time every morning for her tutoring session. My ability to use the teachable moment surprised me. Chenlei examined the unexpected delivery in silence as she listened to my words. With barely a grasp of the language, I marveled at her concentration for a six-year-old. Her adopted parents were my best friends. Elise owned and ran a bookstore on the Bay. Quinn was an associate at the private university where I taught. My little pupil had come to them from China, with a mysterious past of her own to sort out.

"Teak wood was introduced to the Western world by Portuguese seamen." I'd gone into educator mode to prevent the dammed-up wall of my emotions from crashing forward. I enunciated each word properly, slowly, hoping Chenlei might absorb their meaning while I refused to let the reality of this moment fully seep into my consciousness. I hadn't yet hinted to my young neighbor the true significance of this chest, but my face must have shown my pain, because Chenlei was even more somber than usual.

"This particular wood is great for marine use because it repels insects and fungus and is not harmed by acids or alkali," I added, a tear trickling down my face, which I didn't wipe away. As a university professor of communication studies (which led to my obsessive reading about foreign cultures) I knew a multitude of seaworthy facts, but not who delivered this teak wood chest to me from Lahaina Harbor on the island of Maui.

I held up the document crumpled in my hands, and looked at Chenlei. Her eyes showed apprehension, just as they always did. I longed for that day when those vulnerable dark pools of sadness would reflect contentment or joy. I saw Journey's eyes flash in the corners of my memory, on fire with an unadulterated love for life, twinkling precociously on those sultry sun-drenched days of our past. We must have built hundreds of sandcastles together along our beachfront playground before she turned fourteen and Mama died.

Then I married Chase, and Journey's life fell apart slowly, like high tide creeping into our sandcastles until they finally collapsed. That's why at sixteen she left and never called or wrote. How could I tell Chenlei the tragedy this chest represented? Sitting cross-legged in front of it, I pulled her petite body into my lap. "This teak wood chest belonged to a young woman named Journey," I began. "She was my baby half sister."

Chenlei turned around in my lap and hugged me tightly. "I . . . am sorry, Auntie Kylie." Her words broke the dam of my tears as I held her to me, inhaling the sweet fragrance of Jasmine shampoo and raspberry chapstick. It was Elise's idea for Chenlei to call me Auntie. She thought Miss or Mrs. would be too formal for a best friend and neighbor.

It seemed odd to me no one in her own country wanted this precious little girl, bright and full of love, especially when I would have given anything to hang on to the child Mama left in my care while working at the hospital. The same young woman who slipped through my grasp on a hot humid night that kept even the island birds quiet for want of a breeze.

Her duffel bag was gone that morning. Soccer gear was strewn about the bed when I went to wake her for school, and I shivered, just as I had when I saw the chest placed before me. It was a premonition that made me shake so. Teak chests don't come from sailors sharing stolen treasure. They come from missing pieces of your past.

Where we lived, where I still lived, had been a summer home for those visiting the wealthy Claiborne family further up the hill. Their estate sat on a cliff overlooking the Pacific, whereas this white-framed cottage my mama rented was nestled on a lower slope. There was a short winding path to the sea with a steep stairway at the end. Shiny green island foliage and sweet plumeria flowers invaded all but the narrow path. Bird-of-paradise blooms shot up randomly throughout the lush hill, their striking shape and color adding drama to the otherwise serene slope.

I used to see imaginary glimpses in my mind of Journey stealing away into the night, making quick glances over her shoulder with eyes that flashed defiance. Despite her boldness of spirit on that fateful evening, the vision that often haunts me still is of a vulnerable young woman. I knew all too well what she ran away from, but what had she run away to? And what caused her untimely death?

After several minutes of endless tears washing my face in a warm salt bath I stopped rocking back and forth with Chenlei in my lap. I quit stroking her dark head of chin-chopped hair and willed myself to keep control, for the sake of my little neighbor, if not to preserve my own sanity.

"Let's see what's in the chest," I said, while drying my face with the sleeves of my shirt. Chenlei stood to peer inside as I opened the lid. My sister's scent of island flowers, often worn in her hair, mingled with the teak like an exotic perfume. I inhaled several times with closed eyes and tried to find the courage to explore her years without me. After we visually examined its contents, I reached for a rolled canvas placed on top. My hands shook as I untied the twine that held it and gave one end to Chenlei. We slowly unraveled a portrait done in acrylics. Chenlei tilted her head to view the upside down painting of a brown-eyed cherub with mocha skin, similar to how my sister looked as a young girl.

I unwound the last bit of canvas and a letter fell to the floor. It was a single sheet of parchment paper. I let go of the painting and it curled up tightly again. Chenlei held it to her chest while I stared hesitantly at the letter. As I reached for it I could see Journey's distinctive penmanship of long narrow strokes and delicate curves.

I looked at Chenlei, whose eyes were questioning, her mouth frowning in wonder. We sat on the hardwood floor again, Chenlei still clinging to the painting while I touched the words on the parchment paper and thought about Journey writing them. The long curvy letters were nothing like my petite delicate ones. We were such opposites. Her eyes a warm vibrant brown; mine a pale blue. Her hair was all wild ebony waves; mine straight and blonde. Our fathers were of different heritages. Hers a native Hawaiian with dark eyes, mine a lean fair-haired German.

These might have been her last words put to paper. I began to read out loud, slowly. There could not have been a greater incentive for

Chenlei to understand English. The child listened attentively to every word read from the peach scented stationary.

*Dear Kylie,*

*I have asked Grayson Conner to send you my few possessions, as my demise is now inevitable. Regardless of my fate Alana will be safe with her father. Can you believe I have a seven-year-old, Kylie? She was not planned of course, and I have had my moments of sheer despair, but she has been worth every second of worry. Grayson doesn't know Alana is his. In fact, he has not seen the child until now. I was only in his life briefly, long ago, and have returned like a bad dream.*

*I have missed you, my dear sister. Remember those endless hours we spent on the shore, swimming with the turtles and collecting coral? Oh to have back those days of warm sand between our toes and salt on our lips from the ever soothing sea. To run from you, shrieking and giggling, while playing hide and seek. Oh to braid flowers in our hair again! Remember how we would wish every day for a regular mother and father to come home and read the paper, cook our dinner, and take us to town for ice cream? Even the life of neglect we had is better than what I have known since, and now my days are spent.*

*My doom is of my own doing, and the end is near. Then Grayson is all Alana will have, although I dream that she will meet you, but what are the odds you will get this letter? I cannot bring myself to call. I feel so unworthy of your love. Sneaking away in the dead of night. Never letting you know if I was all right. Well, the truth is, Kylie, I am not all right. I have not been since the day I left.*

*Grayson never meant for me (or Alana) to be in his life, and I at least, won't be for much longer. So I am packing this chest and hope it reaches you. I can nearly feel the darkness surrounding me now, beckoning me to cross over into its cool and soothing arms. I sadly long for it, long for relief at last.*

*Your loving sister,*
*Journey*

Chenlei and I stared silently at the words and I could only think of one thing at that moment. *Journey had a child.* For all of the ten years since my little sister's parting, Chase and I had tried to have a child of our own. We still clung to the hope that one day it would happen and I'd become pregnant. We debated fertility treatments and fought about possibly adopting, reaching no conclusion we could both live with. I was desperate to be a mother and after knowing Chenlei, I was especially open to adopting a child as remarkable as she, homeless and without hope unless claimed for love by a foreign shore. But Chase was stubborn and determined to have his own children. I knew he would never easily accept my sister's child, only because Journey and he had been like oil and water in the short time we'd all lived together in this cottage.

Chenlei glanced into the chest again but neither of us, it seemed, were up for the task of exploring the contents any further. I carefully replaced the rolled up canvas and shut the lid. Then I put the letter in my purse with the death certificate and walked Chenlei home. Her father, Quinn, would be back from the university by now.

I watched Chenlei disappear through the open front door, and saw Quinn wave at me, but I couldn't speak to him. How much had Chenlei understood? How much could she retell? For now, her summation would have to do.

I needed to tell Chase.

Walking back over the hill I kept seeing visions of Journey picking flowers, which grew in abundance on the grounds surrounding our little house. She would put them in a vase and fuss over the richly colored bird-of-paradise and white plumeria blooms until perfectly arranged.

Once home again, I went straight to my jeep, fumbling for the keys to start the engine. On the narrow winding road that led to town another wave of emotion overtook me. I pulled to the side of the road and nearly choked on my own tears as I asked God why he would do this to me. Take someone I loved beyond measure and reason, take her without warning, without my saying goodbye, or I'm sorry, or I love you. This time my rage was not quiet. I sobbed loudly and pounded on the steering wheel with my fists. But such release did not abate my pain. It only fed it.

Wiping red and swollen eyes again with my shirtsleeve I thought of Alana and how I needed to find her. Indeed, I *needed* her and wanted to believe that she needed me too. It didn't lessen my pain about losing my baby half-sister, but it made me able to drive to town and tell Chase, who would no doubt try to talk me out of searching for Journey's little girl.

But how could I not?

# CHAPTER TWO

*Elise took a good look at this foreign daughter of hers,
more foreign for their inability to bond than for place of birth.*

I laid the death certificate on Chase's desk without saying anything. His eyes met mine. He must have noticed I'd been crying. With obvious concern he skimmed the document. Chase was tall and lean with disobedient brown hair that fell haphazardly across his forehead. It was symbolic of his entire existence. He was always in the middle of a deal, or on his way to or from a helicopter project, and never followed any rules but his own when fighting death-defying fires from the air.

"Where did this come from?" he asked. Not, "How could your baby sister possibly be dead?" But then Chase was probably not surprised by her death. He never knew the sun-browned barefoot child that strung shells into necklaces and played with hermit crabs in tide pools on long summer days. The Journey he knew was a veritable confusion of hormones and hard life lessons. When Chase met Journey she had already started down the tumultuous road of a troubled adolescence partly because of Mama's death, and partly because her Hawaiian father was not even a name on a birth certificate, let alone instrumental in her life.

"It came with a teak wood chest, delivered early this morning from a harbor in Maui." I walked over to the window and with raw glassy eyes peered out at tourists on the boardwalk. "You could at least pretend to be sorry, Chase."

"Of course I'm sorry." I felt him staring at the back of me, heard the defensiveness in his tone. He would be the first to admit my little sister

*Journey* **11**

drained him of his stoic patience during the two traumatic years she lived with us.

"This is tragic, Kyl. She must have only been, what? Twenty-six?" He walked over and put his arms around me. I let Chase hold me, grateful to be engulfed by his warmth and strength, and the scent of bar soap mixed with sea air that was uniquely his. Chase ran on the beach every morning before showering for work. Somehow the salty breezes from off shore had permeated his hair and skin, reminding me of sun soaked days romping the tideline with Journey.

Remembering the letter in my handbag, I pulled away and retrieved it for him to read. I stared blankly at glossy wall posters of helicopters hovering over an enticing blue sea and forested cliffs while he read, my mind confused and numb from the morning's events. The posters defined what Chase did. He had his own helicopter business—C. Hudson Helicopters—and although he mostly did scenic island flights for tourists, the big money was in fighting fires, especially in Colorado, where Chase was from.

I would never forget how we had met. He and his family were visiting the Claibornes at the top of the hill. Chase's father and Mr. Claiborne were old college buddies. I remember looking up from my book one day, while propped against the wall of our private sea cave on what Journey and I had come to believe was also our private beach, and there he was. Staring at me from the entrance.

Chase fell in love with me that day, and I with him. But neither of us were willing to admit it for quite some time. Not until after he had graduated with his bachelor's degree that spring, in business, from Colorado State and returned to the island for his MBA. He claimed he'd fallen in love with Hawaii. Chase moved in with the Claibornes, more because we could rendezvous on the private beach between his classes and mine, than because of the free room and board.

The one spectacular picture of a helicopter dumping water on a raging fire reminded me of the dangerous work he did outside of tourist runs. As if I could forget the danger involved in his business of choice.

But that was Chase. His entire heritage was based on gutsy macho nerve.

He sat down again behind his desk tucked away in a corner and scratched his head as he studied the letter. A few wooden chairs neatly placed for meeting with clients completed the sparse furnishings.

"Is Grayson Conner the person who sent the chest?"

"I think so."

"Did he know about the letter?"

"I doubt it. It was rolled up, hidden in a painting."

"I see. Well, clearly she committed suicide."

"You don't know that, Chase."

"I think the letter makes it pretty clear, Kyl."

"No. I don't believe it."

"You mean you don't want to believe it."

I collapsed into one of the wooden chairs. He'd bought it at a flea market for ten dollars. I told him it was an antique and worth a lot more than what he paid. It was solid oak, solid like Chase and his family. All American. No tales of troubled teens with dead mamas and absent daddies. No devastating divorces or dramatic moves from the Midwest to an island in the Pacific, leaving only memories of my daddy, coupled with a longing to have the early years back, those innocent years when moving out and across the ocean wasn't even a consideration yet in my mama's thought process.

What did Chase know about being forced to transform mid-childhood? My large extended family that came to our home for early Sunday suppers disappeared from my reality and were replaced with endless isolation on a lone stretch of beach. Abruptly my mama went from a full-time mother who had not used her nursing degree to a virtual stranger working afternoon and evening shifts at the local hospital, leaving me a baby sister in need of constant care.

He could not relate to that in the least.

"Journey did not commit suicide, Chase. I know my little sister. She would never have done that. She had an enthusiasm for life everybody wanted to extract from her just by being near, as if through osmosis they could become infected with her energy." I sighed. "That's why she always had an entourage of followers, made up of her little misfit classmates." It hurt me to admit it. I had been jealous of her charisma. My little sister fit in everywhere she went, and I did not. My skin was too fair, my hair too light, my accent too Midwestern. But she was an island girl through and through. Taller and slighter of build than most, but with bronzed skin and dark curly hair, and that island heritage you must be born among the palm trees to possess.

"You haven't seen her for ten years," Chase reminded me. "A lot can happen in that amount of time."

"You haven't said anything about the child." I studied his expression, changing the subject on purpose before our disagreement became a heated debate. "Her daughter, Alana, would be my niece. And she is about the same age as Chenlei."

"Half-niece," Chase corrected me. As if there were such a thing, as if it would make me want her less, or need to find her less. He had to know I would look for her, had to already be afraid of this inevitable consequence of the letter.

"Chase, you can't be a half-niece."

"Why not? Journey was only your half-sister."

"Only?"

"You can't seriously be thinking about traipsing through all the yachts harbored in Maui to find your half-niece."

"Why not?" I stood up and stared at him, my adrenalin flowing, my emotions ready to short circuit from an overdose of recent realities.

"Because." Chase paused there, perhaps hesitating to say what he wanted to say in favor of a more correct response. "I know you, Kylie. You'll want to keep her. Raise her like you did your sister."

"And what would be wrong with that?"

"Grayson Conner may have other ideas. He didn't ship her to you with the chest. Maybe he knows she's his own flesh and blood after all."

I leaned on Chase's desk, planting my face inches from his. "Well, there's only one way to find out, isn't there?" I purposely was intimidating him with my try-and-stop-me attitude. It came in handy a lot as a kid, when bullies bothered Journey or me, but it wasn't such a bad thing for leverage in a marriage either.

"Fine. Go look for her." Chase handed me the death certificate and the single-page letter. I sat down again, wishing this conversation had not dissolved into an emotional battle.

"We've thought about adopting a child, Chase. Journey doesn't imply anywhere in her letter that Grayson wants to raise Alana. A child he doesn't even know is his."

"Okay, fine, but you can't morally take this child from him without letting the man know he's the father, and then letting him decide if he wants to raise her." Chase furrowed his brow. "That is, if he still has her."

I folded my arms and studied his eyes. They were as aqua as the deep sea and melted my resolve on a regular basis. But right now I wanted divorce on demand. I wanted to throw his laptop at him. *I wanted this little girl my sister left behind.*

I wanted Chase to want her, too. I wanted him to tell me to find her and bring her home to the Big Island where we would treasure and spoil her forever as our very own. I wanted him to spew rich superlatives about what a tribute it would be to my beautiful baby sister tragically lost to us too soon. But I knew better. Chase didn't want to adopt. He wanted children of his own and I wondered of late if he'd given up on me, turning his efforts to more fertile pastures.

I envisioned him alongside his only female copilot. Were they more than a flight team? He and Meagan Cole laughed too hard lately when they were together. They finished each other's sentences. Most distressing of all was how they avoided conversation about their next layover location during fire season. I didn't want to believe anyone could come between the great love Chase and I shared, but it was getting harder to pretend Meagan was just a work associate.

I crammed the letter and death certificate back into my purse, wishing it hadn't awakened this ongoing battle over my baby half-Hawaiian sister. She always stood squarely in the middle of our ability to reason, and often snuffed out all but the most meager pangs of lust and love we shared so generously when her name was not on our lips. I walked out the door with no further comment and left to Chase's imagination how long it would take me to pack and catch a shuttle plane to Maui.

I had to know what happened to Journey. I needed to find Alana. I would deal with Chase later. Maybe when he returned from Colorado he would have a change of heart. Maybe once I found Grayson Conner he would be happy to pack Alana up and give her to me on the spot. Who was this man anyway? Did Grayson have anything at all to do with my sister's death, or the misery she obviously felt that might have led to it?

When I returned to our home on the sleepy knoll tucked away from the mighty cliff above the sea, Chenlei was waiting for me. Quinn must have let her walk over to sit there and watch for my jeep. She sat gently rocking on the swing Chase had built. A smile crossed her face. "Teak wood!" she exclaimed, and patted the swing slats.

Until that moment I had felt no joy on this gloomy day, despite it being full of bright sun in a cloudless sky. Now I smiled despite my heavy heart. "Yes, it is teak wood, Chenlei. Good observation." In theory I was only Chenlei's friend and neighbor, but in truth, I felt more like her mother. Somewhere in my emotionally deprived maternal mind, I thought of Elise as her Auntie and me as her mama.

I knew thinking this way was not good. Not for me, not for Chenlei, and not for the Damask family. If Quinn and Elise knew how attached I'd become, they would distance her from me out of concern for my wellbeing, and hers. That's why I was careful not to appear too involved, too in love with her. It is also why I needed to get away, find Alana, and convince this Grayson person that she would be better off with me. What kind of home could a boat be? If indeed, he even still had Alana.

I hugged Chenlei, and sat on the swing beside her. "I'm going to be gone for a few days."

She peered up at me, her eyes wide-open in disbelief. "Gone?"

"Yes, Chenlei. But just for a short time." I tried to explain how I was going to search for my niece, who was just a year older than her. And if I found Alana, and brought her back here, Chenlei would have someone her own age to play with. Someone besides her big brothers, Austin and Wyatt, who were eight and ten, and wanted to teach her soccer, and how to climb trees, and refused to play house.

Chenlei looked away from me and stared blankly into space. I could see her receding into herself, into that place no one could penetrate, that place of fear and uncertainty. I studied her little round face as if it were a map to her psychological makeup. The set jaw and furrowed brow worried me.

I pulled Chenlei onto my lap and we rocked together as one, the swing creaking on each forward thrust. I didn't say anything, but we sang the songs I taught her. Simple repetitive songs that helped her learn the difficult language. Funny songs that made her smile despite her sudden onset of anxiety. Afterwards I brought her inside and gave her peanut butter cookies and milk. When she was finished she helped me fold my clothes and pack them into the suitcase. Before I shut it, I had her run and get the snapshot of her I kept on my desk in the den. It was from the party I'd had for Chenlei and the Damasks when they first returned from China.

Chenlei's beautiful little face was quite serious in the picture, not sure of what to expect. She looked frozen inside, afraid to feel anything because feelings only made you vulnerable and were best kept at bay. That's how she looked now, while handing me the snapshot. I placed it in the suitcase and told her I would think of her every day until I returned. She smiled and I could see that comforted her a little. Then I took her hand in mine and held the suitcase in the other as we walked over the hill to her home, the only other house nearby on this stretch of shoreline. It was Elise's inheritance from her grandparents.

My best friend had just pulled up when we arrived. Seeing her broke the dam of my fragile emotions. Tears stung my face and I was surprised that any remained by this time, eight hours after the arrival of the chest. What would Elise think or say when I told her about my sister? That last summer before Journey had walked out of my life, Elise had walked into it. We'd bonded while I helped her unpack boxes and rearrange furniture until it fit well. Tea, books, humor, marital challenges, hopes and dreams for a family were among the initial topics that made us kindred spirits. My new neighbor was an instant best friend and a godsend for helping me cope after Journey left.

"Kylie? What's wrong?" Elise closed the car door.

Austin and Wyatt bounced out the other side of the SUV. They scrambled after a soccer ball flying across the knoll and down the grassy bluff. The Damask boys lived mainly for sports and video games but were also good students. Quinn and Elise had taught them to be responsible and kind. I was grateful they looked out for Chenlei at school, even though they didn't seem to have much use for a younger sister.

Chenlei hid behind my back, as she always did when Elise returned to collect her at the end of the day. Classes at the university had just ended for the summer when the Damasks went to fetch her from China. Upon returning Elise was behind with taking inventory and restocking her bookstore. Quinn was teaching for the summer session. I had eagerly volunteered to be Chenlei's caregiver and tutor on the days Quinn taught.

"What's happened?" Elise asked, embracing me in a tight hug.

"It's Journey, Elise." I paused, another wave of disbelief flooding over me. "She's . . . she's . . . passed away."

Elise let go of me as her green eyes widened. "Not Journey! Oh Kylie, I'm so sorry." She hugged me again and I wanted to become lost in her scent of old books mixed with Plumeria lotion. My friend and neighbor was a tall skinny French woman, with chin length hair in a shade just a tad darker than the ordinary brunette. It somehow alerted you to the fact there was nothing typical about her.

"How?" Elise asked in a muffled tone, her head buried in my hair. "Did someone call you? The police maybe?" She pulled back and studied me.

"No. I received a delivery early this morning. A teak wood chest."

I was speaking as if in a fog. "There was a death certificate. And then Chenlei and I found a letter written by Journey in the chest. Rolled up in a painting."

I looked down and felt for Chenlei behind me, pulling her gently to my side and stroking her silky hair, pushing her bangs back to reveal a high, flat forehead. I knelt beside her and looked directly into those dark eyes that were so compelling.

"Chenlei and I found the letter in a painting of an island girl. Didn't we, Chenlei?"

Chenlei nodded, her dark eyes staring hard into mine. What was she thinking? That I was getting ready to desert her? That everything would change again, *yet again*, for this little girl, who had never known the comfort of stability?

"In the letter Journey revealed that she has a daughter." I looked up at Elise, who was blurry through my wet eyes. "Alana is seven. Can you believe it? I have a niece," I whispered, nearly choking on the last few words.

Elise knelt beside us. "That's incredible, Kyl. It's wonderful news. Journey has left a part of herself behind for you to love." She hugged me, and Chenlei's dark eyes stared blankly, showing her uncertainty of what to think about all this. Elise took a good look at this foreign daughter of hers, more foreign for their inability to bond than for place of birth.

"How exciting and upsetting your day must have been, all at the same time, Chenlei." Elise looked at me after speaking to Chenlei. It was an insecurity she had about how to approach the child, how to communicate with her. What Elise didn't understand was that she didn't need to worry about approach, or speech, or anything else a tutor would be burdened by. She needed only to love the child with abandon. But Elise was not comfortable with Chenlei. I wasn't sure why yet, but I was determined to find out before they were both beyond any hope of bonding.

Chenlei didn't respond to what Elise said. Instead she stared past her new mother into the blue sky behind us, and then hugged me with all her strength, as if afraid someone would try to pull us apart.

*Journey* **19**

"Elise, I'm leaving this evening. I'm taking an island shuttle to Maui, to look for Alana."

"Yes, of course." Elise began nodding her head while pulling her hair back from her face. It was a habit born of stress. The thought of caring for Chenlei alone the next few days apparently triggered it.

"I'm sorry about the last minute notice. I'm sure you and Chenlei will have fun together at the bookstore." My tone was encouraging for Chenlei's sake, but Elise just kept nodding, hands glued to her head on either side as if keeping her hair from falling off until finally she responded.

"This is all so overwhelming, Kyl. But please don't fret about us. We'll be fine."

"Elise, I'll be back before you know it." I looked down at Chenlei clinging to my leg. "If I call maybe you'll let me talk to our little angel here?"

"Yes, definitely." Elise smiled tensely, her brows furrowed. "Kyl, if there's anything I can do for you, anything at all, let me know." She hugged me again and I sensed she needed whatever strength I could give her as much as she was offering me hers.

"It's okay, Elise." I gently squeezed her shoulders. "Everything will be okay. I just need to find out what happened to my baby sister, and to see who has Alana. Perhaps bring her back with me," I added timidly, not daring to hope.

"Oh, Kyl, that would be so wonderful, to raise your little niece. If there is no father to raise her, that is." She said that last line cautiously, as if to be sure neither of us got our hopes up too high, just yet.

I kissed Elise on the cheek and Chenlei on the top of her head, reminding both how much I loved them. Secretly I prayed they would find a way to bond while I was gone. I put Chenlei's hand in Elise's and observed their tearful eyes.

It was a parting picture of uncertainty that haunted me during the entire flight to Maui.

# CHAPTER THREE

*His calm expression replaced my anger with a need to beg forgiveness, for not being present in Journey's hour of need.*

I checked into a motel in Lahaina where Chase and I stayed as newlyweds. The room had a picturesque view of the harbor and brought back faint memories of a less complicated time between Chase and myself, although Journey was between us even then. There were moments when I thought her the bane of my existence. And yet, despite my resentment for Journey's intrusion into my childhood, I had needed her as much as she needed me. If my little sister had not been there to nurture and set an example for, I might have been the runaway at sixteen. A white Midwestern transplant does not blend well into a sea of native Hawaiians. Being bullied at school was a daily event.

With a determined shove I slid open the window overlooking the harbor. A full moon reflected off the water. Boats bobbed up and down while water lapped at their hulls. From somewhere in the night a faint melody being strummed on a ukulele drifted in with the sea air. Was Grayson Conner's boat out there, anchored in the harbor, not far from where I stood staring into the night?

Part of me wanted to slip down to the docks right now and face this man who got Journey pregnant, and may have had something to do with her death. But it had been a long day and I was exhausted. I changed into my nightie, brushed my teeth, and fell into bed. Harbor sounds from the open window filled my head, along with flashes of Elise and Chenlei looking terrified to see me leave them alone, together.

I awoke early and watched the sunrise over Haleakala, tinting the sky rosy pink. By the time I showered and drank a cup of coffee, I was eager to approach the docks and discover the whereabouts of Grayson Conner. I grabbed my baseball cap and sunglasses as I headed out the door. Journey's letter and the death certificate were in my straw bag.

I suddenly wished I had unpacked Journey's things from the chest in search of more information about her ten years apart from me, and especially the past few months.

But I couldn't stomach the thought of dissecting that final shrine, the symbolical representation of all she had been, or ever would be, in her short tragic life. Someday I would go through it, and perhaps I would let Chenlei help. My somber little friend, struggling to make sense of her own fragmented life, might give me the courage to prevail until every last piece of Journey's keepsakes had been examined.

The first boat I approached had a young man on the upper deck, sweeping with a straw broom. He had shaggy blond hair protruding from a battered woven hat.

"Can I help you?" he asked, stopping the rhythm of his broom to observe me.

"Maybe." I hesitated. "Do you know a Grayson Conner?"

He laughed. "Everyone knows Grayson Conner, at least everyone who lives here. Are you from the mainland?"

"No. I live in Kona."

We stared at each other for a few seconds.

"Which boat is his?" I asked.

He scrambled down a ladder and hopped off what appeared to be a diving boat.

"May I ask why you need to see him?"

I adjusted my ball hat and looked out to sea. There was no short answer for that.

"It's just that Grayson's kind of a loner. He's a very private person, although sometimes the locals need him in a hurry." He began tossing scuba gear onto the lower deck from a weathered box at our feet.

"Why?" I asked, puzzled.

"Grayson's a doctor. You didn't know that?" The scruffy young man with broad tanned shoulders and baggy board shorts gave me his full attention. "He's a surgeon. Grayson's well known for the work he does here at the local hospital, and the outpatient clinic."

"I see. Well, it's my little sister I need to speak with him about. Is this a diving boat?" I asked, evasively, not sure that I wished to discuss Journey with this young man.

"We make our main money escorting divers to good locations, but we do a little fishing on the side. Does your sister need to see Grayson?"

"No. My sister . . ." it was hard to finish the sentence. My eyes wandered to that endless expanse of water gently moving up and down. "She's passed away."

It was frustrating to discover Grayson Conner was a doctor. I had found doctors to be an annoying breed of people. First there was Journey's father, who left my mother to pursue his career on the mainland and never looked back. Next there was Mama's final boyfriend, a heart surgeon who crashed his private plane somewhere over the Pacific, taking Mama from me prematurely and leaving me alone to finish raising Journey.

And now there was Grayson Conner, who lived on a yacht in the Lahaina harbor from which he delivered my sister's chest of possessions without so much as an explanation.

"I'm sorry." I could see a barrage of questions forming in the young man's pale blue eyes.

"My name is Kylie Hudson," I offered up, extending my hand.

"I'm Alex Preston." He shook my hand firmly as we briefly studied one another. "Grayson could be back this afternoon, or five days from now. It's just that he never tells anyone his plans and he has other harbors he can tie up in." Alex pointed and stared at the furthest dock from where we stood. "That's his slip, on the far end. I'm sorry I can't be any more help to you than that."

"Thanks, Alex. Maybe I'll see you around. I'll be here for a while. At least until I have a chance to speak to Dr. Conner."

Alex took his hat off and scratched his head while staring at Grayson's empty slip.

"Listen, Kylie, I'm sorry about your sister. Why don't you meet me around five at the Hula Grill, right there across the harbor." He pointed to an unassuming building with a sign out front that had faded from the sun. "It's the best restaurant here in the harbor, a well-kept secret from mainlanders." He put his hat back on. "If Grayson ties up here tonight he'll probably eat there."

I told him I might just do that and left the docks to spend the day art browsing in the Lahaina shops. At lunchtime I fed half my fish sandwich to the gulls on the peer, having no appetite for art or food, although both helped pass the time. The rest of the afternoon I read a novel beside a Bonsai tree without being able to retain a single thing I'd read.

By happy hour I had entered the Hula Grill and ordered a Mai Tai to wait for Alex. He showed up right at five p.m. in fresh Hawaiian shorts and a clean t-shirt. I smiled and asked how his day's excursions on the boat had gone to which he politely answered well. It was the end of our small talk.

The waitress asked Alex if he wanted his usual beer, and then left us alone to quiz each other silently for a few awkward seconds until I delved into my difficult interrogation. "My sister apparently spent time on Grayson's boat, Alex. You might have met her."

"Grayson's never had anyone live on his boat that I'm aware of, except Journey and Alana. Alana still does, actually."

My breath caught in my throat and I must have become pale, because Alex asked if I was okay.

"I'm fine, really. It's just that, Journey was my sister."

"Oh my God. Where've you been? Why weren't you here for her?" Alex straightened up in his seat.

"What do you mean, here for her?" I asked, my voice nearly breaking.

Alex stared past me, as if questioning whether he should be the one giving me these answers.

"Kylie, do you know how she died?"

"No. The death certificate is vague. It says 'cause of death undetermined.'"

I grabbed the document from my straw tote just as the waitress served Alex his beer. He took a long drink as if he'd need it and then studied the death certificate carefully.

"This is signed by Grayson," he said without looking up.

"Let me see." I took the certificate from him. Sure enough, Dr. Grayson Conner was scrawled across the bottom in the unreadable fashion every doctor is known for.

"How did she die?" I asked, looking up at him, right into his soft blue eyes that showed all the vulnerability I felt.

Alex ran shaky fingers through his mop of straw colored hair. "Grayson's right. It would be hard to say exactly what she died of. Journey was found in the water."

"She drowned?" I whispered. Chase's words about suicide flashed through my mind. That can't be, I thought, because Journey could swim like a dolphin, like the dolphins we often swam with ever since she was five years old.

Alex leaned forward in his chair and studied his hands. "It's hard to say because she had so many drugs in her at the time."

"Drugs?"

"Painkillers. The next morning after they found her floating near the shore, they checked her pill bottles and she'd consumed quite a few before entering the water." Alex nearly lost his composure. He cleared his throat and added, "Later, the toxicology report confirmed that she'd taken too many, but it wasn't unusual for her to consume more than the conservative recommendation."

Tears streamed down my face. It was obvious he had known my sister quite well, and I found comfort in that, in knowing she had not died among strangers.

"She'd built up a tolerance for them, the painkillers," Alex added. "No one knows if she fell in or jumped. She loved to swim. It sort of eased her pain and always cheered her up. Anyway, she resurfaced with the morning tide."

My stomach lurched and I thought I might be sick. Why hadn't I been here for her? "Alex, I had no idea. I haven't seen my sister in ten years. If only I'd known where she was. Why did she need painkillers?"

We both looked up as someone approached our table.

"Grayson." Alex stood and shook his hand.

I had no preconceived idea of what Grayson Conner should look like, but I didn't expect what I saw. He wore khaki shorts with a navy blue t-shirt and sport sandals, which made him look more like a tourist than a doctor. There was nothing to distinguish him except for an interesting watch and a gold signature ring of some type. His hair was prematurely gray, and his eyes a stunning blue. He observed me carefully and didn't say anything. His silence was intimidating. I wanted to ask a string of demanding questions. Instead I just sat quietly and waited to be introduced.

"Grayson, this is Kylie Hudson. Journey's sister." Alex said it with disbelief. As if I had been the one missing all this time and not Journey.

I studied Dr. Conner while he ordered a beer from the waitress, who obviously knew Grayson well. He was not a large man, but he had a large presence about him. He was of medium height and build, obviously strong, and in excellent condition. Alex looked relieved to have him there to answer my questions about Journey. But suddenly my questions were all different, and they weren't fully formed, because my mind was stunned by all this shattering information from Alex.

Our silence became awkward as my unasked questions evaporated. Grayson was not the monster I'd envisioned. His calm expression replaced my anger with a need to beg forgiveness, for not being present in Journey's hour of need. I took a deep breath and tried to compose myself, tried to find the words to speak. "How did my sister die, if it wasn't from drowning or overdosing on painkillers?"

"She had cancer, Ms. Hudson." Grayson's steady blue eyes looked straight into mine.

"Cancer?"

"Yes. Your sister had a brain tumor."

Alex handed me a napkin for the onslaught of tears I could not prevent. Both men were quiet. Perhaps they didn't feel it appropriate to ask me any questions yet. I was grateful they didn't, because their questions would probably demand answers I didn't want to face.

"How long was Journey here, in Lahaina, on your boat?" I asked.

"Journey came to me in late spring, and spent the summer here, her last."

I shook my head slowly. I wanted to scream *why did she come to you and not home to me?* But I knew the answer to that. Grayson was Alana's father. Journey needed to leave the child with him. And the letter clearly stated why she didn't come home to me. But I suspect not wanting to come between Chase and me, not wanting to deal with Chase period, is what kept her away more than guilt.

Before I could ask another question, a small child came walking up and leaned against Grayson. I didn't have to wonder who she was. Even if Journey hadn't mentioned Alana in her letter, there was no mistaking this child was hers. The curly hair and sweeping lashes were trademarks of her mother, as were the soul-searching brown eyes.

I froze in her presence, and recalled Elise and Chenlei, and how I left them together, looking uncomfortable. For the first time I could empathize with Elise's awkwardness. I wanted to gather this little girl in my arms and tell her how much I loved her mother, tell her how sorry I was she died. But instead I just drank in her unbelievable resemblance to Journey.

"Did Makana feed you anything but shrimp back there in her kitchen?" Grayson asked. He put his arm around the child as a greeting. She muffled yes into his shoulder. "Alana, I want you to meet someone. Look up and say hello to your aunt." Alana peeked out of her hair, not lifting her head from Grayson's shoulder.

"I am your mama's sister, Alana. My name is Kylie." I put out my hand to shake hers. She looked at Grayson, and he nodded. Hesitantly she shook my hand before sitting down on the outer edge of the booth, next to Grayson. She stared at me quietly, with brown curls falling over her face and arms.

Grayson still looked outwardly calm, but I detected some nervousness beneath his cool façade. Something gave that away. Perhaps it was the glint of fire in his eyes, hot with too much thinking behind them. Did he believe I had come for Alana and would he fight for her? Did he know she was his? Had Journey told him in the end, after the letter was written, before she took the pain pills and was consumed by the sea?

There was so much unspoken between us, but I needed space, a chance to collect my thoughts. All I could think of was getting out of there and going down to the beach, where I could gather my wits about me, maybe take a long walk by the shore. I stood and smiled, looked directly at Alana, and willed myself not to fall apart.

"I'm so happy to meet you, Alana," I somehow muttered softly. "And I'm so sorry about your mama. I loved her very much. When she was your age we would swim together in the ocean by our house, and build sandcastles on the shore."

I felt my oppressive sadness lift a little as her warm brown eyes peered up at me. A spark of hope and light entered my miserable dark world of grief. A piece of Journey lived and breathed within this child. I could see it in her similar features, and feel it in my heart.

"Tomorrow I will come visit you, okay? Where are you staying?" I looked at Grayson, who was staring at me. His facial expression was pleasant enough, but there was no hint of a smile.

"Alana lives on my boat. Why don't you come by in the morning? Anytime you want. We aren't going out until afternoon."

"I'll be there."

Neither of us discussed where his boat was. He must have assumed if I didn't already know I'd find out. I said goodbye to Alex, and then I left, walking away with more questions then I came with. But the biggest question of all was about Alana. Could Grayson really be her father and not know it?

Or did Journey only wish it to be so?

# CHAPTER FOUR

*I looked into Grayson's eyes reflecting the clear sky perfectly and felt as if my hurt and confusion were as obvious as the sun dancing on the water.*

Once outside the restaurant I nearly sprinted to the beach down beside the docks, dodging several people on the way. I took off my sandals and walked for a couple miles, letting the incoming waves splash about my ankles. All I could think of was that precious little girl and what a spitting image she was of her mother. My thoughts stretched to encompass Grayson and his obvious affection for Alana. What kind of a relationship did he have with Journey?

I sat down to watch the sun set in all its orange and amber brilliance, and was still sitting there listening to the soothing waves as an inky blackness filled the sky. But soon the stars began to wake up and twinkle merrily above me, joined by the sliver of a moon. I walked back under its dim light, with no answers to my questions. Had Journey suffered long? Had her heart ached for me as mine did for her? Apparently not, I decided, because she didn't come home to me, unless it was truly Chase that kept her away.

When I reached the shore by the docks I glanced at the outermost slip, where the silhouette of a white yacht stood between the moon and me. On the top deck was a shadowy outline of someone. It had to be Grayson. I almost believed he would not be there in the morning, that his boat would disappear into the dark horizon and leave its mooring space vacant permanently. I would lose Alana as I had lost Journey.

Impulsively I wanted to camp on the beach and watch the boat until dawn for fear of its leaving in the dead of night, just as Journey had done ten years ago. I sat in the sand and wondered if I really should keep an eye on this intriguing man, who might breathe life into my worst fears. I must have been in deep thought considering it, because when Alex walked up behind me, I nearly jumped out of my skin.

"I'm sorry. I didn't mean to startle you."

"No, that's okay. It's good to see you."

Alex sat next to me and we both watched Grayson, leaning on the railing of his upper deck.

"Are you going to take Alana away from him?"

I didn't know what to say. I wanted to adopt her with all my heart, but the truth of the matter was whether he knew it or not, Grayson had every right to keep his daughter.

"Do you think Grayson wants to raise her, on his boat all by himself?" I asked, hoping he would see how unreasonable that was.

"I think Grayson and Alana are as close as any natural father and daughter might be."

*Alex didn't know.* I was upset with myself for what I was thinking, sitting there in the cool sand, watching the water tumble in at our feet. I could adopt Alana out from under Grayson and no one, including him, would be any the wiser for my deceit. It would serve him right for not knowing he was the father. How could he not know? How truthful had my sister been in her letter?

"Alex, do you know who Alana's father is?" I asked, innocently enough.

"No." He sighed, and leaned back on his arms in the sand. "Journey told me once Alana's father didn't love her, and didn't have any idea he was the father."

"Did she love him, Alana's father?" I asked. I should have hoped Journey loved Grayson, and that was why she chose not to come home to me and deal with Chase. But I felt uneasy about her loving this man. Something about him made goose bumps appear on my arms.

"No, she didn't love him. And she didn't love Grayson either, at least, not like that. I think he was the father figure she never had. I know Journey relied on him heavily with her illness these last few months, and she trusted him completely with Alana."

"Did you love my sister, Alex?" I couldn't help but ask. It was so apparent he had feelings for her.

Alex sat up and looked over at me. "Is it that obvious?" He shook his head and stared up at the stars. "I only wish it would have been as obvious to her."

"Maybe it was," I answered softly, not needing to explain why, in her condition, Journey may have chosen not to acknowledge his feelings.

Alex began to swipe at silent tears with the back of his hand, and my own started to flow again. We sat there and cried beneath the stars while Grayson left his perch on the top deck and disappeared somewhere into the belly of his boat.

Soon thereafter Alex and I stood to leave. We hugged each other tightly, newly bonded by our grief. Then we went our separate ways, myself to a restless sleep that couldn't bring morning soon enough.

I arrived on the dock at eight a.m. and walked straight to the furthest slip, relieved to find the boat still there. Grayson was drinking coffee on the lower deck. He put a hand out to help me come aboard. I was ushered to a redwood table with matching deck chairs.

"Please, have a seat." Grayson poured me coffee while I sank comfortably into a royal blue cushion with the entire Pacific Ocean before me, as far as one could see. It was a remarkable view and made me want to live on a boat myself.

"Alana is sleeping," he commented, rather than saying good morning.

I looked into Grayson's eyes reflecting the clear sky perfectly and felt as if my hurt and confusion were as obvious as the sun dancing on the water.

"Why didn't Journey try to contact me?" I asked.

"Journey thought you would be opposed to the way she chose to treat her illness."

"Would I have been?"

Grayson shrugged his shoulders and studied his heavy white mug of coffee. "Maybe. There were lots of reasons she didn't contact you. That's just the excuse she always used."

Grayson sat his mug down on the table. "I wanted her to get in touch with you. She didn't seem to have anyone else, and she loved and admired you a great deal."

"Not enough to come home to me." My eyes stung with the truth of my own words. I couldn't bring myself to add that Journey had not trusted me to care for her young daughter, either.

"Being terminally ill does things to people," Grayson offered up. "We can't ever completely understand their thought processes in that situation."

Grayson behaved as cool as his logic. His every move was slow and calculated, his manners and tone of voice flawlessly smooth. But below the surface I sensed there was a hotbed of emotion, indignation, even outrage for what happened to Journey. It was there in his furrowed brows, the way he tightly cupped his mug.

"If she were taking so many drugs, and her illness progressed so much, why wasn't my little sister in the hospital?"

"Because she didn't want to be."

"Were you her only doctor?" I stood up, feeling restless that I didn't know all of this already, that I didn't know anything at all about my little sister's life in the last decade, or about her death in the last few months. I stood at the rail and focused on the sailboats near the horizon.

"Yes. At least while she was in Maui, I was her only doctor, but we brought several other doctors in for consultation."

"Where was my sister, before Maui?" Tears spilled down my cheeks, and I didn't care, because with Grayson seated behind me only the Pacific could see them.

"It is my understanding she came here from Oahu, where she lived with and worked among the artists at Waikiki."

Grayson walked over and stood beside me at the rail, holding his half-filled mug of coffee. I quickly wiped away my tears with shaky hands.

"She talked about an older woman, called Shalana, who taught her how to make jewelry. She apparently helped quite a bit with Alana as a baby. Alana is named for her."

I turned sideways and looked at him. "Why do you live on this boat?"

The question surprised him. I could see a sudden vulnerability in his eyes. Then he was quite frank with me. Perhaps he felt it was only fair since my sister chose to spend her last months, days, and hours with him.

"I didn't know where else to go when I left my wife, eight years ago. All I could think of was the boat for an immediate refuge. I've been here ever since."

"Are you divorced?"

"Yes, we divorced six months later."

"You didn't waste any time."

"No."

"There weren't any children then?"

"Yes. We have a daughter. She was five when I left." Grayson tossed his cold coffee into the Pacific and then stared into the waves.

"She must be thirteen. Do you see her often?"

"No. I haven't seen her since that night eight years ago."

I was shocked by his response. This man was so good with Alana, how could he walk out on a five-year-old and never look back? But I didn't ask him about it. I had pried enough for now. Somehow I felt less exposed, having pulled this painful event from Grayson. But then he counter-attacked with a question that caught *me* off guard.

"Am I going to lose Alana, too? Have you come to collect your niece?" Grayson looked straight at me with those eyes that nearly matched the sea for brilliant blue.

I was ill prepared to answer, not sure myself what my intent was. "Why? Do *you* want to raise her?"

Grayson leaned over the rail again, as if the Pacific could give him the words to explain. "I kept Alana after Journey's death initially, I think, to make up for having deserted Taylor all those years ago, illogical as that may sound even to me. But the truth, I have come to realize since your arrival, is that I have grown to love Alana as my own."

"I see. So what started out as penance has grown into something more." Even I cringed at the cynicism in my voice.

There was no time for Grayson to respond because just then Alana appeared on deck. He turned his attention to her with a cheery *good morning* while Alana wrapped suntanned arms around his leg. She smiled up at him. Grayson smoothed a few rumpled curls off her forehead and asked the child to sit down while he fetched some cereal.

I sat with Alana and we talked for a while, about how she loved to go snorkeling with Grayson, or fishing off the dock with Alex. She seemed to be a happy little girl, full of enthusiasm for life. Her eyes were solemn and betrayed the hurt of recent loss, but we didn't talk about that. We only discussed how she loved to snorkel and fish. Grayson soon rejoined us and I was invited to go to Molokini with them, so Alana could show me where she liked to snorkel. I agreed to go, and was happy to do so, leaving the yacht temporarily to gather my swimsuit and the lunch I insisted on brining.

The sea was calm as we left the marina and headed away from the harbor. I stood at the front rail on the main deck with Alana. Grayson was steering from inside the cabin. It wasn't a big yacht, or pretentious in any way, although the design and stark whiteness of it against a brilliant blue sea was impressive. I admired the teak deck that distinguished it from most boats in Lahaina Harbor, and wondered if Grayson ever sailed the motorized vessel.

We anchored near Molokini and helped each other adjust our snorkel gear. There were other boats in the distance, but not too near. Grayson said this was where the turtles came to avoid tourists. Sure enough, there were half a dozen surrounding us before we had wandered far from the boat.

Alana seemed in her element playing with the gentle creatures. Her tiny sliver of a body intensified their massive shells and rough skin. It was apparent how much she delighted in them, and it reminded me of times past when Journey and I would play with these sea creatures for hours on end. We had no fins or masks, but swam and dove with them as if it were the most natural thing for two little girls to do. It was soothing to have these memories come flooding back to me as I watched my sister's child wiggle her way among the tortoises.

Afterwards we lounged on the upper deck and let the sun dry out our drenched bodies. Grayson and Alana made lemonade and we ate the Ahi tuna sandwiches I brought from the Hula Grill. They went down well with the salty Hawaiian chips and sweet ripe mangos I'd also bought.

It felt as if I had done this snorkeling excursion many times with Grayson and Alana. There was no awkwardness, no formality to it. I marveled at Alana's ability to accept a near stranger so quickly into her trust. Like her mother, there seemed to be no real strangers to her, only friends waiting to be known.

Grayson was obviously at ease commanding the open sea in his yacht. I thought his forthright and gentle demeanor comforting. He manned the boat and cared for Alana in an unhurried way. Sometimes I would catch him looking at me and our eyes would meet, his so large and expressive it would nearly take my breath away. I sensed a longing in those ocean-deep eyes, but for what I didn't know.

"Are you ready for a cruise along the shore?" he asked of Alana and me.

"Yes!" Alana giggled and then slipped below into the cabin, perhaps to change out of her wet suit.

I stood at the rail as the boat cut through the water at a steady clip. The peach colored sundress I'd slipped on over my bikini blew wildly about in the wind. It was a spectacular day and cutting through the water at such a pace was exhilarating. I chided myself for having said a boat was no place to live. Quite the contrary, I had an inexplicable urge to never leave this yacht. Despite the warmth of the sun and wind, goose bumps broke out on my arms as I glanced at Grayson, focused on the horizon. The sun was glowing through his silhouette, making him appear to be a god almost, chiseled and powerful—in control of the beastly, untamable sea.

When had I felt this alive? Perhaps never, I decided.

After awhile I peeked inside the cabin to check on Alana, who had not returned to the deck, and found a sleeping angel draped across the sofa. Books and stuffed sea creatures were lying haphazardly about. After returning to the deck I told Grayson we had lost her to the land of dreams. He smiled. It wasn't often he smiled but when he did, his entire face lit up.

Grayson stopped the boat in a cove and silently we stood at the railing, admiring the secluded patch of sheltered sea.

"Do you come here often?" I asked.

"Yes. It's peaceful here, like a refuge from the storms of life. I came here on the day Journey died. I told Alana about her mother here." He took a deep breath of the sultry air. "I will tell you why I walked out on my wife, why I turned my back on Taylor, because you have a right to know."

"I do? And what gives me that right, exactly?"

"Alana. Your connection to her, to this child I would keep forever if given the choice. But it doesn't appear that will be an option."

I stared into the emerald tones shimmering off the Hawaiian Pacific and forced myself not to comment, not to admit to myself Grayson was being entirely more straightforward than I. He was gripping the rail and looked tense, as if this would be painful, and so I gave him my full attention. I did indeed wonder what happened between him and his wife that would cause him to give up his daughter, and live on a boat in Lahaina Harbor.

"I met Gwyneth in medical school," Grayson began. I wasn't prepared to fall in love and was even less prepared to fall for a woman who had her own ambitions in the competitive world of architectural design.

As much as my head thought it could never work between us, my heart didn't listen. Finally I came to the agonizing decision we should end our whirlwind romance. Not just because we rarely saw each other between our busy schedules, but also because I had hoped to marry a woman that would want to raise our children. Gwyneth spoke as if she never intended to have any."

Grayson was silent for a minute, reflecting.

"It was too late," he said with finality. "She was pregnant. We married quickly, quietly, eloping amongst strangers, and then frantically tried to build a normal life in what was not a normal situation. With me working ungodly hours and she having to put her career on hold until our child was born, things were tense."

"Did she stay home with Taylor?" I asked.

"Only the first few weeks. Then she arranged for our neighbor to watch Taylor, and returned to the hectic pace of her architecture apprenticeship. She was also in graduate school for design. We rarely saw each other between her schedule and my internship, except for stolen minutes a few evenings a week, when we were both home at the same time, with Taylor crying between us at the table, and neither of us knowing how to console her. Charisa, our neighbor, knew her habits and desires far better than we did. I often thanked God she was willing to watch Taylor in a loving home full of her own children who played alongside our daughter."

Grayson was silent again, a clouded look forming in those usually bright eyes. I dared not hurry him but waited patiently until he chose to continue.

"It was stupid of me really, not to see the signs, not to pick up on what is so apparent to me now."

"And what is that?" I prodded him, almost afraid to know.

"One day I came home early. My partner left well before me. Michael and I shared a new medical practice and had been close friends since early on in med school. But it was a slow day. The last two appointments canceled."

Grayson paused again, as if this conversation drained his energy. He ran well-manicured fingers through his thick gray hair, obviously stalling. I was sure he had never spoken to anyone about this before. I felt myself become nervous for him. He looked down into the water below, with his perfectly groomed surgeon hands folded over the railing, and continued.

"I couldn't wait to surprise my little family. They were not in the living room when I entered the house, but Gwyneth's car was in the driveway. I didn't want to call out, in case Taylor was napping as she often did in the late afternoon. But then I heard Taylor's laugh. I peered out the window and saw her on Charisa's swing. I decided Gwyneth must still be at Michael's and perhaps he'd given her a ride. My medical partner was not married yet, but he'd recently purchased a small pineapple plantation with an old estate on it. Gwyneth was redesigning the interior as her first independent project."

He stopped there and shrugged, as if to say fate altered the course of his life that day and there was nothing he could do about it.

"I walked into our bedroom thinking I would change clothes while I waited for Gwyneth," he continued. "Maybe we could bring a picnic dinner down to this very boat, an inheritance from my grandfather, who had recently died. We rarely had time to spend on it back then, except for Sunday afternoons."

Grayson was silent for a long second and I was holding my breath.

"And there she was, in the bed, with Michael."

"Oh Grayson, how terrible. I'm so sorry," I whispered, touching his arm to console him.

Grayson laughed. "Michael, of all people, my best friend, my medical partner, someone who hadn't taken the time to look for a girl to settle down with. And no wonder, because he had already fallen in love with my wife."

Alana came walking onto the deck just then, all sleepy-eyed. We both looked at her and it brought us back from Grayson's hellish memory of a time gone haywire. That's what this was, too, I concluded, a time gone haywire, with this child ripped from her mother by the fatal reality of a merciless disease. Not unlike Taylor was ripped from her father on that day he became emotionally unable to cope with his wife's betrayal.

I looked at Alana, into her brown eyes with the curled lashes, and saw my sister there. Whether betrayed by disease or matters of the heart, I sadly realized, once fate plays its hand there is no going back.

That was the hardest reality of all.

# CHAPTER FIVE

*Alana was lost in her imagination with the sea creatures, oblivious to my newly found secret treasure and the pangs of conscience I was having over what to do with it.*

I took Alana inside and got her a snack, while Grayson raised the anchor from our secluded cove. Afterwards we gathered books and animals from the sofa and took them to Alana's private quarters at the other end of the yacht. Her room had a cherry wood bunk attached to the far wall, with a built-in dresser below. Silver-framed pictures of sea creatures hung from oak paneling. A hand-sewn quilt sporting coral fish covered each bunk. I tossed the stuffed turtle and baby whale on the lower bed to join their other ocean friends.

"Who made your room so beautiful?" I asked.

"Mommy did it," Alana offered up, while tossing shorts and a shirt from her dresser drawer onto the bed. I rinsed her suit in the adjoining bathroom, tiny but efficient.

"Did your mommy pick out all these books?" I asked, admiring the collection on the shelf beside the bed. It had a front panel to keep the books from spilling out in rough seas.

"Sometimes Grayson and Alex buy me books." Standing on the bed she took a few from the shelf. "These are my favorites. Mommy bought them before she got too sick to shop." Hugging the books tightly to her chest, Alana stared out the portal as if her mama would be there, swimming beside the boat.

"I miss her too, Alana."

"Yes, but she's with the turtles," Alana informed me. "I know she is."

I hugged her and wanted to cry, but thought better of it. Instead I sat on the bed and we leaned against the wall, where Alana cuddled beside me to share her favorite books. One was about an old lady that swallowed a trout. It made us laugh and cheered us up a little. The other was a poetic tale about a mother and daughter who became sea turtles. They escaped pirates that seized their fishing boat. It was beautifully illustrated and I could see why Alana related to it so completely. If only she and her mommy could have become gentle giants beneath the sea, where bad things like pirates and cancer can't harm you.

"Let's comb your hair, Alana," I suggested after admiring the illustrations. They were prints made from original paintings, I noted, and a local author wrote the story. I put the books back on the shelf and reached for the hairbrush when my eye caught something wedged between the wall and dresser. It was an envelope. Carefully pulling it out with my fingernails, I saw Grayson's name written across the front, in Journey's handwriting. Alana's delicate voice was ringing in my ears as she chattered away, but I didn't hear what she said. I felt the boat slowing to dock and there were shouts from above. Suddenly it was very warm in the little room, even with the round porthole window fully open.

Alana was lost in her imagination with the sea creatures on the bunk; oblivious to my newly found secret treasure and the pangs of conscience I was having over what to do with it. Before I could convince myself otherwise my hand shoved the envelope halfway into my white bikini bottom, beneath the bright peach sundress.

I quickly combed through Alana's curls before we appeared on deck, looking fresh and ready to go fishing with Alex, who had generously offered to take us when done snorkeling. Grayson decided he would bow out of that activity, but we agreed to meet him for dinner at the Hula Grill.

"I'll see you later." Grayson bent to kiss Alana on the forehead. He looked at me and I felt him study my expression. Did he know I felt guilty about something? Could he sense my discomfort? If he did, nothing indicated his concern.

Alex bounced onto the deck when he finished tying the ropes securely. "Are you ready to catch some fish?" He looked at Alana who nodded her head enthusiastically. Alex laughed. "Let's go then."

I pulled the letter from my bikini bottom and hid it in my straw bag, telling myself I could still give it to Grayson at an opportune moment.

The water was so clear beside the dock you could see the fish hovering below the surface. Alana and I admired them while Alex baited our poles. It wasn't long until my little niece hooked a tiny silver fish and squealed with delight. We slipped it into a bucket where it happily swam around in circles. When done admiring her catch, Alana put her newly baited pole back in the water and sat beside me on the dock.

I already felt so close to Journey's daughter, having bonded more in a day than Elise and Chenlei had in three months. But my conscience was nagging me, telling me I had become a desperate and conniving person of little ethics for taking the letter.

I aggressively reeled in the extra line on my fishing rod, and Alex laughed.

"It doesn't help to lose your patience with fish."

I smiled and adjusted the brim of my hat. "I know. It's just that my line had too much slack in it."

The more I thought, the angrier I became with myself, and then somehow I managed to redirect my unhappiness toward God, who had not allowed me the opportunity to bear children. He had given me plenty of children to love, just none of my own. There had been a baby sister to care for when only a child myself, and there was Chenlei but she belonged to my best friend, who unfortunately was frozen with fear in her presence. And now Alana, my little niece, who just so happened to be living with her natural father, only neither of them knew it.

All I needed was one tiny excuse to whisk her away from here, from this dock we dangled our lines over, this harbor and this man with the yacht, who was as complex as they came. One tiny excuse and it would be done. I became restless waiting for lazy fish to bite, and after announcing a need to freshen up before dinner, asked Alex if he would return Alana safely to Grayson's boat. Then I gathered up my things to take off for my room, where in the privacy of my own guilt I could read words not meant for me, but for Dr. Conner, who was quickly becoming my nemesis.

Before leaving the pier, I took a long look at Alana talking to the tiny fish she had caught, swimming in Alex's bucket. Her long brown curls fell haphazardly into the metal pail and reminded me of her mother's wildly wavy locks that had been strikingly similar. As I walked back to my motel room across the harbor all I could think about was Alana and how in a way, it was like having Journey back. How could I not be a part of her everyday life? How could I ever part from Alana at all, now that I had met her, and fallen in love with my little niece?

I took a shower and then sat at the table by the window where I rummaged through the straw bag until finding the letter I had shoved to the bottom. It hurt to look at Journey's beautiful penmanship scrawled across the front of the envelope. I couldn't bear the reality of my unethical motives for stealing this letter she had written for someone else. Glancing out the window I could almost see the furthest slip where Grayson moored his yacht. How unfortunate for him this letter had slipped behind the dresser.

I began pacing the small room. All this thinking was giving me a headache. Maybe I needed caffeine. Grabbing a diet drink from the mini fridge I flipped the tab while staring at my stolen treasure there on the table where I'd left it. Half of the fizzy cola was gone before I dared touch it again. I held the envelope up to the late afternoon sun streaming in the window, but the additional light did not reveal its contents.

I reasoned with myself that I could put the letter in a new envelope, and give it to Grayson as if I'd never read it. Somehow that seemed less devious than all other options running through my mind, like never giving it to him at all, and using the contents against him if I could. Feeling as if I had a plan for possible redemption, I carefully ran a fingernail along the inside of the top edge. I pulled out the single sheet of white stationary and unfolded the middle crease, while holding my breath.

There were tiny purple flowers dancing across the paper, and it smelled like lavender. I admired my sister's beautiful curvy and fluid handwriting. Everything she did had an artist's flair, whether arranging flowers, building sandcastles, or writing letters. I remembered Grayson telling me Alana was named for a Shalana who taught Journey how to make jewelry. I could only imagine how striking my little sister's handmade jewelry would be.

Knowing this letter was not meant for my eyes somehow made me stare at the words for the longest second and not really comprehend their meaning. But then the sentences began to flow easily, one into another, like the tears I shed while reading it.

> *Dear Grayson,*
>
> *I am going for a night swim. I realize the foolishness of this considering the many drugs I have ingested to dull this throbbing in my head, but I am a good swimmer. I want to see the turtles one last time to say goodbye. They are all around the boat tonight, calling to me, requesting a final swim for old time's sake. Kylie and I swam for hours with the turtles as children. They would linger as we romped together in our ocean playground.*
>
> *Maybe I will become one of these tortoises like in Alana's storybook, and then I can roam the sea forever, keeping watch over my beloved daughter. Alana is why I write this. In case I cannot will my weakened limbs to bring me safely back from my late night swim. She is yours, Grayson.*
>
> *I have wanted to tell you many times, but it is difficult. You do not remember our one night together. You had just left your wife weeks before. Your yacht was full of partying neighbors, and rum your only friend. I was barely eighteen, emotional and confused, upset that my boyfriend had found someone new. This is how I came to be in Maui and on your boat partying with virtual strangers. I snuck into your*

*cabin to find refuge from the merry crowd up on deck.*

*You collapsed beside me sometime in the night. I was crying softly, feeling sorry for myself, as full of rum as you were. I was not frightened when you clumsily put your arm around me, having observed all evening what a kind and gentle man you were. Sympathetic about my broken heart you told me how young surfer boys should be tied to their boards and whipped for how they treated women. I smile now at your telling me the best I could hope for would be to swear off all men forever, as you had sworn off women.*

*We fell asleep that way, lying there together, and sometime during the night we made love, perhaps to forget our misery and ward off our pain, perhaps to feel anything at all again. I left at dawn, more sober than not. When I discovered I was pregnant, I knew immediately it was yours. I have never regretted it. Not my night of comfort in your arms, or this beautiful child we conceived, whom you have come to know and love as I do. I leave her now in your good hands. I envy you the chance to watch her grow into a woman.*

*~Journey*

I folded the letter and placed it back in the envelope, set it down on the table and stared out the widow. I couldn't bear to dwell on it, dwell on how I read something meant for another, had betrayed not just anyone, but my precious, dead sister. At least that's how it felt. Grayson didn't matter. I didn't want him to matter. I didn't want him to be Alana's father. I refused to believe it completely. Journey always tried to wish into being things that simply were not so.

As a child her imagination often obscured the truth. She would pretend we had normal parents and normal lives, where the mother fixes dinner and the father reads the paper, and I would play along with her game. We would give names to these fictitious parents, and make up pretend conversations, and then we would get silly and be funny, but the intent and the longing was serious. Sometimes, when we met strangers in town, they would ask about our parents, and Journey would paint the same picture with the same names we had invented on the beach while walking in the wet sand at high tide. I would look at her, shocked and dismayed. But she never indicated remorse for her imaginings.

Perhaps this was more of that. I decided right then I would investigate where she had been and what she had done in the last ten years, before giving Alana up to Dr. Grayson Connor on no more evidence than this poetic and possibly make-believe letter. It seemed fair enough since she hadn't told him, hadn't established a relationship with him beyond her need of his medical attention and a roof over her head. The night could have been a rum induced dream, or the letter a final wish helped along by heavy painkillers, a wish that this generous and passionate man would provide for Alana.

I found myself pacing again in the little room, pondering my next move when the cell phone rang. It was Elise.

"Kylie, how are you? Did you find Alana?"

"Yes." I sat on the bed heavily. "And she looks just like Journey, Elise. I can't believe it."

"That's wonderful. I bet you're dying to bring her back here."

"I am going to bring her, for a visit anyway," I said without confidence, since I didn't know what Grayson or Alana would think of such a plan.

"What do you mean, for a visit?" Elise sounded confused.

"I mean, I don't want to just uproot her from everything she's familiar with. And then there's Grayson."

"What about Grayson? Is he the father?"

"No one seems to know who her father is," I lied. "But Grayson would like to keep her."

"You're not going to let a stranger raise her, are you?"

"Lot's of things are up in the air right now, Elise. I need time to think."

Journey **47**

I hoped that would appease her. I couldn't bring myself to admit I might not end up with Alana because my conscience might not let me.

"Someone here wants to talk to you, Kylie."

I knew Elise meant Chenlei. It was touching to hear her try and speak clear English to me. I kept my sentences simple and basically said I was bringing Alana home to play with her for a few days, hopefully. I almost cried when she said *I love you* before giving the phone back to Elise.

We no sooner said goodbye and I realized it was time to meet Grayson, Alana, and Alex for dinner at the Hula Grill.

I prayed my guilt about the letter wouldn't show.

# CHAPTER SIX

*I wanted to give back the letter while begging forgiveness, but instead I calmly took Alana by the hand and held her suitcase in the other.*

I waited at a table for four and tried not to think about what I had done, opening Journey's letter meant for Grayson. I wondered what her birth certificate said, and where it could be. Perhaps in the chest, I decided, which made me a little more eager to go through Journey's things. I wanted desperately to bring Alana back with me for a visit, and was hoping that would not upset Grayson, or Chase. He could be as unhappy about me bringing her to the Big Island as Grayson would be sorry to see her go. But he was still in Colorado until tomorrow, and not reachable by cell phone, so it would be a coming home surprise.

It would be up to Alana of course. I was not going to force the trip on her, so soon after losing her mother. There was plenty of time for a Big Island visit, or perhaps a move there permanently. I felt a twinge of longing overshadowed by guilt as Alana came running up with a big hug. She began telling me all about the *very big fish* Alex caught off the dock. She held her hands out as far as they would stretch.

I looked up at Alex, and his broad grin told me it was true.

"It was a fluke, really. The big ones never come that close to the pier. I threw it back with Alana's baby fish." He mussed her hair and we all laughed about her tiny fish swimming happily in the bucket.

Grayson was quiet while we were being seated, giving me the courage to blurt out what was on my mind. "Would you like to come to the Big Island for a few days, and see where your mama and I grew up?" I asked, my eyes darting from Alana to Grayson and back again. Alana grinned and clapped her hands.

"I was thinking four days, just a long weekend really." I studied Grayson's face, trying to read his thoughts.

"If it's okay with Alana, then I have no objection," he said quite civilly.

"I leave in the morning," I added, still looking for the slightest hesitation from any of them, even Alex, but there was none.

Grayson shrugged his shoulders. "It would do her good to spend time with her aunt and uncle, see how land people live."

Alex and Alana laughed. I smiled. "Okay then, we need to pack your things, right after dinner." I winked at Alana.

Grayson and I worked out the details during dessert.

I followed them back to the yacht, where Alana and I packed her little suitcase with clothing, a few small sea creatures, and two of the more treasured books from the shelf. When finished we went looking for Grayson. He was on the top deck by the railing, as he had been my first night in Lahaina.

"Alana, are you sure about this?" he asked with fatherly concern.

She nodded enthusiastically.

"Well then, give me a big hug to last until you return." He knelt down and scooped her up. I wanted to give back the letter while begging forgiveness, but instead I calmly took Alana by the hand and held her suitcase in the other. I thanked Grayson for allowing this visit on such short notice. He nodded and bent down one last time to whisper *I love you* in her ear.

It nearly broke my heart to know he meant it.

Alana and I slept cuddled together in the queen-size bed and checked out early to catch the first flight to Kona. My little niece was used to sleeping in like a pampered princess on Grayson's yacht, and so she dozed in her seat across the Pacific.

When we reached the house on the bluff beside the sea there were no signs of Chase having returned yet. I decided it was time to meet

Chenlei who was at home with Quinn, and was expecting us. We walked over the hill hand in hand and occasionally stopped to pick a pretty flower until we had a bouquet of the tropical delicacies. Our beautiful arrangement had a strong sweet scent that enticed every bee in the field to buzz near us. We would run from them squealing, and then laugh, out of breath.

Once we reached the Damask home Alana was eager to show Chenlei the flowers. She knocked enthusiastically on the door. Chenlei answered it, her small presence in the doorway seeming more delicate than I remembered. I knelt down and we hugged tightly. Then we both looked at Alana, who handed the bouquet to Chenlei. Her eyes lit up with delight as she stared appreciatively at our fragrant gift.

Quinn stood in the doorway beside Chenlei and smiled. "So this is Journey's child." He bent down and gently shook her hand. "Welcome, Alana. Chenlei's been waiting for you."

The little girls looked at each other and giggled. They seemed destined to be kindred spirits, despite the physical differences between them. My Asian friend was quite petite, and starkly pale. Her jet-black hair fell into place with a discipline few people have, whereas Alana's long tanned limbs and unruly curls appeared unstructured and somewhat on the wild side.

"Why don't you show Alana your room, Chenlei?" Quinn suggested as he motioned us into the house.

Chenlei reached for Alana's hand, and they walked together down the hall.

"I bet they don't come up for air until lunchtime," I said while flopping into an easy chair. It had a perfect view out the window of lush green hills rolling slowly into the sea.

"I bet you're right," Quinn laughed. "Chenlei's been more excited about your return and meeting your niece than she was about coming to America." He sat on the sofa and put his feet up on the coffee table.

"What could be more exciting than being adopted and moving to America?" I asked.

*Journey* **51**

"Feeling accepted by your new mother." He sighed. "I'm not sure Elise will ever warm up to her."

"What do you mean?" I appeared puzzled, but I knew exactly what he meant.

"I mean, Elise is so reserved around Chenlei. It's as if a part of her is afraid to fully embrace the child."

"That's your professional analysis of the situation, Dr. Damask?" I asked, making light of Quinn's very real concern. I didn't want him to become any more worried than he already was, so I didn't let on that I was worried, too.

"Okay, well, what do I know?" Quinn answered defensively. "But I think Elise spends every waking minute at her bookstore in order to avoid Chenlei."

I leaned forward in my chair and looked right into Quinn's eyes. "Elise just needs time. It's not like she carried this child for nine months. Some people adjust much more slowly to new situations, and adopting a child is a life-altering event. That's why they screen you carefully and it isn't for everyone."

"I hope you're right." Quinn stared past me, out the window. "This is more stress than I need, with my busy teaching schedule at the university this fall." He rubbed his temples. "I don't known if we've done the right thing, bringing Chenlei here," he confessed.

"What do you mean, Quinn? You adore her, and Elise will come around."

"I don't know about that, Kyl."

I stood to leave. "Quinn, I promise to do everything I can to help. I'll talk to Elise, and don't worry, have a little faith. It's only been three months."

After consulting with the little girls it was decided they would stay at Chenlei's until after lunch. I promised them we would make a trip to the bookstore this afternoon to see Elise. Quinn reminded me about the faculty get-together later this evening for the fall kickoff. I told him that's why I returned home this morning.

My next concern was Chase. Hopefully, he had arrived back from

Colorado by now and I could see him alone before Quinn walked the little girls over after lunch. I could only imagine what his reaction would be. Especially once he saw Alana's strong resemblance to Journey. I could only hope he would become as attached to her as I already had. Chase was a reasonable man, and he loved children, despite his difficulties with my sister. These thoughts were heavy on my mind as I walked over the hill toward home.

And then there he was, all six feet of him, the dark hair falling across his forehead mischievously, just as always. Standing in the doorway he looked at me carefully, as if checking my emotional pulse. I walked up to him and put my arms around his neck.

"Welcome home, stranger," I whispered in his ear.

"I missed you, Kylie."

"Alana is here for a visit. I left her at Elise and Quinn's to play with Chenlei for a while." I offered this up while sitting down on the porch swing, where just a couple days ago I had told Chenlei about my plans to find Journey's child. And now they were playing together as I had suggested they might.

Still filling the doorway with his tall lanky frame, Chase stared at the blue sky. "So I take it you found Grayson and he had Alana?"

"Yes, and he still has her, technically. She is only here for a visit. I wanted you to at least meet her, Chase. And I wanted Alana to see where her mother grew up." I stopped swinging, not taking my eyes from him, disturbed by the tension in his body. He was angry and being careful not to betray this emotion to me, but I could tell by the tight shoulders, the set jaw.

"Did you tell Grayson he's the father?"

Guilt made my heart pound. "No. I'm not sure *he is* the father. I need to do some investigating."

"You think your sister lied in her letter? Why would she do that? I mean, I know she was head strong and stubborn, but she was more than happy to be honest to a fault." Chase walked over and sat on the porch step, not interested in being cozy with me on the swing.

"Journey was honest with you, Chase, because her frankness upset you. But she was always confusing fantasy with reality as a child."

I began rocking again, while Chase sat very still on the porch step.

"If you'd realized it was her goal to make you angry, you'd have understood her better." I jumped off the swing and sat beside him. "Chase, I want to raise a family and we may never have children of our own."

"We don't know that, Kyl. I don't see any reason to adopt yet. Damn, we still have a couple of years to get pregnant. Maybe we should at least visit a fertility specialist."

I nodded, even though I didn't want in vetro fertilization, especially since both of us checked out okay after extensive tests. There were no physical reasons interfering with natural conception, except that time was running out on my biological clock. All I could think about was how many Chenleis there were who needed a home. And now there was Alana.

"Chase, this is my sister's child, not a reincarnation of my sister." I paused there and took a long slow breath, not wanting to seem agitated. "Can't you understand what it would mean to me for us to raise her?"

"Even if I did want to raise Alana, it's wrong to keep this child from her real father." Chase turned and looked at me, his eyes flashing with frustration. "My God, Kylie, you're so obsessed with this whole idea of raising her, you can't even admit he *is* the father, or that you're wrong to do this to him."

The silence at my end was as heavy as my heart. I knew Chase's words might be bitingly correct. But I wouldn't know for sure until I at least saw this Shalana and spoke with her about Journey's decade away from me.

Chase stood up. "I need to go into the office for a few hours and catch up on some things."

"Okay," I said, happy to change the subject. "When the girls get here I'm taking them to Elise's bookstore, so she can meet Alana."

I stood up and hugged him. He didn't resist and it wasn't long until his body softened and melted into mine. Thoughts of love making later that night crept into my conscience and made my libido race.

Chase kissed me lightly on the forehead and headed for his pickup. I waved him off and then went inside to unpack for Alana, and make sure the spare bedroom was inviting for our little guest. I was taking chocolate chip cookies from the oven when I saw Quinn smiling through the kitchen window. The girls came skipping in the door, full of giggles.

"Well, it would appear you two are fast friends already," I commented while pouring them a glass of milk. They each chose a cookie and sat daintily at the table. I smiled, thinking what a contrast they were to Austin and Wyatt, who would have tumbled in the door like wild cubs—grabbing a cookie for each hand.

"Where are the boys?" I asked, knowing they should be home from school by now.

"They're waiting in the SUV." Quinn reached for a cookie but didn't sit down. "We're headed to soccer practice," he said with his mouth full.

"Here, take these." I handed him a napkin filled with warm cookies.

"Thanks, Kyl. Elise is expecting you. I called her on the cell phone."

We watched him leave with his special bundle for the boys.

"Well, girls, what do you think? Would it be fun to visit Chenlei's mama at her bookstore?"

They looked at each other and grinned widely, cookie crumbs sticking to their bottom lips. After the snack I showed them where Alana would sleep, and for a while they fussed with the dolls and animals on the bed, little treasures from my own past. Before heading out the door for our bookstore adventure, Alana stopped in front of the teak wood chest under the living room window. I stood beside her and we stared at it, while Chenlei quietly took hold of Alana's hand.

"Do you want me to open it and we can see what's inside?" I asked, almost reverently.

Alana shook her head no.

"If you change your mind, you let me know, okay?" I rubbed her shoulders lightly.

"Okay," she agreed.

We positioned ourselves in the jeep and clicked on our seatbelts,

*Journey* **55**

each lost in our own thoughts as we headed for Elise's shop on the main tourist strip, which ran parallel to a bay full of boats. I had already decided to buy each of the girls a book, and after a while I cheerily asked what they might pick. Chenlei couldn't decide what type of book she wanted without seeing them, but Alana knew immediately she wanted another book about sea turtles. I hoped Elise's store was well stocked with aquatic stories.

    I didn't want Alana to be disappointed.

# CHAPTER SEVEN

*I looked into her dark eyes and saw the many
ways in which she could relate to being lost.*

The sun reflecting off the ocean was especially brilliant as we drove past the bay. A stone wall cushioned pedestrians from waves, and a cement sidewalk led to endless shops. It was known as *the strip* with delightful wares ranging from exquisite art to the humblest of tourist paraphernalia. Boats were speckled in the sea and dwarfed by a huge cruise ship farther out. Some tourists were walking about, but were scarce for the most part with school having resumed on the mainland.

The girls scrambled into the bookstore a few paces ahead of me, all giggly and unaware of those few patrons browsing the shelves. It was a moment that stuck in my memory as Chenlei's first display of uninhibited behavior. She was simply glowing with happiness. This was not the guarded child of only yesterday. A milestone had been reached, and all because of Alana.

"Hi girls!" Elise said as she walked up to greet them. "You must be Alana." Elise pushed some of the brown curls off my little niece's shoulder. "You sure do look like your mother." My best friend appeared almost mesmerized by the resemblance. It took her back as it had me, to when Journey was still filling our lives with her energizing presence. Alana had inherited that ability to command attention without making an overt effort.

"I told the girls I'd buy them each a book," I said while putting a hand on Chenlei's shoulder. She was noticeably subdued in her new mother's presence.

Elise kissed her foreign daughter on the cheek. "Are you having fun playing hooky?" she asked.

Chenlei smiled and nodded.

"Well, tomorrow it's off to school with you, but I did check with your teacher, and it will be fine for Alana to visit." Elise looked at Alana. "Would you like to attend school with Chenlei tomorrow?"

My niece peered up at me.

"I realize you're in second grade and not first like Chenlei, but I bet you'll be a big help to the teacher," I said encouragingly, knowing Chenlei would be disappointed if Alana didn't come to school with her.

The girls glanced at each other and giggled again, a form of communication common to all little girls regardless of where they were born. I showed them the children's book aisle and they delved into the task of finding the perfect purchase, while Elise and I sat at an antique table for two in the corner of the shop. Sun streamed in the window and lit up a small crystal vase filled with deep purple flowers placed in the center of it. Elise gave attention to detail few others were capable of. Her shop was cluttered but comfortable, giving a sense of order and purpose to every book and antique it housed.

She had brand new books and very old books, and all of them were for sale. Like the antiques, the books she sold were handpicked for good variety and excellent quality. Of course a lack of space forced her to be discriminating, but Elise liked it that way. It gave her an excuse to be a literary snob without having to admit her reading biases.

I handed her a latte out of a white paper bag I had placed on the table when the girls and I came in. "It's your favorite," I said. "Fat free hazelnut with extra foam."

"Gee, thanks. What else you got in that bag?" Elise pulled out two raspberry muffins while I took the lid off my latte to help it cool. Raspberry was our favorite, and the perfect special indulgence for this memorable day, Alana's first in Elise's bookstore. I could only pray it would not be the last.

Elise studied me over her steaming latte. "Kylie, tell me about Alana.

And this man with the boat, Grayson is it? Did he send the chest?"

"Yes, he did. He's a doctor." I paused there, my emotions welling up.

"What is it, Kyl?"

"Elise, Journey had cancer, a brain tumor."

Elise shook her head in disbelief. "I'm so sorry. I can't believe it."

"I know." I swallowed hard. "Grayson is a surgeon, and he lives on a yacht in Lahaina Harbor. He let Journey and Alana live on his boat all summer, knowing that my sister was dying." I paused there. "Why didn't she contact me, Elise?"

"Kyl, you know Journey would have run home to you in a heartbeat. It was Chase that kept her away. She feared coming between the two of you, and it isn't really Chase's fault. Some things just are the way they are."

"Chase got home this afternoon from Colorado, and he wasn't pleased about the surprise guest. He wants nothing to do with Journey's child."

"Who do you think is the father?" Elise asked.

"I'm not sure. I need to make a trip to Waikiki and talk to a woman named Shalana. That's supposedly where Journey spent all her time after she left here."

"Did Grayson tell you that?"

"Yes. Grayson wants to keep Alana."

"You'd like to come up empty handed in your search for Alana's father, wouldn't you?"

"Yes," I confessed. "I want nothing more than for her to be an orphan and for Chase to fall in love with Alana in the next few days."

We were both silent a minute. I knew Elise had a million questions she wasn't asking out of respect for my feelings. I thought it an opportune time to change the subject.

"How is Chenlei adjusting in school?" I asked, almost afraid of what I would hear.

Elise shrugged and glanced at the girls. "About as well as you could expect. She is shy and withdrawn, and Miss Roberts was afraid at first her pained expression meant she might break into tears at any moment. But I think Chenlei's teacher is figuring out that beneath that somber face lives one tough little girl. Chenlei is a survivor."

"Whatever she is trying to overcome is what obviously haunts her. I would love to know what that is," I confessed.

"I don't know, Kylie. No one can give me any details about her past." Elise stared out the window at the cars driving by. "I've been all through the limited information on Chenlei at the Hope Adoption office and there is no background on her to speak of. She came to the orphanage from a street vendor who was using her to solicit sales, before he was arrested for stealing those wares he was selling."

Elise rolled her eyes and nibbled on her muffin while I tried to imagine what all Chenlei might have experienced in her six short years.

"And before the street vendor no one knows anything about her?" I asked, finding it hard to understand how there could be no records about her birth, or her family.

"We think her mother died in bed one night and Chenlei was there, sleeping beside her. She's been having nightmares ever since she arrived and is finally able to communicate well enough to tell us that much."

"Do you really think that happened?" I asked.

"Chenlei told Quinn one night after waking up screaming that her mother was sick. And that she lost the baby inside her, not yet big enough to be born." Elise smoothed her hair back, obviously uncomfortable with this information. "Chenlei burst into tears when she told Quinn this. I was standing at the foot of the bed, watching Quinn comfort her. Chenlei went on to say when she woke up in the morning her mother didn't move beside her, and there was blood everywhere."

Elise paused, fighting back tears. "Chenlei began to shake when she spoke of the blood and Quinn just held her until she calmed down."

"How terrible for her," I said under my breath, while observing the girls on the floor paging through a book together. "I wonder if that's when her mother died, and she ended up with the street vendor."

"Probably," Elise answered. "Kyl, I've longed for a little girl ever since Austin was born and we nearly lost him, and Dr. Lang told me there would be no more children. Once I got involved with Hope Adoption, and helped Edward start their office here in Kona, it became clear to me I would love to have one of these foreign children, an older harder-to-place child like Chenlei. I knew it meant there would be a history there to deal with, but the ghosts that haunt Chenlei may be more than Quinn and I can navigate through."

"What do you mean, Elise?"

"I mean this child is coming between us."

"How?" I asked, surprised, and yet Quinn had seemed equally frustrated with Elise earlier when we spoke. It puzzled me that this sweet child, despite her tragic past, could cause such turmoil in a relationship as strong as theirs.

"Quinn absolutely adores her," Elise shared, wiping away a tear.

"Isn't that a good thing?" I asked.

"It is and it isn't. I mean, he is so protective and possessive of her."

I stared at Elise for a minute. "It sounds as if you're jealous of Chenlei's relationship with Quinn. That doesn't make sense, Elise. You aren't an insecure person."

Elise stared back at me. "Well, I hadn't thought of it that way. Every time I try to discuss his obsession with her, he becomes defensive and turns it all on me, saying I'm the one with the abnormal response to Chenlei. But she doesn't let me in the way she does him."

"Maybe that's out of loyalty to her mother, whereas she never knew her father, at least, that we know of."

Elise shrugged. "I don't know why their relationship has affected me this way. I guess because I feel left out in the cold wondering how to fit in. So, I just dote that much more on the boys and leave them to their private world."

We drank our warm drinks in deep thought, observing the girls sitting cross-legged on the floor, mismatched pair that they were, yet completely aligned through tragic loss.

I wondered if Quinn was really being so unreasonable, or if that was just how it appeared through Elise's bright green eyes. Green with envy it would seem at the moment, for Quinn's displaced affection.

Elise got up and tossed her empty cup into the trash just as the girls came skipping over, each with a book in their hands.

"Well, what did we decide on?" I asked enthusiastically.

Chenlei handed me a book about a little girl whose family lost her for a short time at the zoo. The animals took care of the girl, and helped find her family. The words were just challenging enough for my approval. I looked into her dark eyes and saw the many ways in which she could relate to being lost. What a dream come true to have zoo animals help you locate your missing loved ones, not to mention calming your fears of abandonment.

Alana had chosen a book about her precious sea turtles. It was written by a Hawaiian and was filled with beautiful illustrations just like the book her mother had bought her. The tale was charming and based on a legend about the gentle creatures of the sea.

We purchased the books and Elise hugged each girl goodbye, saying she'd see them later while Quinn and I attended the faculty meeting. They nodded and ran out the door to sit on the bench by the front window.

"Elise," I whispered, "I'll talk to Quinn tonight, I promise."

"What could you say that might make a difference?" Elise whispered back skeptically.

"Just that you're feeling a little left out, with his doting on Chenlei every second."

"That makes me sound pathetic, Kyl."

"No. He'll see how insensitive he's been. And how he needs to back off a little as the overprotective dad, so you and Chenlei can have a chance to get to know each other."

"Kylie, I almost forgot to tell you, I think you're getting closer to being approved for adopting a child. That is, if you still want one."

We both glanced at Alana out on the bench.

"You're kidding? Yes, of course I still want to adopt. There is room in my heart for more than one little girl. Besides, I don't know yet what will happen with Alana."

"I thought so." Elise smiled. "Your name has come up again for review, and as always I put in lots of positive strokes for you and Chase. It's just that . . ." Elise stopped there mid-sentence.

"What Elise? What's holding everything up?"

"Chase's traveling. There's a concern about him being gone too much."

I sighed and looked at the girls again. They were reading their new books.

"Can't he travel a little less?" Elise questioned.

I leaned on the counter and looked frankly at her. "Elise, if Chase had his way we wouldn't adopt at all. He wants to have his own children."

Elise slowly nodded. "Well maybe he would change his mind if we had a child for him to consider. I'll do everything I can for you, Kyl."

"I know you will." I hugged Elise tightly and left as tears welled up and blurred my vision. Luckily the girls didn't notice.

On the way home I tried to recall when Elise first became involved with Edward, who ran the adoption agency. He had been in the bookstore a few times and then one thing led to another until little orphaned girls from China became Elise's sole hope for a daughter. Soon she was volunteering all her free time to help Edward open and run the Kona office.

I listened to the little girls chattering in the back of the jeep, and tried to think of a way to plead with Chase to cut back on his helicopter jobs in other locations. Why couldn't he hire someone else to run operations outside of Hawaii?

Elise had offered to keep the girls all evening, thinking it would be awkward for Alana to be alone with Chase. Of course, it shouldn't be awkward. It should be the most natural thing, wanting to get to know my sister's child. But that was not the case. I didn't want to admit Grayson would make a far better choice for a father figure in Alana's life than Chase at the moment. But I also knew Alana needed a mother, and judging by Grayson's trauma with Gwyneth, it didn't appear he'd marry again any time soon.

*Journey*

I could only hope that once I found Shalana, she would shed light on the truth, and the truth would be that some random surfer boy was the dad. Some free roaming spirit who would be glad to never know. Someone Journey wished to conveniently replace with a responsible man like Grayson. My little sister was a brilliant storyteller, and no one believed her tales more than she did.

Once we were back at the house on the bluff the girls climbed onto the front porch swing with their books, while I mentally planned my visit to Oahu, to speak with Shalana.

# CHAPTER EIGHT

*"Had I known she wouldn't return on her own, I would have chased her to the ends of the earth," I said, wishing I had done exactly that.*

In the late afternoon I walked the girls over to the Damask home and asked Elise to bring me some books on brain cancer from her store. I wanted to be informed about what Journey had died of. After many hugs and kisses, and promises to Alana that she would meet her Uncle Chase tomorrow evening, I took off for the university. The girls had talked me in to a slumber party at Chenlei's for the night, and in the morning Elise would deliver them both to Chenlei's school.

The campus was no different than when I'd last seen it, despite my personal life having changed significantly. Classes started in a couple weeks and I wanted to spend a few hours preparing lesson plans before attending the staff meeting. Hoping not to see anyone else arriving early, I slipped into my private office. It was quite small but had a big window looking out over the grounds. The window gave a much larger feel to the tiny space.

Quinn had introduced me to the idea of teaching on this campus. He moved here from the Big Island to be full time faculty at the university. We both met Elise that same summer at her bookstore. She had arrived all the way from France to live in the summer home her grandparents had willed to her.

At first I thought they seemed like a mismatch. Tall slender Elise was fastidious, forever planning and prowling about. Even when her body was still, her cat eyes bounced from one shadow to the next. She sought perfectionism in every aspect of her life. Whether buying antiques and out-of-print books, or assembling her personal wardrobe, details mattered to Elise, whereas short stocky Quinn always wore t-shirts and cross trainers. His wardrobe matched his laid-back attitude and subtle humor, which served him well as a history buff and soccer coach.

I think what I liked the most about Quinn was his steadfast humility. He was a favorite history teacher at the university and a superb athlete, but you would never know these things about him unless you saw it for yourself. He and Elise turned out to be perfect for one another, and I envied them that, since Chase and I always seemed to create continual friction rather than balanced harmony.

Of course Journey had been a major reason for the disharmony in our newly merged lives. My sister had never shared me with anyone before, and had never experienced having a father or brother, or any male presence in her life. It was not surprising that she resented Chase, especially since he tried to intervene and change the course of her rebellious teenage behavior.

I pondered all this while sitting at my desk achieving nothing but these recollections while the sun set in its usual spectacular fashion. Just as the last stream of light left the horizon a gentle knock preceded Quinn popping his head in and asking if I was ready for the meeting.

"I was just thinking about when you first came to the island and met Elise. It wasn't long after that when Journey left."

"Are you feeling remorseful about the way things turned out?" Quinn sat down and sighed. He seemed weary rather than rested, not having much turnaround between the summer and fall session. He usually taught somewhere out of the country in the summer, on exchange from the university. At first it was a way to visit his mother's homeland of China and stay connected to extended family there, but then he quit going to China at some point and began traveling to other foreign shores instead. He'd said those he'd known and cared about had passed on and he needed to expand his knowledge of other locations, to enrich his lectures. It didn't give him much downtime between summer and fall sessions.

"Had I known she wouldn't return on her own, I would have chased her to the ends of the earth," I said, wishing I had done exactly that.

"There is just never any way to know what the future holds, is there?" Quinn shook his head. "None of us could have known Journey would raise a baby on her own or get cancer and die. Not even Journey knew, when she left, how the hands of fate would shape her decade away from us."

"I still don't understand the part Grayson played in all this," I admitted. "Elise is getting me some of the latest books on brain cancer. I want to know more about how he treated her disease, and why he said Journey thought I wouldn't approve."

"Is that what he said?"

"Exactly. It isn't like he'd tried to hide anything, but he didn't offer up much information either."

Quinn slid down sloppily into the leather chair facing my desk as he mulled over this information. "Why is Alana just visiting, why hasn't she come to live with you permanently? Is Grayson her real father?" Quinn looked at me carefully and I wondered if he somehow knew all my secrets kept from Grayson and Alana.

"He has said nothing about being her father, if indeed he is," I retorted. "I don't want to uproot her so suddenly. Dr. Conner and his yacht have been her only home since Journey became terminally ill, and my sister died while living on the boat. Besides, they are very close. It seems wrong to sever their ties right now."

Quinn shrugged. "I have to commend you for your patience and sense of fairness. Especially knowing how badly you want children, and how much you loved your sister."

I stood to leave, not wanting to accept his praise, which I did not deserve. If Quinn had any inkling as to my true colors on the subject he would raise his eyebrow in that particular way of his that let you know important things like honor and an obligation to do what is right were at stake. There was no whitewashing such issues for the steadfast Quinn. I grabbed my portfolio of information for the staff meeting and walked out the door hoping he would change the subject.

Quinn walked beside me and asked if I knew the university had received a grant to design a big resort on the island. I told him I hadn't heard, and he informed me that the art department hired someone to work with a group of our best design students. They were going to help construct the interior of a multimillion-dollar hotel going in along the coast further north.

"Who did they hire?" I asked, as we crossed the grounds of low, sprawling buildings with many open courts and thick greenery. The layout of the campus blended well with the tropical environment, giving the college a reputation for their natural and eco-friendly design.

"Someone named Gwyneth James. Her husband is Dr. Michael James and they have a daughter, Taylor."

I stopped dead in my tracks while Quinn stumbled forward a few steps, then turned and looked at me. "What's the matter? Do you know her?"

"That's Grayson Conner's ex-wife. I'm sure of it. They have a daughter named Taylor and his partner's name was Michael." I stared at Quinn as if he were a ghost. "And she was into architectural design."

"She married his medical partner?" Quinn looked surprised and dismayed at the same time.

"You don't know the half of it." We walked slower as if suddenly there were an oppressive need to delay our arrival at the faculty meeting. "Quinn, don't say anything, okay? I mean, Gwyneth has no idea I know her ex-husband, let alone why."

"My lips are sealed." Quinn smiled a warm everything-will-be-fine smile as he opened the door to the meeting hall. We sat in the middle of the room lined with padded folding chairs. Most of the staff had arrived and were busy swapping summer vacation stories. As is customary on the island, windows and doors were open wide. Sweet scents from island floral growing nearby wafted in with the warm evening breeze.

I put my leather bag on the floor beside me and scanned the room. I wanted to see Gwyneth, although I had no idea what the woman looked like. Grayson hadn't described her, yet there she was. Seated upfront near the podium. It had to be her, because she would be speaking to us about the grant project. Gwyneth was not the bigger-than-life blonde I'd envisioned, with long curled lashes over sleepy blue eyes.

Her ability to break hearts was much less obvious.

Grayson's life-altering ex was a brunette, with delicately carved features beneath a white linen suit. Her hair was pulled back into a twisted knot and she looked quite professional, ready to take on the whole design department, or at least, direct its top students. A casual observer wouldn't easily see how this well put together woman had once caused her own life to completely unravel.

Quinn nudged me as he finished speaking to fellow teachers on the other side of him and whispered, "Is that her?" He nodded toward the podium.

"Yes, it must be," I whispered back, although I wasn't sure why we were whispering. Voices and laughter escalated throughout the room as the rest of our colleagues arrived. Soon our Dean of Faculty appeared from a back door and everyone became quiet as he welcomed us.

I barely recall the rest of the meeting. But I was right about Gwyneth. Her presentation was as charming and confident as her appearance. There wasn't an academic in the room that would be less than shocked by the sordid tale Grayson shared with me on his boat.

During the buffet dinner I managed to always be where Gwyneth wasn't. Others were all too happy to welcome her and get acquainted, making it easy for me not to. But I knew it would be rude to avoid her the entire evening. At some point I would have to introduce myself. I dreaded that moment. And then there she was, extending a hand and a smile. "Hello, Kylie is it?"

"Yes, Gwyneth, how nice to have you as part of our faculty this year. What a wonderful experience this project will be for our design students." I looked her in the eye and realized we were the same height and nearly the same build, but the similarities stopped there. My eyes were a soft blue, hers a warm brown to match her hair. In contrast to Gwyneth's professional attire and pulled back tresses, my blonde locks spilled over the shoulders of a bright blue sundress and matching sandals.

While we briefly studied one another I had a flash of Grayson's boat before me, clipping through the calm sea at a good pace. I tried to picture Gwyneth on the railing with her knot untwisted and soft brown hair dancing in the breeze, but she didn't fit the scene.

"Your colleagues have nothing but the greatest admiration for you and the work you do with the communications majors." Gwyneth smiled while I blushed at her compliment.

"I enjoy what I do. From what I've heard here this evening you must enjoy your work as well. You've worked on some impressive design projects," I said while smiling back at her, feeling awkward about the whole experience of meeting Grayson's ex.

"Well, thank you. Unfortunately my work has caused me to somewhat neglect my daughter this past year. She's at that impossible young adolescent stage." Gwyneth paused there and her pretty face no longer showed any hint of a smile. "Taylor's thirteen, and very bright, but last year she became quite rebellious and got behind in all her classes. Apparently, she skipped a lot of them."

Gwyneth pushed a stray hair off her face. I didn't say anything but waited for her to finish.

"English is the one subject she hasn't caught up in over the summer. I was wondering, well, everyone here has said you'd be the perfect tutor for her." Gwyneth shot me a quick little half-smile and added, "I can't tell you how much I would appreciate it."

I stared into the eyes of Grayson's nemesis. They had lost their feisty spark flashed over the crowd of teachers when speaking. The confidence shown earlier on the podium all but evaporated while sharing her daughter's needs, which obviously were less clear and precise than any of the design plans she had created.

"You want me to tutor your daughter in English?" I said, as if repeating the request might help it sink in, for the preposterousness of this development was almost overwhelming. How could I tutor the daughter Grayson abandoned, while he vied for custody of the niece I wished to adopt? I smiled my best smile and tried not to think of her in bed with Grayson's best friend and medical partner. It felt wrong to not at least mention how I'd recently met her ex, but the words wouldn't come.

We decided I would meet with Taylor on Monday, one week before classes were to begin at the university. I felt sympathy for Taylor, knowing her seventh grade had ended badly, and that she did indeed have huge expectations to live up to. Having spent a few hours with her mother told me as much, and then there was the fact that Grayson walked out on her when just a young child. No matter how big a presence Michael might be in her life, he couldn't be expected to make up for Grayson's abandonment of his daughter.

Once my appointment with Taylor was set, I excused myself and went looking for Quinn. I found him at the dessert table near the back of the room, eating cake off a paper plate.

"Quinn, I had a talk with Elise today."

"Did she tell you about Chenlei's nightmares?"

"Yes, how often is she having them?" I asked, wondering why this was the first thing on his mind when I mentioned Elise.

"More often all the time. She wakes up almost every night now and I'm thinking of getting her some counseling."

"I see." My next question was hard to ask. "Quinn, do you think her more frequent nightmares have something to do with my abandoning her, in a way, when I went to Maui?"

"They probably would have started happening more frequently anyway, so don't blame yourself, Kyl."

I nodded, feeling little relief. "Quinn, what happens when she has her nightmares? Does she come into your room? Do you go to her?"

"I go in and lie beside her until she falls back to sleep. I just put my hand on her head and tell her to wake up, that she's having a bad dream, and everything will be okay. What else can I do?"

"Why doesn't Elise go to her?"

Quinn shrugged. "I don't know. Maybe because I always hear Chenlei first and don't see any reason to wake Elise."

"Quinn, that might be a way for them to bond. Maybe you should wake Elise, let her be the protective mama. She's at a loss for how to do that. Apparently you're going for an Oscar, playing both parenting roles to perfection."

"Is that what Elise said?" Quinn sighed.

"What Elise said is that you always seem to be there, like a knight in shining armor, and that may not be what's best for Chenlei."

Quinn stood up and threw his plate and fork away in the trash bin behind us. He lifted his satchel from the floor beside me while I stuck my tote bag on my shoulder. "Quinn, don't be hurt, and don't go home and confront Elise. Just think about it, and I'm sure you'll see the importance of backing off a little, and how Chenlei needs her mama to come to the rescue once in a while."

"Kyl, I'm just doing the best I can with a tense situation. Elise might perceive it to be me always taking front and center with Chenlei, but the truth is that she's not the same with Chenlei as she is with the boys. She hesitates, questions her own instincts, she's awkward as hell with Chenlei."

Quinn and I left the multipurpose room and nursed private thoughts as we crossed the campus to our cars in the parking lot, where we cheerlessly said goodbye. We were more upset with our personal situations than with each other. I wondered if Chase was waiting at home for me or still at the office catching up on things.

Part of me regretted letting Alana spend the night with Chenlei. I missed her terribly and wanted to hug her, snuggle up and watch a movie together. We'd talked on the phone numerous times throughout the evening. I wanted to be sure she was comfortable staying with her new friend, and in a strange home for the night. Elise and Chenlei had managed to make Alana feel secure and loved in her new environment. I knew they would. They were both caring and gracious beyond words. If only these traits they shared could form a bond between them.

The porch light was on when I came up the hill, telling me that Chase was there. He'd fallen asleep on the sofa with the stereo playing soft jazz. A book rose and fell on his chest rhythmically with his breathing. I removed the book and awakened him with a kiss. It led to a night of long-overdo lovemaking.

At breakfast Chase took my hand and shared how much he hoped our night of passion would result in a pregnancy. Adoption did not cross his lips, and probably did not enter his thought process. I squeezed his hand and he kissed the back of mine. I looked into his eyes with tears in my own and did not tell him they were out of frustration for not sharing his impossible dream. We ate in silence, both lost in our own thoughts until he left for the office. I spent the day planning our first evening together with Alana. I wanted it to be perfect.

I wanted him to step into my dream, and let go of his.

# CHAPTER NINE

*I needed to believe it was Journey's wild imaginings, or drug-induced hallucinations that led her to claim Grayson as the father.*

Chenlei spoke more English on the drive home from school than she ever had at one time. It made me smile to hear her stutter occasionally, groping for the right words to communicate with Alana. Their happy chatter warmed my heart and made me realize how much they'd each needed a friend.

"Who takes you to school, Alana?" I asked, while glancing at her in the rearview mirror.

She looked out her window as if the answer would be there. "I take the bus with Jay."

"Is that Makana's boy?" I asked. Alex had mentioned that Makana had a son who helped out at the Hula Grill after school. I could see her nod and smile as I looked over my shoulder. "So you take the bus, and that's the only difference?" I prodded.

It took her a minute to respond, but her answer had been well thought out. "My class is smaller and my teacher is Hawaiian."

"I see. That would make quite a difference, wouldn't it? Do you like your teacher?" I asked.

"Yes. She's very nice." Alana looked at Chenlei. "So is Miss Roberts." Chenlei grinned widely.

Miss Roberts was not from the island. She was a mainland import, something rare in the public school Chenlei attended. Perhaps it was a good thing to have a little diversity. It could only help Chenlei fit in better.

When we arrived at the house on the hill by the sea, filled with memories of my little sister, the girls gobbled down the last of the chocolate chip cookies I had baked for them on Alana's first day here. After their snack, they skipped into the living room, new books in tow. I thought I'd find them cuddled together on the sofa reading, but the chest under the window must have beckoned to them. Silently they stood together staring at it.

"Do you want to see what's in it now?" I asked.

They looked at each other and their eyes met, but it was Alana who responded.

"No."

"Me either," Chenlei added.

"Let's watch a movie," I suggested and both girls enthusiastically agreed. After finding the perfect one they sprawled out on the floor in front of the TV while I curled up in the big comfy chair by the window. I began to read one of the books Elise gave me on the type of brain tumor Journey died of. It was depressing at first, reading about invasive abnormal cells that take over and suck the life out of someone you love. But after a few pages it became only dry clinical information leaving no room for emotion.

Before I knew it the movie was almost over and Chase was walking in the front door. My heart began to beat faster when I realized the love of my life and my beloved sister's child were about to meet for the first time. Neither of them had any idea what this moment meant to me. I didn't know myself until they were both there, in the same room together, in the same house I had helped to raise Journey in. In the same house she had felt the need to leave, because of Chase.

While standing quietly in the doorway, Chase observed the little girls watching their movie. His look was not one of dismay. What I saw there in his eyes was wishful longing, perhaps to come home one day and find his own children lying on the floor watching a movie. It made me want to cry, knowing how disappointed he was that I had not become pregnant yet with his child, and for that matter, would probably never bear his children.

He walked over to the desk and set his briefcase down just in time for the movie to be over. The girls jumped up to turn off the television and then stared at Chase, who smiled warmly.

"Well, Chenlei, who is this little friend of yours?"

They glanced at each other but didn't say anything. Instead they giggled, which had become their signature reaction when feeling shy.

"Could this be my niece, Alana?" Chase leaned down to her eye level and offered his large hand for Alana to shake. Hesitantly at first, but then with a burst of confidence she reached out and firmly shook Chase's hand.

I quickly wiped away tears while praying their relationship would have an opportunity to develop as steady and sure as that handshake.

"It's nice to finally make your acquaintance, Alana. I am so sorry about your mother."

Alana looked down at her bare feet as if to study her toes, while Chenlei stared at her new best friend. There were no giggles this time.

"Do you girls want to pick flowers on the hill for a while?" I asked, as we all looked out the window at the endless white and yellow blooms entangled thickly with the grass, as far as the eye could see across the sloping field.

They eagerly nodded their heads in agreement.

As soon as the little mismatched pair of kindred spirits had hurried out the door, Chase whistled low under his breath.

"Wow, she's the spitting image of Journey."

He collapsed onto the leather sofa while I watched the girls from the front picture window. They fluttered like butterflies from one blossom to the next and diligently gathered their fragile bouquets. Chenlei looked small and delicate with her dark hair shining in the sun. She chose her flowers carefully and studied each one as she added it to her cluster. Alana's long brown curls bounced in the air and her lean tan limbs swooped everywhere at once. She picked the brightest flower in each location she lit upon. They couldn't have been more different, these two little girls, and yet they were so much alike.

"Kyl?"

I turned my attention to Chase.

"I know. She does look like Journey, except that Alana's eyes, hair, and skin are a lighter shade of brown."

What I didn't say is that Alana had Journey's same intellect and love of life, with that same twinkle in her eye. I didn't say how she exuded the same warmth and ability to draw in everyone around her, as if we might catch that bright shiny twinkle in her caramel colored eyes and the world would suddenly be a nicer place to live.

Chase reached for the paper on the table in front of him and stared blankly at the front page. I sat beside him.

"Maybe you could play some games with them, when they come back in. I picked up several appropriate for their ages."

"Sure. I thought you and the girls were making pizza."

"We are. But I think it would be good for you to spend some time with Alana before dinner, get to know her a little, don't you?"

"Why not?" Chase gave me a strained smile and began to read his paper in earnest. My eyes strayed back out the window where the girls were still romping about. I wondered if anything at all could change the hard line Chase had already drawn where adopting Alana was concerned.

It had been more than unfortunate that Chase and I became serious at the same time Journey entered her troubled adolescent years. It had ended up being tragic. It had resulted in her running away from the guidance we tried to give after Mama died, and in her never returning home again, not even to die. And now, there was my growing resentment about it.

I left Chase to his paper and began puttering around in the kitchen preparing ingredients to assemble the pizza. I kept remembering how I had let Chase come between Journey and me, had always taken his side in arguments, had always agreed with his house rules for her. It was suddenly clear how I shouldn't have let him or anyone else come between us. I didn't see it like that at the time, or during all those years I prayed and dreamed, and watched for her return. But it was true nonetheless. Falling in love with Chase had caused me not to see how I was driving Journey away.

Glancing over at him absorbed in the evening paper I felt a chill. Of all my emotions and reactions ever caused by him, this was the first not born of love. Whenever I was frustrated or upset with Chase in the past, my feelings were strictly rooted in affection. These were not. And it scared me.

I couldn't allow him to let Alana walk out of my life forever just as Journey had done. It wasn't fair that Grayson might raise Alana by default, on a boat in the outermost slip of Lahaina Harbor. How could I know for sure whether or not he was her father, and more importantly, how could I make Chase want to be?

The next day was Saturday and the girls were excited about taking the trail down to the beach. We packed our things in my large fuchsia bag. I'd included the reference books from Elise, carefully sliding them down the side so as not to smash our picnic lunch.

"Wait for me at the stairs!" I shouted to the girls, who ran ahead. The steps were rough-cut and sculpted out of hard earth by someone who lived in our house above the bluff well before my time. They were beginning to crumble, having been there probably fifty years or more, and being constantly abused by coastal winds.

Chenlei and Alana waited patiently for me to catch up and we descended the stairs together. Once our sandaled feet were firmly on the beach, I led them to a cave beneath the cliff, not far from where the stairs were carved out. It was cool inside, with a compacted sand floor, and just enough light for me to read.

The girls laid out their towels, already calling it their own private beach house. I was pleased they preferred it to the scorching sun nearer the surf. I could easily see them splashing in the waves and was close enough to save them, should I need to make a mad dash on their behalf. So I settled against the lava wall with a towel between my back and the

*Journey* **79**

hard surface, and began to read one of the medical books Elise had given me.

I'd read many a book in this very position, while watching Journey splash alone in the waves. She would have loved a Chenlei to play with. Being nine years older than my sister, I often bowed out of swimming and sand play, for more serious endeavors such as reading and thinking.

By this time I had read enough about Journey's illness to be appalled at the approach Grayson took with her treatment. I'd learned the most aggressive way to deal with a brain tumor such as Journey's included surgery, to remove as much of the offending tissue as possible, and then chemo to destroy it.

I wished Grayson were there in the cave with me so I could quiz him thoroughly about how he treated my sister's cancer, which apparently was not to treat it at all, other than with enough drugs to tolerate the pain. I shuddered at the realization she might still be alive had I been there to help her decide on a more aggressive plan, to beat her disease rather than succumb to it.

Putting the book down for a minute, I stared at the girls laughing and running in the waves. It seemed like only yesterday Journey had been Alana's age. What would I have done differently had I known my beloved sister would run away at sixteen, and die of cancer at twenty-six? Suddenly I was glad Grayson was not present, because I wasn't sure yet what approach I wanted to take with him. I wasn't ready to confront this man about his medical ethics. In the end, I probably would have let Journey handle her disease as she wished to, which is ultimately what Grayson did.

I wished Chase had come to splash in the waves with the girls but he had tourist runs to make in the helicopter. He'd been so good with them when playing the games I'd bought. I could tell they thought he was funny, and witty and clever, and he was. I had watched them from the kitchen as I put away the leftover pizza. Chase was charming and they were charmed. What a good daddy he would make, I concluded, if only fate would allow us the opportunity.

By now the girls were crouched in the wet sand, building castles. Alana glanced at me and waved. I waved back, my heart aching for her to always be there, on the beach building castles below our little white frame house where her mother had been born. Was it so wrong to believe living with us would be best for her? To conclude that fate wedged the letter behind the chest of drawers, where I, of all people, would find it? Perhaps it was God's way of telling me, *Yes, I want you to have Alana to raise as your own.*

Could Chase and I keep the flame of our love burning bright through whatever decisions we would finally make about Alana?

I walked down to where the girls were busy sculpting and admired their work. Both of them were familiar with the surf and knew their creation would only last until midway through high tide. But then the water would creep in, delicately at first, properly filling all the fissures they'd created for that purpose, until finally it raged with a stronger force and collapsed the walls.

When their castle was finished we gathered in our cozy cave to eat the peanut butter and honey sandwiches I'd packed in the fuchsia bag. There was bottled water, sliced kiwi, and leftover brownies from the night before to complete our picnic lunch. Afterwards I reminded the girls that this was Alana's last evening on the Big Island and asked what they'd like to do.

"Why don't we have a slumber party in the living room, and watch movies all night?" Alana offered this suggestion while clapping her hands and jumping in place. It was the same enthusiasm Journey always had when sharing her ideas.

"That sounds like fun. What do you think, Chenlei?"

With a big smile our little neighbor nodded in agreement.

"Okay then. I will talk to Elise and see if she minds you staying over."

The girls ran from the cave and down to the shoreline shouting *Hurrah! Hurrah!* I soon joined them and suggested they search for sand crabs to live in their castle, before the tide chose to reclaim it. I showed them which lava rocks protruding from the shore had dozens of the little creatures hiding beneath them, where the surf splashed and echoed.

Later in the afternoon, I swam with the girls and then we walked a couple miles down the beach. It was barren and devoid of tourists, with only a few locals scattered about, just as it had always been for Journey and me.

The girls and I saw dolphins off shore and sea turtles where they could usually be found, beside the smooth rocks just below the surf. The sea turtles brought a haunted look to Alana's face, and it was painful to observe. I wondered if she thought of her mother. It made me think of Alana's favorite book, where the mama and little girl became sea turtles to escape pirates. Even I wanted to believe it, that Journey was a happy turtle with one eye above the surf to watch over her daughter.

When our day at the beach was over we climbed the steep, rough-cut stairs, wet, weary, and trying hard not to lose a foothold. Chase was not at the house as I had hoped he would be when we arrived. I tried not to show my disappointment at his working late on this particular Saturday, with our special guest here.

We cleaned up and crossed the hill to Chenlei's house, to ask permission for her to spend the night. Elise was just returning from the market and we happily helped carry groceries in. Wyatt and Austin were polite but mostly ignored the girls until Elise gave them all popsicles to eat on the front porch.

"The boys are glad Chenlei finally has a friend. So am I." Elise smiled. "I think they feel bad for her, always tagging along behind them everywhere."

Elise began to put the food away. I sat at the table and watched as she unpacked the bags. "Chenlei will make friends at school soon and you can have them over for her to play with," I suggested.

She stopped putting canned goods on the shelf and looked at me. "Wouldn't it be wonderful if Alana lived with you? I don't just mean for Chenlei's sake. I've never seen you so at peace with yourself, and the world. Motherhood becomes you."

"I'm not her mother," I quickly pointed out, trying not to think about the one living parent she might have, and how I was hoping to take her away from him.

"But you want to be, don't you?" Elise stared at me, as if the answer would be written on my face.

"It doesn't matter what I want, Elise. What matters is what's best for Alana." What I didn't say was that I had no right to break up the relationship between Alana and Grayson, if he really was her father. I didn't say it because I wanted to play God for at least a little while longer.

Maybe forever.

# CHAPTER TEN

*Slowly I walked back down the long dock and stopped
close enough to see his face in the fading dusk, out of words
and out of breath from my own fear, of myself.*

Chase ran helicopter tours until sunset. It was ten o'clock before he returned home, after being persuaded to have drinks with his last client. By then the girls were nearly asleep, their movie droning on without them. They had munched their way through a bowl of popcorn and sipped grape juice until their lips were purple. Blankets were snuggled around their curled up bodies, and stuffed animals carted over by Chenlei were making little bulges in the makeshift bedding.

Chase tiptoed around the disarray and met me at the bedroom door. We left it slightly ajar in case the girls should need me. Whispering a conversation about our very different events of the evening didn't cover any of the subjects on either of our minds. I read one of the books on cancer for a while, annoying Chase, who wanted the light off. The information was as difficult to understand as the man lying beside me, snoring despite the lamp being on.

When I finished my chapter I tucked the girls in and turned off the television. Light streamed in the window from the full moon and made shadows across their faces. I fell asleep thinking about how close Journey and I had been at one time, when it was her face I saw in the flickers of light as I covered her up late at night. I awoke around midnight feeling strangely sorrowful and immediately thought of my first morning after Journey's departure so long ago, when I first realized she wouldn't be seated beside me at breakfast, perhaps ever again. But then I became aware of a moaning in the living room and jumped out of bed. It was Chenlei having a nightmare.

I knelt beside her and began to rub her back. "Chenlei, wake up. You're dreaming, honey." Her eyes flew open and stared blankly into space. I pulled her gently into my lap. "Are you okay, sweetie? It was just a dream."

Alana sat up groggily and asked what was wrong.

"Chenlei was having a bad dream. I'll lie between the two of you and we can go back to sleep." Neither of the girls objected as I tucked us all in together. Staring out the window I observed how the moon had shifted, leaving us in a thin fog of eerie light. Chenlei began to speak in a voice as frail as the fog.

"I cannot help her."

"Help who?" I asked in a whisper.

"My mom. She is . . . she is . . . not moving. Not warm. Her hands are . . . cold." Chenlei quivered.

I hugged her closer to me. "Shhh, Chenlei, picture your mama when she was smiling and well." I kissed her softly on the cheek.

"I . . . I cannot help her . . ."

"Chenlei, it's not your fault. There is nothing you could do."

Alana snuggled up closer to us.

"Both of your mamas loved you very much," I assured them. "They didn't want to leave you, but they are in a place now that is free of pain, a happy place where they can look down and keep watch over you."

They were quiet as I stroked and patted their arms, hoping sleep would overtake them. I stared at the ceiling and remembered what Elise told me about Chenlei's dreams. I tried to visualize waking up next to a cold body—eyes wide open, staring at the ceiling. Dark sticky liquid everywhere . . . a little fetus, purple, perfect . . . but not developed enough to live on its own. I could only wonder what Chenlei did with such horror. Scream, perhaps, until her voice was too hoarse. Or maybe she cried in raking sobs until her tears ran dry. Did she withdraw without a single sound or tear, pulling up and into a dark place deep inside?

How did Alana react when she learned of her mother's death, there in Grayson's arms beside the rail of the boat, moored in the cove? I couldn't help but picture Alana there, surrounded by the Pacific, with the hot sun beating down on her as relentlessly as the glaring truth of her mama's death.

It might as well have been yesterday for all the healing either of them had experienced as of yet. Maybe the pain of their loss, and mine, would just simply never abate.

And so we slept, each of us surrounded by our own sadness.

Chase had left to fly helicopter tours just as the little girls began to stir in the living room. I was already making them pancakes as they slid onto the kitchen chairs, looking up at me sleepily.

"Good morning, girls," I said cheerfully while they yawned and sipped their juice. "After breakfast we'll walk Chenlei home, and then it will be time to head for the airport."

"Will you spend a few days with us?" Alana asked.

"I can't, honey. I have to prepare for my classes, which start soon."

Chenlei was quiet. No smiles or giggles this morning. Her only friend was leaving.

After breakfast we put the living room back in order, and I couldn't help but glance occasionally at the chest under the window. I noticed Alana and Chenlei doing the same. Chenlei's eyes would widen when she looked at the chest, as if eager to discover its treasures. Alana would furrow her brow, perhaps afraid to embrace the finality of it.

As for me, I wasn't sure what kept my body from running over to pull out the contents in a desperate search for some different answer about Alana's father. Part of me thought it would be there, the *real* truth, buried where even Journey had forgotten she'd put it.

Although no one spoke of it, the teak wood chest made its presence felt until we had picked up the last popcorn kernel and headed out the door for Chenlei's house.

Elise was cleaning up after the boys' breakfast when we arrived. The girls ran off to find them, and I poured myself a cup of coffee.

"So, how'd it go?" Elise asked.

"I think they had a lot of fun. I ended up sleeping between them on the floor, after Chenlei awoke with a bad dream."

Elise sat down heavily in the chair across from me, gripping her coffee mug tightly. "So she had her nightmare, then. I was hoping a change of environment might make a difference."

"Does this happen every night now?" I asked.

"It's beginning to." Elise was staring at the children running through the field out front, where the girls had found Wyatt and Austin playing soccer.

"Maybe she needs counseling, Elise. Quinn told me you were looking into that."

Elise sighed. "Yes, we are."

I nodded approval. "I think whatever happened that night is something she hasn't dealt with in a way she needs to, in order to put it behind her."

Elise got up and took my empty mug with hers to the sink. "If only there were a way to look behind those big, dark eyes and see her thoughts, so I could understand what she needs from me, and how I can help her."

"Just love her, Elise. That's all she needs from you. Bake cookies together. Help her with homework. Pick flowers in the field. Read her books. It's not rocket science."

"Maybe not for you." Elise turned around and I saw tears in her eyes. My best friend was not one to quit on a project, or give up on a task, no matter how daunting. Why did it appear that this little girl was defeating her?

I rose to leave and gave her a gentle hug. Without a word I left.

It was time to head for the airport with Alana.

When we arrived in Maui, Grayson was waiting for us in a little gray sports car which I assumed was his. We barely fit, with Alana wedged between us. The top was down and our luggage thrown haphazardly in the small space behind the front seat. Despite how impractical it was, the little sports car was admittedly a lot of fun to ride in. Grayson was quite eccentric and yet he was so unassuming. He was not like anyone I had ever known.

Alana spoke nonstop during lunch at the Hula Grill, telling Grayson all about her Big Island adventure. I asked if she might have missed anything important in school the last two days, feeling guilty about having kidnapped her. Grayson informed me our little shining star would not suffer educationally, because she was well beyond her classmates in every subject.

We decided to spend my remaining time on the yacht, cruising along the shore. I helped Alana unpack her things and she chose to stay below for a while to look at her books. When I checked on her a few minutes later she was sound asleep. Apparently the Big Island visit wore her out.

I stood beside Grayson at the wheel and admired the white caps foaming over like translucent clouds in the dazzling blue sea. Sailboats were interspersed along the shore with leisurely kayakers. It was a typical day in paradise for those few lucky souls escaping mainland mayhem.

Grayson anchored and offered me a drink, which I readily accepted. It was a Mai Tai made with some type of smooth rum that far exceeded the standards of most island bars. I savored it, knowing in a few hours I would be on a plane, and would not be back for a while, with my busy teaching schedule to look forward to.

"Grayson, I've been reading about Journey's illness. My friend Elise runs a bookstore and lent me several of the latest publications about brain tumors."

He nodded, waiting for me to ask my questions.

"I was wondering, I mean, I know very little about Journey's particular condition, but isn't the standard treatment usually surgery, and then chemo?"

"Kylie, your sister was well informed of all her options. I made a point to keep her abreast of every detail concerning her condition as it changed. All the latest tests were done on her and many conversations on this very deck centered on options for treatment."

"Is no treatment really an option? Or just a death wish?"

"Are you suggesting your sister didn't want to live?"

"What exactly did Journey mean to you, Grayson? You obviously weren't romantically involved."

"I believe that I was like a father to her."

"And that role wasn't a burden to you?"

"No, not at all. She was very much like a daughter to me. Journey was so naïve for a runaway, so hungry for someone to care for her. Not at all worldly or independent."

"I would have done anything for her, Grayson. There wasn't a day I didn't think of her, or wasn't tempted to try and find my little sister," I said meekly, feeling ashamed that she had been a runaway without even a heart for it.

"Then why didn't you? Try to find her I mean? She never went all that far, or tried to be all that invisible. She didn't change her name, or go underground or across the sea. My God, she died right here in this harbor, one short flight on a commuter plane from your home on the Big Island."

I digested his hurtful words while staring out to sea. I couldn't look at him. Finally I spoke because his silence was deafening.

"Our mama died when Journey was only fourteen. She had no other family except for me. No other adults in her life, for that matter, if you don't count schoolteachers."

I paused there, unsure if I wanted to continue unraveling realities I'd never spoken of, just as Grayson had never verbalized his moment of no return with Gwyneth.

Only the gulls responded, prompting me to continue.

"Truthfully, we saw those schoolteachers more than we saw Mama, who was usually working endless hospital shifts to make ends meet. Occasionally she would go on a date with an off duty doctor. Mama crashed in a private plane over the Pacific on one of those dates. I was twenty-three by then, and had just eloped with Chase. She died that same Saturday. Funny how I had dreaded telling her what I'd done, only to find out I would never have the chance."

Grayson quietly refilled my drink. I swirled the ice, leaning there on the rail, the wind in my face, the big vast ocean before me. I wanted to jump overboard rather than explain what happened, if I even knew what happened. I could not be sure why I never looked for my little sister, whom I loved so much.

"Journey started spending all her time with a group of school friends. Chase moved into our little home on the bluff with me, and we tried to rein her in, but she wanted nothing to do with us. She was angry and confused. In a way I had abandoned her by marrying Chase, as much as Mama had by dying. When she left at sixteen, there was a sense of relief underneath my panic. I couldn't admit that even to myself. It was like having someone die whom you have poured you heart and soul into keeping alive, only to find that once gone, you can live again."

I finished my second Mai Tai and swiped at stinging tears. Then I looked at Grayson, staring out to sea.

"I thought she'd run away with one of her friends, someone from her little band of misfits. I wanted to believe they'd return when the outside world proved to be less tolerable than what they'd run away from. I did look for her, Grayson. I banged on every door of every friend she'd ever had. I went to the local authorities. And then I . . . just waited. Waited for her to come to her senses, waited for her to miss me. Waited for an act of God."

I finished my Mai Tai, glad that my senses were blurred, and collapsed into a deck chair.

"One day turned into another," I continued, "and it got easier and easier to believe that she would grow up, want to reconnect, and come back. But then one year became two, and then three, until one day I realized that too much time had gone by. Sadness and regret crept in like high tide, washing away any anger or indignation I might have felt about what happened. But I never stopped believing she would eventually return, not until the teak wood chest showed up. Not until then did

I give up on recovering the true treasure I had lost."

Grayson and I watched the sailboats bobbing up and down between us. He kept a fresh drink in my hand. Where had the time gone? Alana had slept through dinner, and although my gracious host had provided a tray of bread, cheese, and smoked fish, I had no appetite. Now a fireball of a sun was slowly setting.

"I can see how this happened, now," he admitted. "Journey would never talk about why she left, or about your home situation. She always spoke very highly of you, and about how much she missed you. The closest she ever came to criticism was telling me about the long hours you spent studying, constantly, from after high school until receiving your doctorate just before she ran away. Nonetheless, Journey was so proud of you getting all those scholarships based solely on academic merit. She truly admired you, Kylie."

Grayson shook his head. "She never mentioned Chase. Not once, or that you were married. She did say her mother had died unexpectedly when she was fourteen and she didn't know who her father was. Kylie, she always blamed herself for hurting you, for leaving. And her only explanation was that she had to break out of her little world and find a wide open space to breathe in, lest she suffocate and die before she truly ever lived."

I looked closely at this man whom I now felt so connected to, because of Journey. He sat across from me and clearly his expression had relaxed, for the first time since I'd met him. Kindness was swimming in his large blue eyes instead of storms at sea. All the guarded agitation of my unwelcome appearance in his life, perhaps to irrevocably change it, was gone.

I suddenly felt awkward at having bared my soul to him, more awkward than when I stole his mail to help me steal my sister's child.

"Who is Alana's father, Grayson?"

"I don't know, probably some surfer boy. Maybe the one she was grieving for that first night I met her, here on this boat, drowning my own sorrows with loud music, unruly friends, and too much rum."

I nodded. He really didn't know. How could he possibly not remember? There wasn't enough rum in all of Maui for a man to forget he has slept with a beautiful young woman half his age. Maybe he was right. Maybe the father really was a surfer boy long gone, just as I hoped.

I needed to leave before I confessed I'd taken his letter and had every intention of taking Alana, too. I mumbled something about needing to catch my flight home.

Wordlessly Grayson took us back, while I planted myself at the front rail and refused to turn or look at him again. Finally we arrived at the dock where he flawlessly steered the boat into the outermost slip and tied the ropes as I gathered my things for a fast exit.

I jumped ashore asking him to kiss Alana for me when she awakened, and was almost halfway down the dock when he shouted, "Wait!"

Turning around I stood still to observe his shadowy figure in the near dark. Slowly I walked back down the long dock and stopped close enough to see his face in the fading dusk, out of words and out of breath from my own fear, of myself.

"Alana has an open house at her school the end of October, and she would love for you to come. It's on a Thursday night." He paused, but didn't move so much as a fraction while standing there in front of me. In our silence I could hear the water lapping against the boat, and then he added, "You could stay the weekend if you wish. There's a guest room next to Alana's."

His voice was quite inviting, and I realized for the first time just how deep and warm it was.

"The child has grown attached to you, I can see. It would be good for you to be there. Especially if you intend to . . . have custody of her."

"Yes, I'd like that."

Grayson nodded.

I turned and left again, unsure as to whether or not spending a weekend on Grayson's yacht was a good idea. My instincts were on red alert, although I couldn't pinpoint why. All the way to the airport I watched palm trees barely moving in the night air outside my taxi window. Time

*Journey* **93**

seemed that way sometimes, to barely move. Like a moment stuck on rewind. Grayson standing on deck with his disarmingly knowledgeable eyes penetrating through me was a continual instant replay in my mind. Hard as I tried, I couldn't let it go. It haunted me as I flew over the Pacific, and all the way up the winding road to the house on the bluff.

Even then, Grayson was on my mind as I lay down next to Chase, who was sound asleep.

# CHAPTER ELEVEN

*Whether standing beside Gwyneth, or within a sea of strangers,
I would have known this was the child of Grayson Connor.*

Chase and I argued before breakfast, causing me to burn the toast and undercook the eggs. He didn't understand how I could have spent so much time on Grayson's boat the day before and not address the possibility of him being Alana's father. I tried to explain how awkward it would be to suggest such a thing when Grayson believed the dad to be a clueless surfer boy.

We gulped our coffee down silently and didn't touch the unappetizing food. I mentally planned the details of my trip to Waikiki while throwing away our disastrous breakfast. The door shut rather firmly and I realized Chase left for his office without so much as a goodbye kiss. Part of me knew I had earned his dismay. There really was no excuse for clinging to the hope of finding a father Journey conveniently buried somewhere deeper than the letter in the rolled up painting.

If I truly believed I'd find telltale clues of a surfer boy dad in the teak wood chest I would have examined every dark corner by now.

Running into Gwyneth while I parked at the university reminded me of my first meeting with Taylor later in the day. We were to spend some time together on the beach before the university's fall kickoff event. Gwyneth looked ever the perfectionist in a matching ensemble of beige silk, with her hair tied back smoothly in a heavy gold clip. I wore a clingy lavender sundress, and although I usually felt overdone in my little dresses and heeled sandals, Gwyneth dwarfed that concern in me with her tailored summer suit.

Quinn's office door was ajar when I walked by. I stood there and watched him reading one of his textbooks. There were papers strewn about his cluttered desk and except for different motivational posters on the wall, his office mirrored mine in every way. It had the same perfect little square of space and large window looking out onto the campus.

"Are you ready for your first class of the semester?" I asked, sinking into his leather chair across the desk from him.

"Excited, really."

I laughed, grateful to have a colleague who could change my mood instantly. "I'm excited, too. We're just a couple of sappy nerds, aren't we?"

Quinn smiled. "I like nerds. They never hurt people, or start wars."

"Speaking of wars, Chase and I get closer to one every day over Alana."

Quinn shut his book to give me his full attention. "We talked about that a little, while you were gone this weekend."

I knew they'd been fishing in Quinn's boat. But I hadn't talked to Chase about it. It seemed fighting took priority over sharing events of the weekend. "What did Chase say?" I asked.

Quinn was slow to answer. I supposed he was choosing his words carefully.

"He feels very threatened by Alana."

"That's ridiculous." I rolled my eyes.

He shook his head. "Not really, Kylie. Think about what a strain Journey was on your marriage. And think about how you aren't any more objective about her daughter than you were about her."

I stood up and glared out the window, trying to focus on the palm trees, swaying slightly in the morning breeze. Not even their gentle motion could temper my anger. I took a few deep breaths as Quinn continued.

"Kylie, this child is probably with her real father, according to Chase, and yet you seem bound and determined to steal her right out from under him. Is that fair to either of them? Is that even rational thinking?"

"He isn't necessarily the father, and I am planning a trip to Waikiki this weekend to try and find out for sure."

"And what if you discover he isn't, and who the real father is? Then what?"

I turned and looked at Quinn, my arms folded in defiance.

"Kylie, you're only hoping to discover some doubt about Grayson being her father. You don't want to uncover her real father no matter who it is. Because in the end, you only want an excuse to take her as your own, even though your husband isn't in agreement."

"That's the part that hurts. If Chase really loves me as much as he says he does, why wouldn't he want us to raise Alana? Why can't he see that she is family, and how important she is to me, especially now that Journey is gone?" I sat down again in frustration.

Quinn picked up a pencil, tapping the eraser on his book. "Kylie, that's just it. The whole Journey fiasco is something hurtful to Chase, too. He knows that Alana would be a constant reminder of him possibly causing Journey to leave in the first place. He's afraid you will grow to resent him even more for what happened, rather than putting it behind you."

I didn't respond. Instead I stared at the mountain climber on the poster hanging up behind Quinn's desk. Surely if someone could scale that snowy peak, I could find a way to overcome this heap of obstacles Quinn was summarizing all too well. He took advantage of my silence by continuing.

"You know, from Chase's point of view, he was only trying to keep Journey safe by expecting her home at a certain hour, or not to hang out with certain people. You agreed with him at the time. It's why you didn't take Journey's side in any of it. You were concerned about her safety, too. But see, you've lost sight of all that. Now you're just full of guilt and pain about her death. How do you build a family around regret and resentment, and how can Chase understand you coming between a man and his child when he wants a child of his own so desperately?"

"Quinn, I will think seriously about everything you've said." I focused on his face rather than the mountain climber behind him, and changed the subject.

"Didn't you leave for China the summer Journey ran away?"

He shrugged. "I think so. I went four summers in a row on exchange from the university. I believe that was my first trip."

"I remember because I spent that summer tracking down everywhere Journey might have gone, and then I would check on Elise at night, hold your little newborn Wyatt and cry my heart out." I sighed, hating the memory of that summer frantically searching for Journey at every home of every childhood friend she'd ever associated with. Elise had been the glue that held me together through that summer. "Didn't your connections there help Elise with her volunteer adoption work at Hope International, here on the Big Island?" I asked, mostly to change the subject.

Quinn folded his hands on the desk and stared at them. "We were both involved in the agency at first. We wanted a little girl, but I don't think we dared to believe it might happen, so we just thought of the organization as a worthy investment of our time. And we really liked Edward." Quinn looked out the window. "Elise met him in her bookstore," he added, almost as an afterthought.

"I know. He's the one that got her all excited about little girls from China."

"I hope adoption works out for you too, Kylie, if you and Chase can't have your own kids."

I stood to leave, after glancing at the clock. I needed to get to my first class of the semester.

"I hope so too, but the bottom line, Quinn, is that Chase doesn't want to adopt, period."

"At least a child from China would be neutral ground."

I nodded as I left. I couldn't shift gears in my thinking that fast. My heart was squarely in Alana's corner at the moment. But I loved Chenlei like my own, and knew a child from China could be a dream come true for me, if adopting Alana didn't work out. What I feared was that, in the end, Chase would be as opposed to adopting a child from China as he was to raising Journey's offspring.

Nothing short of me becoming pregnant would make Chase happy.

The grounds of the university had a path that led to the ocean on the south side. Late in the afternoon faculty and students began to gather there for a traditional celebration that marked the beginning of fall semester. I held my heeled sandals and walked along the shore, wet sand oozing between my toes. The lavender sundress played about my legs, teased by a steady breeze typical of late afternoon on the south shore.

I was nervous about meeting Taylor. Unusual for me to be nervous, I chided myself, when meeting a student. I tried not to envision the scene that separated father and daughter all those years ago, and was suddenly annoyed with my conscience. Why did meeting Grayson's child matter a fig to me one way or the other? There was nothing wrong with knowing the man Gwyneth divorced, so she could be with his partner. There was no rule saying I had to confess this information before tutoring their child, who at thirteen obviously had some issues surrounding her past. In fact, there was little doubt those issues were weighing heavily into her present academic dilemma.

I felt as if living in the shadow of Grayson's presence, and it was influencing me to defy my own code of ethics. Shadow indeed. Concern about Grayson's past, present, and future loomed before me endlessly, and this was a man I did not know existed until recently. What tricks had fate come to play on my life?

Because of Grayson I was reliving my last encounters with Journey on a daily basis, those final memories just before she left without a trace. I remember running my hands through the soft wild curls of her chocolate hair, and inhaling the sweetness of her mango-scented lotion. We'd laughed and joked while I trimmed the very ends of her gorgeous mane, and fought later when she insisted upon going out after dark. Her flashing eyes and angered voice were my last memory of her, tempered by the scent of citrus and silky feel of her untamed tresses.

Her departure came rushing back to me nearly each hour of late, crashing out of a distant fog, and landing on hard ground. I recalled those first days, weeks, and months without her. Thoughts, memories, hopes and dreams of her haunted me, taunted my conscience without mercy or relief—then, and now, since meeting Grayson. I had for a second time become possessed by the loss of her, obsessed and consumed by my hurt, by her betrayal, by her cruelty to have left me when I loved her so much.

I stared out into the sea and thought about those endless weeks after Journey had left. They had faded together and turned into months, and then years, yet my pain did not fade, or surrender, or transform into acceptance. It just internalized. It became a part of who I was, this sadness, this inability to ever feel light and carefree again.

There were many more people now gathered on the shore, laughing and shaking hands, drinking lemonade or iced tea, and eating fresh fruit or little pastries from a large overflowing table with a caterer positioned at either end. Taylor stood beside her mother, who hadn't seen me yet, as she talked to several new colleagues. It had to be Taylor. Whether standing beside Gwyneth, or within a sea of strangers, I would have known this was the child of Grayson Connor. For although she had the heart shaped face and delicate chin of her mother, the intensity of her questioning eyes were his alone. The fair skin dusted by a rosy tan, the long body and short legs. On Grayson a broad upper body made him sturdy and strong. On Taylor the broad shoulders narrowed into petite curves.

I stood quietly beside this group of colleagues for one final minute and surveyed my task at hand. Taylor cocked her head and smoothed back her shoulder length hair, as straight as it was blonde. She flashed the intense blue eyes at me, perhaps wondering if I were the dreaded tutor, and I smiled, taking the opportunity to extend my hand and introduce myself.

"You must be Taylor," I said.

"Are you Mrs. Hudson?" Taylor asked, her blue eyes softening, as if I were not the punishment she'd envisioned.

"Yes, but please call me Kylie. Do you have your English book with you?" I inquired, for Gwyneth was to have her bring the text we'd be working from.

"It's in my backpack, in the car." Taylor looked at her mother, who gave her the car key. When she left to get the book Gwyneth thanked me again for coming to her rescue, while playing nervously with the gold bracelet on her left wrist. The vulnerability Taylor brought out in Gwyneth was quite a contrast to the confident, accomplished woman I'd observed mingling with faculty.

When Taylor returned with her book, I snagged her from the crowd and took her down to the water's edge, where we walked barefoot in the warm foamy surf until we reached a long flat rock jutting out above the tide line.

Sitting on it with wet feet and windblown hair, we opened the textbook and began to scrutinize each other, which of course, helped me plot a plan for her tutoring success. I knew instantly this would be my hardest assignment to date, knew in fact before I had met her. From the moment a request for tutoring had escaped Gwyneth's lips at our first encounter, I had wrestled with my ambivalence about this assignment, and indeed, this very moment. And now here I was, getting to know the little girl Grayson had sacrificed to the betrayal gods.

It made the possibility of betraying *him* just a little easier.

# CHAPTER TWELVE

*She hadn't been at ease with me until freeing her heart of its pent up secrets about this mystery father on a boat in Maui.*

Taylor had on ragged, torn jean shorts and a white cotton tank top, with her flat tummy exposed in-between. The new curves of her young body were accentuated by the skintight clothing. Typical at thirteen, she emulated current female rock stars with her straight messy blonde locks and irreverent attitude, but she had no body piercings or tattoos and wore no makeup other than shiny lip-gloss pulled frequently from her jean pocket and slathered on full, well-defined lips—an inheritance from her mother. I had a feeling Gwyneth's strong influence was why wholesomeness exuded from Taylor, despite the attempt at rebellion.

I looked carefully at the chapter Taylor had turned to, while she stared at the breakers just offshore.

"You say there's a paper due on a book you're reading, and this is the essay format you're to follow?" I asked.

"Umhum." Taylor made this almost inaudible sound with a large hint of the apathy her mother had explained was the problem.

"What book are you reading?" I inquired, hoping it was one I liked more than some that were assigned for eighth grade.

"*Running with the Demon.*"

"A fantasy novel?"

"My teacher is a huge Terry Brooks fan."

"I see. Well, it's a wonderful book. So much for the classics," I said to myself more than to Taylor. Secretly I thought bravo for the teacher.

Fantasy was something many kids this age read anyway, yet that particular book was quite literary.

"Have you read it?" I was hoping she had. Gwyneth said Taylor was an avid reader, and soaked up knowledge like a sponge. She made straight A's all of her six elementary school years. Gwyneth felt Taylor's bad grades during this confusing time of adolescence were strictly to punish her for being a busy career woman. Gwyneth never mentioned that Taylor had a stepdad, or that her father lived on a boat in Lahaina, or why. Had I not heard these things from the original source, I wouldn't know at all.

Taylor shrugged. I knew that meant she had indeed read the book. "What did you think of it?"

Another shrug.

"I've read it, too," I confided. Her eyes darted at me, perhaps questioning my sincerity and then stared into the surf again.

"I wish I had magic like Nest," I said. Nest was the main character and heroine of the book. Taylor leaned back on her arms and chose not to answer, squinting to view surfers down the shore from us.

"She was a runner. Do you do any sports?" I was groping for a way to open the door between us.

Taylor sat up straight, folded her legs, and looked at me. "I play tennis, and I'm pretty good at singles, but I have a lousy backhand so I usually lose the big matches. I'd love to make the playoffs someday, but I never will."

"I see." We noticed the sun beginning to set without verbally saying so, but our eyes feasted together on soft glowing shades of orange at the horizon. I knew Taylor went to a small private school, where they played tennis, something unheard of in Hawaiian schools, but then she and other mainland imports like her were not welcome in Hawaiian schools. Native Hawaiians were quite prejudiced against outsiders, especially white people. Alana looked Hawaiian enough to fit in and Chenlei, being Asian, was also strangely accepted. Austin and Wyatt defied reason by being popular, but they were very athletic, confident boys.

Who got picked on was not consistent, but apparently Gwyneth and Michael didn't want to take any chances with Taylor. My mother never knew of the prejudice I had faced as a young girl in the school system of the Big Island. If it hadn't been for Journey, who needed me, looked up to me, and loved me unconditionally, my school age years would have been unbearable.

"I wish I had magic too, like Nest," Taylor offered up, her eyes still glued to the setting sun.

"What would you do with it?"

"I'd make my real father miss me, and want to see me."

I was taken aback by this confession, and chose my response with care. "What makes you think he doesn't?"

Taylor looked at me. "He lives on a yacht in Maui you know. My mom told me that. And he never remarried. He just operates on little kids, and he fishes off his boat." Taylor paused. "I'd love to learn how to fish." She picked up a small rock and threw it into the surf.

It was obvious Taylor had no one to talk to about her dad. Otherwise such confessions of the heart would not be shared with a near stranger. The children I tutored often opened up to me, needing someone to talk to more than academic success, needing to process their personal feelings before abstract knowledge. Taylor had a cross to bear with her childhood that took precedence over everything else right now. Making good grades to please Mom and stepdad Michael was not a priority. Gwyneth had told me by the look in her eyes that she could not deal with her part in Taylor's pain, with the ugly truth behind this father/daughter separation.

"He writes poetry, too." Taylor smiled. She hadn't been at ease with me until freeing her heart of its pent up secrets about this mystery father on a boat in Maui.

"He writes poetry?" I asked. "How do you know that?" I tried hard not to reveal exactly how surprised I was to hear this. But then, there was little I actually knew about him, if I had to be honest.

"'Cause. He wrote a book. It's one of those little poetry books, you know? My mom saw it at the bookstore and bought it for me. Can you believe it? He's my dad and we didn't even know he wrote a book until we saw it for sale." Taylor shook her head, but when her eyes flashed my way they were filled with wonder and respect for this father she longed to know.

"They're all about the sea, the poems. And some are about courage, or pain and dying, 'cause he's a doctor and he sees that sort of stuff." Taylor paused and then impressed me with her uncanny depth for a thirteen-year-old. "He kind of fits it all together with a theme about the human spirit. At least, that's what *I* think."

The sun was truly ablaze now, the entire sky affected by its mission to set. Taylor and I stared at its glorious finale knowing one blink could wash it away into the sea. We didn't comment on the awe of it. When the glow dispensed I knew it was time to look for Gwyneth and return Taylor. I jumped off the rock and smoothed my lavender dress. Taylor grabbed her textbook and we walked together back to the party, where the crowd had thinned and the food had disappeared. Those remaining were more relaxed at this late hour. It was obvious in their hardy laughs and close-knit conversations.

Gwyneth spied us walking up, apprehension on her face apparent even in the dusk. I cheerfully summarized our successful first encounter, and no sooner had I done so than a man who must have been Michael came walking up from the trail to the beach. Before I could ask he held out his hand to shake mine and introduced himself. He told me how pleased he was that I would be giving Taylor the help she needed in English. The looks exchanged between Michael and Taylor indicated they had an amiable relationship.

I could only wonder if that would still be the case, were she to ever find out what had happened all those years ago, when she was only five.

Chase was packing when I got home. I knew he had another big job in Colorado and could be gone a couple weeks, so I didn't want to fight. Making up was more what I had in mind as I sat on the bed and watched him.

"So you, Meagan, and Charlie are leaving tomorrow?" I asked.

Chase glanced up but avoided eye contact with me.

"No, Charlie isn't coming. He's going to do the island runs while I'm away."

"So, it's just you and Meagan going?" Dread set in as I realized why Chase was avoiding eye contact with me. I stared at him while he put shirts into his suitcase on the bed.

"Yes, and we're leaving tonight."

Chase said it with a finality that defied me to question his decision. He closed his suitcase, no doubt hoping to close the subject. Six months ago he would not have made this decision without discussing it with me first. But now things were different. I was more than toying with the idea of adopting Alana, without considering his feelings, and so he was returning the favor.

He sat down next to me on the bed.

"Meagan's been flying with me for over a year now, Kyl. Why the sudden disapproval?"

"It's never been just the two of you, alone, on your jobs away from home."

"You're jealousy of her is irrational," Chase said defensively. "You just need to trust me when I say she is no threat to our marriage. Sort of like I need to trust you about adopting Alana, and how that's not a threat to us either."

"I thought you weren't leaving until the morning," I said, not wishing to bring Alana into this.

"I have to leave tonight. We still need to do a lot of things tomorrow before we start flying."

Before I could think of what to say in the interest of making peace with him, he kissed me goodbye and was gone.

I trusted my husband and tried to talk myself out of being angry. Even though Meagan was single and attractive, Chase had never given me a reason to be suspicious. Quite the contrary, I'd always felt secure in his love for me. Nonetheless I hated that he'd hired Meagan and flew with her frequently. She was obviously flirtatious with Chase, even in front of me. Now they'd be alone together in Colorado for days on end.

In a way I couldn't blame him for doing this to hurt me. I could see the situation through his eyes, see the painting of it Quinn had stroked for me, but I just couldn't accept it. Journey was *my* sister, and I not only loved her like a sister, but like a mother and a best friend. She was my life, and I was hers for many years. Alana was *her* child, a child she didn't live to raise, and I was Alana's *aunt*. I wanted a child to raise more than anything, more than respecting my husband's wishes.

I stared out the window into the darkness, still sitting on the bed, and wondered if my growing resentment towards Chase's attitude was fair. He had only wanted what was best for Journey all those years ago, just as Quinn had pointed out. A tear ran down my cheek as I finally admitted to myself the truth of the matter. Journey left because she believed I no longer needed her. I had a new husband, and she was just in the way with her adolescent traumas and total dependence, thanks to our mother's sudden exit. It wasn't really Chase's fault. It was my fault. I wanted her to not be dependent on me anymore. I probably conveyed that message all too clearly without realizing it. I wiped away more tears as the phone rang, startling me back into the moment.

"Kylie?"

"Hi Taylor."

"My mom wanted me to call you and see if we can meet Saturday. She said you don't mind tutoring on the weekend."

"That's true. I'd be happy to meet with you this Saturday. Why don't you plan on coming by my house around noon? We can go to the beach when we're done. I practically live on the beach," I added.

"Great. I'll be there. What should I bring?"

"Bring *Running with the Demon*."

"Okay. My mom wants to talk to you." She handed the phone to Gwyneth, who seemed to be stalling, waiting for Taylor to exit the room before telling me how excited she was that Taylor had finally connected with someone who could motivate her to bring those grades up. I told her how pleased I was that Taylor and I had connected, because we both knew it was motivation she needed, not skills. The child was beyond smart.

I went to bed scheming a way to introduce her to Chenlei on Saturday. What Taylor needed as much as anything was a reason not to feel sorry for herself. If anyone could make her feel better about her situation, it would be Chenlei, who longed for her dead mother and had a father who was a *real* mystery.

I decided it was time to examine treasures in the teak wood chest. And what better way for these two girls to get to know each other than by going through my sister's things together? If my plan succeeded, Taylor would be the caregiver Quinn and Elise were looking for when I was not available. She would do well with the boys, too, I concluded. It was a great plan. There was no better way to ease personal pain than by caring for others, and empathizing with their struggles, which often proved to be more intense than your own.

I tried not to think about Chase and Megan flying across the Pacific together, for two weeks of Colorado sun and fun between helicopter patrols. I ignored my desire to call Taylor back and have her bring that poetry book her father had written. I drifted off to sleep dreaming about Alana and our day on the beach. Nothing would make me happier than to have an endless number of days on the beach with her.

The teak wood chest was my last thought before deep sleep. Until now I had not been ready to face it, or the truth about Alana, believing the truth could end my hope of adopting her. I planned to fly to Waikiki on Sunday.

Between looking through the chest and meeting Shalana, perhaps my questions about who fathered Journey's child would finally be answered.

# CHAPTER THIRTEEN

*"Mansions on cliffs are built to hold life at arms length, but I've found they seldom keep trouble out, and often don't let happiness in."*

Saturday morning Michael brought Taylor by and I invited him in for chocolate chip cookies warm from the oven. Chenlei was a little shadow beside me, as if fused to my leg. I had been explaining all morning that Taylor was coming and she was excited about meeting this new student of mine, but clung to me despite her enthusiasm. I thought it would be awkward sitting at my kitchen table with Michael, but he soon put me at ease.

"Taylor tells me her father lives on a boat in Maui," I offered up.

"That's true." Michael didn't look surprised that Taylor had shared such personal information. He did look uncomfortable. I suspected to this day guilt rose in his throat like bile whenever thinking of his former medical partner.

"She seems to have him on her mind a lot lately," I added.

"I know." Michael leaned forward in the chair, his hands held together like a criminal getting ready to confess. "Grayson, that's her father, hasn't kept in touch and I think it's hard on her. Especially now, being thirteen and all, she has a lot of questions about why not."

Michael didn't indicate there was any more to say, as if he had severed the *why not* from his brain and couldn't find anything to probe on the subject if he tried.

"Why hasn't he?" I asked, thinking Michael needed to face *why not* or there was no hope for helping Taylor.

He studied my expression. It was as if he knew *I knew* why not. Maybe he just wondered if the question deserved an answer, or if there was an answer he could live with. I explained that if I were to be successful in the long run as Taylor's tutor, I would need to help her understand why her father hadn't stayed in touch.

"Grayson and Gwyneth haven't spoken since their divorce. Taylor is just a casualty in the long cold war between them," Michael offered up rather sadly.

"He shouldn't have let his child get caught in the crossfire," I suggested.

Michael shook his head. "Don't judge him, Kylie. He's a good man. It was just too painful, and now it's too late. At least, he thinks it is."

"How would you know what he thinks?" I smiled.

"I guess I don't." He shrugged his shoulders.

"Have you tried to contact Grayson and let him know Taylor needs him?"

Michael stood up to leave and I had my answer. He and Gwyneth didn't know how to approach this subject, let alone any subject with Grayson after all this time. It was what I had suspected. They were as dysfunctional as he was about confronting one another and moving on. Instead, it was eating them up inside, as much now as then.

"I'm sorry, Michael. It's just that Taylor isn't going to invest in her education as long she believes her father has dismissed her as his daughter."

"Believe me, if I had any idea what to do about it, I would have done it a long time ago. It's just that, well, it's complicated." Michael suddenly looked older, the lines on his forehead deeper than a minute ago. He was a nice-looking man, tall and lean with dark hair and sleepy hazel eyes.

We walked out onto the front porch. I leaned against the railing while Michael lingered at the bottom step, and shared the rest of the story behind this father/daughter non-relationship.

"He set up a trust fund for Taylor as soon as the ink was dry on the divorce papers. Every year he puts a large chunk of change in it. We call it her college fund. She'll be able to attend any university her heart desires, and still have a lot left over for getting started in life. But first she has to make the grades, and she's very capable. It's killing Gwyneth that Taylor's wasting her intellect with this sudden adolescent rebellion."

"Does Taylor know about the trust fund?" I asked.

"Yes. She's always known about it. He puts the money into it at Christmastime and we get a statement to that effect. Somehow he managed to get someone at the bank to send it in a gold envelope with a rather generic Christmas greeting card each year. For her birthdays, books have always shown up. Subscriptions to book clubs, sets of classics, large gift certificates for the local bookstore. Always something to do with books." Michael stared off into the rolling hills between our house and Elise's. "Never a personal note. Not once."

I didn't respond and he changed the subject, instead of making a mad dash for his SUV. "This is a beautiful place. The house, the setting."

"Thanks." I sat down on the top step. "Chase and I recently bought it. I've lived here since I was a little girl. My mother rented it for years, and then Chase and I rented it until the owners made us a deal we couldn't refuse, or more correctly, we could afford." I laughed. "They must have decided we'd get squatters rights soon if they didn't make it affordable." I pointed to the top of the ridge, almost out of view. "The Claibornes, that's who we bought this property from, own the mansion on the cliff."

"I like this house better. Mansions on cliffs are built to hold life at arms length, but I've found they seldom keep trouble out, and often don't let happiness in." Michael put his hands in the pockets of his khaki pants and rattled the loose change.

"It sounds like you've been intimate with one or two mansions."

"I grew up in one. I'll tell you about it over a beer sometime." He grinned sheepishly.

The girls were calling to me as if on cue. It was time to delve into mementos gathered by Journey over the last ten years, after leaving me in the dead of night to grieve for her ever since. Not unlike Taylor was grieving for the father she never knew. At least she still had a chance to know him, but judging by the response on this subject from both Grayson and Michael, it would be no easy task to bring father and daughter together. Not if Grayson and Michael had to communicate with one another in order to do it. Heaven forbid involving Gwyneth.

Michael waved goodbye and headed for his vehicle, while the girls nearly dragged me into the living room. We stood before the chest like soldiers at attention. None of us wanted to make the first move to open the box, despite Taylor and Chenlei barely being able to contain themselves only a few seconds ago.

Finally I knelt before it and unfastened the latch. The three of us stared at the silk scarves lying about the top of the chest. Journey's personality was in those scarves, in the soft greens of the sea and tumultuous blues of tumbling surf. I remembered how she had worn them around her waist as a cover-up for her bikinis, and tied her long hair back with them on hot afternoons.

"Are these real silk?" Taylor asked. She picked one up carefully and admired the swirling pattern of palm leaves and plumeria flowers. Chenlei draped one around her neck and smiled at the silky feel of it.

"Yes, they are real silk. You look beautiful, Chenlei." I tied the scarf in a loose knot, and admired how the bright colors brought out her dark features. Then I pushed the scarves remaining in the chest aside to pick up a wooden box. It was simple and square, but well designed and obviously meant to hold jewelry.

The girls were all eyes as I opened it to reveal silver bracelets, lots of them. I knew immediately Journey had made these. She'd had an interest in making jewelry all through high school, and had taken some classes. Shalana was a jewelry maker, and I wondered if these pieces had her influence in them. It was a more polished and sophisticated look than what I had seen of Journey's high school handiwork, but Journey's signature was somewhere on the back of each piece. "JLT" for Journey Luvay Tyner, was carved with three straight lines and a slight lilt to the curve on each letter. The *J* curved out slightly on the bottom left, the

*L* on the bottom right. The *T* curved slightly down on the top left and right.

We each held a bracelet and admired it. Every piece of jewelry had either a different design embedded in the precious metal, or a special twist to the silver strands. Many had jade or onyx stones soldered into them. Some had topaz or garnet. There were a couple heavy silver rings with tiny turquoise stones, and two necklaces of silver loops with inlaid emeralds. Journey's signature was in the rings and the necklaces, too. I was elated to see these works of art carved by my sister's own hands.

"Did Alana's mama make these?" Chenlei asked, her eyes sparkling as she admired them.

"Yes, she did," I said and adjusted the bracelet she held on her arm. It tightened enough to fit her slender wrist. There were little red garnet stones embedded in it. The stones were small and delicate like Chenlei.

"It fits you perfectly," I commented.

Taylor looked over and agreed. "Your sister made these?" she asked, surprised.

"Journey was always creative. She liked to paint, and took jewelry-making in high school."

"These all look professional." Taylor carefully set down a bracelet and slipped a ring from the wooden box onto her finger, holding it up to examine the oval turquoise in the center. It fit her finger perfectly, and the blue stone was stunning next to her light features. I decided she should have it one day, because her father had done so much for Journey. Eventually I would tell her how my sister found a refuge in him, and how she came to die on his boat. I had no timeframe for when this truth would surface. I had barely begun my tutoring with Taylor, and yet I already felt our trust was at risk because I had not confessed to knowing her father.

"That ring looks like it was made for you," I said.

She laughed. "It *is* pretty."

Chenlei walked around me to see it more closely on Taylor's hand. I wondered if Journey were hovering above us somewhere, able to see

*Journey* **115**

these two little girls mesmerized by her handiwork. She would have loved Grayson's daughter like a little sister, and her heart would have gone out to the orphaned Chenlei. Journey had thought of herself as somewhat of an orphan. Sometimes she would ask me about her father and if I knew him, if there were any pictures, to which I replied no. But I had seen him at the house on several occasions and I could tell her that he looked strong, with beautiful curly hair like her own. We never knew his name, and it wasn't on the birth certificate, of course, because my father's name was there. We both asked Mother once, to which she replied *it doesn't matter*. It seemed as if she had wanted to block him out of her mind and heart, and saying his name would make it that much harder to forget.

"Let's put the jewelry away and see what other treasures are waiting for us," I suggested. Taylor slipped the turquoise ring off and Chenlei pulled at the bracelet I had tightened to fit her. I put my hand on hers. "Chenlei, you may keep this bracelet. Alana would want it to be yours."

"Really?" She spoke with painstakingly perfect English. "I may keep this bracelet Alana's mama made?"

"Yes. It's perfect on you," I said, tightening it back up.

Taylor agreed.

Chenlei was beside herself. "I never take it off!" she said, leaving out the *will* in her excitement. Taylor and I laughed, despite that very issue being my angst with her learning English.

Besides the jewelry box we discovered several sketchpads filled with drawings, a couple well-loved teddy bears from her childhood and some soccer mementos. Soccer was the only sport Journey played at school. Some of her best memories were on the soccer field with me cheering from the sidelines. There were two albums filled with photographs in the bottom of the chest, and a box of loose pictures.

We sprawled out on the living room floor and looked through the photo albums. The girls especially loved the pictures of Journey and me as children. There were pictures of us taken with Mama during holidays. Next we looked through the sketchpads. I was overwhelmed to discover most of what Journey drew while away depicted our childhood together, on the beach building castles or walking in the surf. There were two that I kept out to have framed, one in charcoal and one in pastels.

The charcoal picture depicted the two of us leaning against our favorite boulder, on our private beach playground. The pastel was of us sitting in the sand building castles. Her style was soft, with long flowing strokes and delicate shading, but exquisite detail. I wondered what she might have accomplished had she lived.

We set aside the album of pictures that began with Alana's birth, to bring when I returned to Lahaina. I was disappointed not to find any trace of who Alana's father might be, if not Grayson. There was no birth certificate. Taylor and Chenlei, however, were far from disappointed in any aspect of unpacking the chest. They had thoroughly enjoyed examining every soccer trophy and photograph, while hugging the raggedy bears and trying to guess what their names were. I told them one was Pooh, and the other Honey.

We hastily made some peanut butter and peach jam sandwiches to take to the beach, after carefully replacing the items in the chest. Chenlei was proud to show Taylor the cliff steps. Like a model child she waited for me when reaching them, she and Taylor having run ahead on the path. We descended together, Chenlei between Taylor and I, in case she were to slip. The girls spread our humble feast of sandwiches and sliced papayas on a tablecloth in the beach cave. We drank bottled water to wash it all down and then took a walk along the shore. I had Taylor fetch the backpack with her notepad and *Running with the Demon*, knowing we planned to do some work when finding a suitable place up shore for our classroom.

The girls ran to the water's edge and squealed as the tide chased them. They were fast becoming friends as I'd hoped. Taylor looked out for Chenlei like a big sister, and Chenlei mimicked her every move with true little-sister admiration. After a while of beachcombing and tide chasing we crawled upon an outcropping of rocks and pulled out the books we brought. Chenlei had her own stack of books to read. She gathered them in her arms and climbed to the far side of the rock from us.

"Here's my rough draft." Taylor handed me her notebook, filled with small cramped longhand scrawled across five sheets of paper.

"Did you use the persuasive format?" I asked, noting this was the type of essay the teacher required.

"Yep."

"What are you trying to persuade the reader of?"

"That the advantages of magic do not out-weigh the disadvantages, and so we are probably better off without magic."

I thought about that while Taylor pulled her silky blonde hair into a ponytail and tied it with a cloth band from her pocket.

"Really? So, if you had magic, and could make your father reach out to you, what would the problem be with that?"

Taylor stared at me, and I could almost see her thinking. "Knowing it hadn't been his own choice, and that I'd messed with his free will. That's huge."

"That *is* huge," I admitted. "But what's the harm in it, if you're both benefiting from the results?"

Taylor twirled a piece of hair with her finger. "Well, I would never know if his feelings were sincere."

"And that doubt in your mind would make all the difference?"

"Right." She kept twirling her hair, making it conform to a tight circle. I wondered how strongly she believed that if given the choice, she wouldn't sprinkle a little fairy dust on her father.

"Free will is really an absence of magic in a way, isn't it? Not being able to control others, not completely. It's a blessing and a curse, free will, don't you think?"

Taylor nodded.

"But the good news is, I believe your father *does* want to see you, and I think he loves you very much. We don't always behave according to our feelings. Sometimes we choose to do what is right despite our feelings, and sometimes we choose to do what is wrong because of them."

"You think my father wishes he could see me? But he can! I'm right here, and he knows it because he sends money to me every Christmas." Taylor pulled a little book from her backpack. "I don't think he misses me at all. I think he's too busy fishing, and fixing up the locals, and writing his poetry." She handed me the book. It had a picture of a choppy Pacific on the front with a title that read: *Storms at Sea By Grayson Conner.*

I opened it at random and found a poem there that broke my heart. It spoke of a dying baby and a grieving mother, but mostly it was about how the wake of such a death storm leaves irreparable destruction in the human heart. The wounds never truly heal. They are invisible scars, revealed through the eyes, always the eyes.

I glanced up and saw Chenlei approaching. She dropped her books into the backpack and sat beside us. She looked at me with her dark, pain-filled eyes, just like in Grayson's poem. Even here at the beach with her new friend Taylor, the pain was evident. And then there was Alana. I pictured her caramel eyes and the grief that spilled out from them. It was so obvious she had known recent pain, and nothing would ever make it fade or wash away. Not any amount of time. Not the entire Pacific Ocean. Grayson had captured that truth in a few words.

It brought him to a whole new level in my mind, and possibly in my heart, had I been willing to admit it.

# CHAPTER FOURTEEN

*And then I found her, in the thickest part of the vendors, where the heavily twisted limbs of a banyan tree as ancient as the marketplace hovered overhead.*

Gwyneth picked Taylor up and we talked more about her project at the university than about Taylor. In one minuscule moment vulnerability entered her eyes and she asked how it was going with Taylor. I told her we were working on a persuasive essay, and it was shaping up nicely.

Taylor shouted an enthusiastic goodbye from Gwyneth's Z3 convertible as they drove down the long narrow lane. A flash of pulling over to beat the steering wheel of my jeep in a grief-induced rage on a day not long ago crossed my mind. I could not understand why a beautiful young woman would be stricken with cancer and taken just as her life was beginning, or why I had been cheated out of making peace with her.

Right then, at that moment, I decided to find a way to bring Grayson and Taylor together. I wanted for them what I couldn't have. A chance to make amends, to forget and forgive, to start anew. It did occur to me that, ironically, I felt compelled to return one daughter to Grayson while feeling just as adamant about taking the other. Gwyneth's Z3 sped out of sight, leaving a cloud of dust in my ability to reason clearly.

I walked Chenlei home and couldn't help but notice the silver bracelet on her tiny wrist. It reflected shimmers of light as she stooped to pull flowers. It seemed uncanny that this one bracelet had been tinier than the rest; its delicate red stones a perfect compliment to Chenlei's dark hair and eyes. It was as if God knew for whom my sister created it, guiding innocent hands to form the precious metal for a sole purpose

*Journey* **121**

of delighting this child. Elise noticed the new addition to her young daughter's arm the minute we entered the house.

"Look at you, little one. Where'd that pretty bracelet come from?" Elise took the small bundle of flowers from Chenlei and put them in a vase of water.

"Alana's mama made it." Chenlei's eyes danced as she said it. I had never known anyone to show more emotion through the eyes than Chenlei. You could take her emotional pulse by looking into the round dark pupils, which I often did. If Elise would only learn to read the map of Chenlei's eyes she could open the door to her heart. I wondered if Quinn had learned to decipher her moods by those inky pools fringed with straight black bangs. Maybe that was how he had come to bond with her so soon, and so completely.

"I gave it to her, Elise. I knew Alana would want her to have it."

Chenlei smiled, revealing a straight row of tiny white teeth. I had forgotten how perfect they were. It was only the second time I had witnessed such delight in my little neighbor, the first being with Alana at the bookstore. It was heartwarming to see Chenlei during these rare moments, overcome by happiness to the point of having it bubble up and spill out of her.

"Hmm . . . I see." We all sat at the table and Elise took a good look at her adopted daughter. "Well, this pretty new bracelet has certainly made you a happy girl, hasn't it?"

Chenlei giggled. "When is Alana coming back?"

I watched her toy with the bracelet, her head bent, revealing a straight part in her shiny black hair.

"I'm going to visit Alana next week, for her open house at school. I bet she'd love it if I brought you along." I glanced up at Elise.

"What would Grayson think?" she asked, skeptically.

"He'd be pleased to meet this friend Alana talks about nonstop."

Elise raised an eyebrow. "How do you know Alana talks about Chenlei?"

"When I called to confirm my plans to stay with them, he told me so."

Chenlei looked at Elise with an odd expression, as if wondering what this new mother would do. It occurred to me that Chenlei had no road map to read Elise either, that somehow she intuitively translated Quinn's every mood, every emotion, but not Elise's.

"Let me talk to your father, and if it's okay with him, then you can go."

Chenlei clapped her hands together and slid from the chair. She disappeared around the corner of the kitchen, and Elise shared with me that Chenlei would read books on her bed until dragged away to do something else.

"She loves to read. Ever since you got her English skills to the point where she can do it fluently, we can't keep her supplied with enough reading material." Elise said it as if she wasn't sure whether that was a good thing. I knew what she was thinking, that Chenlei was already withdrawn, and now her favorite activity would keep her living in a fantasy world through books.

"I doubt that she ever knew Chinese print to any extent," I said. "That made learning to read in English much easier. She does an excellent job. Chenlei is very bright, Elise. She's reading at a fourth grade level."

"I figured as much." Elise looked serious rather than pleased. "Her teacher says she is a veritable genius with numbers, and even word problems, despite being so quiet and withdrawn."

"It's not that unusual, to be smart and withdrawn. Look at your own husband. He was painfully shy and the head of his class all through school. Isn't that what he tells us when he's had too many Mai Tais?"

We both laughed.

Elise sighed. "Chenlei still has the nightmares."

"Are you taking her to counseling?" I asked.

"Yes, but so far Brandon hasn't been able to get Chenlei to open up."

"Dr. Chambers?" I was surprised, because he was the counselor for the university, and dealt mainly with college students.

"Quinn believes Brandon is an excellent counselor, and of course, they are friends so that makes it even better."

"I agree," I said. "Brandon is the best."

I stood to leave. "I'm headed to Honolulu in the morning, Elise, to

*Journey* **123**

find out what I can about the time Journey spent there."

My best friend studied my expression. "You're hoping to find out who Alana's father is or isn't, aren't you?"

"That's right. And whatever else I don't know about her years apart from me."

Elise nodded, staring out the window at the field between our houses on the bluff. "Edward's associate has told me someone came forward with information on Chenlei."

I sat back down. "Really?"

"Really. Someone who taught at the college." Elise continued staring out the window, her mood suddenly dark and sullen, as if this information was more disturbing than enlightening.

"How intriguing, Elise."

"I know. The street vendor told the orphanage her mother had worked at the college, but he wouldn't say where he picked Chenlei up, only that her mother was dead. It's partly how we chose her. Quinn felt a connection to Chenlei through the story given by the vendor, since he had taught quite a few summers at that college."

"You never told me about the connection with the college," I said, surprised.

Elise shrugged. "I might have forgotten to mention it because it was just a dead end until now." Elise continued staring at the field outside the window. Her low, raspy monotone was eerie, and obviously, my friend was quite disturbed by all this new information.

"Why would someone come forward after all this time?" I asked, thinking it odd.

Well, Edward's associate just got back from China, checking on available children there at the orphanage, and he had promised me he'd try to get some information that might help with Chenlei's nightmares, since Edward hadn't come up with anything. So he went snooping around the college asking questions, and Professor Laura Jennings remembered Chenlei's mother, Ling. She did filing for Laura and a couple other professors, in exchange for the opportunity to audit their classes."

I smiled. "So her mother's name is Ling?"

"Yes."

Elise left the window and began to busy herself in the kitchen, where she made us each a glass of iced tea. I couldn't resist staying to hear the whole story.

"How did Professor Jennings know Ling was Chenlei's mother?" I nearly whispered, while glancing down the hall to be sure Chenlei was still in her room. She had shut the door and I could hear her music playing.

"Laura had met Chenlei. Ling had brought her by several times as a baby, because they had become friends, or at least more than acquaintances. Laura also said that Ling was beautiful, intelligent, and quite young, maybe twenty. Her father was killed in a work related accident, in one of the manufacturing facilities. Laura said Ling's family all worked several jobs to make ends meet."

Elise was emptying the dishwasher as she spoke. She was strangely detached from the information. I decided all of this had become overwhelming for her, and I hoped that it wouldn't be long until we could all more forward, and Chenlei's past would no longer adversely affect her present, or her future.

"So Ling wasn't married. What else did Edward's associate find out? Did he say where Ling was when she died?" I drank my tea absentmindedly, engrossed in this tale of tragedy and triumph. Chenlei's adoption by Elise and Quinn was a triumph, and for Ling, too, who was surely looking down at her daughter from above somewhere. What better parents could she have picked, but ones that were obsessed with books, and higher learning, just as Ling had been?

"Ling was eventually laid off when cutbacks were made. A businessman in the community had noticed Ling at the college while taking some accounting classes. When he heard she'd been laid off, he took her and Chenlei in. Supposedly Ling had become pregnant with this businessman's child, I forget his name, and then he turned her out. Or more specifically, he sent her and Chenlei to a wealthy client of his, who needed another servant and wanted a child for his own daughter to play with."

*Journey*

Elise had been drying silverware from the dishwasher, slowly and carefully with a dishtowel, and then putting it away as she shared this information.

"Chenlei was four at the time," Elise continued, the same age as this wealthy client's young daughter. Edward's associate found the businessman, who did not object to admitting Ling had been his mistress, and who she'd been working for when she died. He swore that Chenlei was not his and had merely been a servant's helper alongside her mother in his home."

"That's quite a story, Elise. I bet this businessman was married and saw an opportunity to bring his wife a couple servants, while having Ling as a mistress, too."

"That's not all," Elise said. She sat beside me again and looked into my eyes. "The wealthy family that Ling worked for did confirm that Chenlei slept with her mother in a small servant's room off the back of the house, and they found her there, dead one morning, blood all over her and Chenlei from Ling having lost the baby."

I shook my head, not able to speak. My eyes filled with tears and so did Elise's.

"The family Ling worked for would have frowned upon her having a baby to care for. It would have affected her ability to work the long hard hours required to keep a mansion clean, linens washed, and food prepared for many important business guests. If the work she was doing while pregnant didn't cause a miscarriage, then threats to abort her baby might have caused her to purposefully lose the child."

I handed Elise a tissue from the counter and took one for myself.

"I'm sure Ling's living, breathing little girl was more important to her than the unborn child," Elise speculated, dabbing at her eyes. "Chenlei was welcome there, to play with the owner's daughter. She had a bright future for being clothed and fed, possibly even educated alongside his daughter while Ling worked in the many rooms of the estate. Edward's associate said that was not an uncommon scenario."

I nodded, slowly. It was difficult to listen to this information that affected someone I had grown to love so much.

"And then," Elise continued, "with Ling dead, Chenlei was given to the street vendor. No saying goodbye to her mother, I am sure. No seeing her buried, no finality in the way of a funeral. Just warm blood followed by cold flesh and then carted off to sell trinkets on the streets for a stranger."

I rinsed out my tea glass, taking a long time while the hot water rushed into it and spilled over the sides. My mind kept flashing back to Journey's days away from me, away from her home. How frightening it must have been to find out she was pregnant with no family to help her, and then to learn that she had cancer. Leaving Alana with Grayson must have given her enormous peace of mind, whether he was Alana's father or not.

Elise and I agreed that Brandon Chambers would be a better help to Chenlei with this information. I left, stunned by the story of this small child, whose intellect was becoming increasingly more apparent as she mastered the language of our country. Crossing the field back to my house I wondered what Ling might have accomplished, given the opportunity, with her passion for learning. She was probably as bright as our little Chenlei. I thought about how her life was wasted on menial tasks and hard labor.

Later that evening I packed for an overnight stay in Honolulu and worried about what stories I might discover concerning my own beloved sister, who was about the same age as Ling when she died. Ironically, I knew and loved both the young daughters they had left behind.

By the time the commuter plane landed the next morning, I was more fearful of what I might learn than hopeful. I checked into a hotel on the Waikiki strip and headed for the International marketplace. Slowly I passed by the stands of jewelry and leather goods, brightly patterned clothing and island trinkets, all scattered beneath a sprawling umbrella of ancient banyan trees. They seemed to serve as a canopy for the cluttered freestanding stalls, congested with tourist shoppers and local merchants, all bantering among themselves.

I studied the many faces behind the displays, looking for someone to engage in conversation about where Shalana might be located. For an hour I scrutinized the many stands full of unique silver pieces picking up specks of filtered sunlight through the canopy of heavy limbs. It began to feel more and more like a futile effort, and I finally tired of this search for a match to the pieces Journey had in her chest, or a face to fit the name Shalana. Feeling somewhat discouraged, I decided to rethink my plan over a plate of ginger chicken with sticky rice.

What if there was no Shalana or she was no longer here, I asked myself, feeling desperate and miserable. How odd it would be to have no trace of Journey's past, no idea of what she did and where she lived during her time apart from me. A hollow feeling grew in my stomach and did not mix well with the spicy Asian food as I began again my search through the silver stands.

By mid afternoon tears of frustration and disappointment began to sting my eyes, causing all the vendors to bleed into one, much like a watercolor painting. It suddenly seemed impossible to believe that I would find one particular jewelry maker amongst all these artists selling their wares, while countless tourists bantered for the best prices. And then I found her, in the thickest part of the vendors, where the heavily twisted limbs of a banyan tree as ancient as the marketplace hovered overhead.

So dense were the pewter gray arms as to let little light through, but even in the dark shadows I knew it had to be Shalana. Course black hair, shiny and braided into one long woven piece, framed a broad face with kind eyes. Her bracelets were what gave her away. They mirrored what Taylor, Chenlei, and I had discovered in the wooden box of Journey's handcrafted pieces.

Our eyes locked, and when extending a hand, my name raised her already dark, curved brow. "You look like Journey. Your coloring is different, but your face . . . I knew when you recognized my silver I had found the long lost sister." Shalana spoke to another woman who sat beside her in the booth, and then she came to walk with me beneath the ancient banyan tree, away from the congested merchant stalls.

It seemed strange to be considered the long lost sister. That's what Journey had been, from my perspective. We walked in silence, side by side, and I realized we were leaving the marketplace and heading toward the beach of Waikiki. Honolulu traffic was soon buzzing by us. It would have made conversation impossible. I knew Shalana was taking a dinner break, and letting me invade her private space while doing so.

It wasn't long until we entered a small, simple frame home and she offered me fresh pineapple juice. I accepted readily, surprised at my need to take everything in without asking any questions. A peaceful feeling settled into my soul as I sat down and watched this sturdy middle-aged woman with her round curves, small waist, and very Hawaiian features, make us each a generous sandwich from fresh tuna.

When finished, she sat beside me at the square wooden table, its light oak finish faded from constant wiping with a soapy sponge. Shalana sat and took a long second to really look at me, into my eyes, searching for something I had already found in her. Decency. My peace came from the realization that Journey had a home here, genuine love and caring. She fit in, I am sure, with all the artists of Waikiki at the Asian marketplace. Journey would easily have thrived in this environment, and with this talented and maternal woman, who was no doubt more of a mother to her than I, for all my futile efforts.

Shalana gave me a tour of where Journey had slept, and had given birth to Alana. The handmade crib was still there, compliments of a woodworking friend. I ran my hand along the smooth wood of the side rail and tried to picture my sister's baby girl tucked there beneath a pink blanket.

I also saw where Alana had slept when no longer an infant. Her small bed still sat on the screened-in porch, which Shalana told me was not used for anything but Alana's bedroom. I stood in the center of the screened porch for several minutes and felt the presence of Alana there, among the stuffed animals still scattered about in the wicker rocker and on the quilted cover over the bed. I had no doubt a friend hand stitched the quilt. It must have been sad when Alana and Journey left, not just for Shalana, but also for her many artist and neighborhood friends.

When we parted it was clear to each of us that Journey had been in our lives for a purpose, and taken away for one just as important, but unfortunately, we couldn't know what that was. We were only left to sort through the maze of her short life that had impacted each of us so deeply. Shalana was not able to shed any light on Alana's paternity. The surfer boyfriend did exist, was Journey's first true love, and yes, he had broken her heart. She went to Maui the weekend Alana was conceived in order to watch the annual surfing event that her ex-boyfriend participated in, despite his having jilted her several months prior. Journey had hoped they might reconcile.

On the commuter plane back to the Big Island the next morning I felt uneasy knowing Shalana, like Grayson, had found it odd I hadn't looked for Journey, who'd made no attempt to hide her life in Honolulu. The truth was that Chase did not prevent me from searching. It was pride that did that. It hurt like hell to love her so much and have her reject me so completely by running away. It screamed to me that I had failed her both as a sister and a mother.

And now there was no undoing it. No revisiting my decision to let her see how hard the world could be so she'd return to my open door, which I literally did not lock for the entire decade of her absence. If only my heart had been an open door. Surely that had been the missing key to unlocking our stubborn standoff.

Yet Shalana didn't appear to be as judgmental of me as I was of myself. Grayson hadn't been either. They believed that as a troubled teenager whose mother had recently died, her running away from authority was typical, and what Chase and I might have done differently was not an easy question to answer.

I had been convinced fate was the villain here. Fate took my mother's life just as my own was opening up before me through marriage. At the time I believed that newfound loyalty for someone other than my little sister is what kept me from searching the globe for her, or even the island for that matter. I had believed that she would return on her own, or someone would tell me they had seen her. It did not occur to me that she would be gone indefinitely.

And then there was that small part of me that was happy to finally be free of her, forced upon me at such a young age. After our mother's death, Journey became even more of a relentless responsibility, complicating the tenuous bond I was creating with my new husband. She must have sensed this, sensed the resentment, and out of love for me she vowed never to return or be a burden again.

By the time I had landed I felt my wings of righteousness clipped forever. Journey's leaving me was clearly no one's fault but my own. She had no recourse, and neither did Chase. Only I could have paved the road between them, had I wanted to badly enough.

And furthermore, without a doubt I knew now that Grayson was the father of her child.

# CHAPTER FIFTEEN

*It seemed unfair to have studied the intricacies of his mind without his knowledge or consent, even though he had put his thoughts in public view for just that purpose.*

The week after my return to the Big Island went quickly. I shared what I had discovered with Elise, who was happy to learn that Journey had a real home and some true happiness while she was away from us. Elise had thought of herself as a second sister to Journey in that last summer before she ran away. She'd give her books when overstocked with inventory and they'd discuss them over iced tea.

By Friday I felt the need to confess to someone my thoughts on Alana's paternity. Quietly slipping into Quinn's office I sunk into his leather chair, feeling like a child that needed advice, admonition, or both. I waited for him to glance up from his laptop. When he finally did, Quinn smiled and asked, "To what do I owe this honor?"

"I need some advice, Quinn, and you're the wisest history teacher I know."

"I'm the only history teacher you know, at least on this campus."

"That's true enough. Did Elise tell you about my trip to Honolulu?"

"She did. Especially the part where Journey and Alana had a comfortable home, and friends that loved them. Artists, actually, that showed Journey how to make fabulous jewelry, like Chenlei's bracelet."

I nodded, and then remembered what Elise had said. "Is it true that Chenlei hasn't taken the bracelet off?"

Quinn laughed. "Yes, it's true. She bathes with it on, sleeps with

*Journey* **133**

it on." His face became serious. "You know what? She hasn't had any nightmares since you gave her that bracelet. Did Elise tell you that?"

I stared into Quinn's eyes, and saw relief there. I'd been aware of how tortured he was by his young daughter's dreams. The nightmares seemed to disturb him as much as they did her.

"Elise said Chenlei would start to moan and move her head from side to side as usual," I said, "but then she would rub the bracelet in her sleep, unconsciously, and not fully awaken. As if the silver piece was a security blanket of some sort, a way to soothe her mind before it became too inflamed with the memories of her mother's death."

Quinn nodded. "That's right. That's exactly what happens. Isn't it funny how we both run to her side now the minute we hear the moaning? Elise and I have become obsessed with her nightmares, while Chenlei has become not only accustomed to them, but resourceful in helping her trauma pass."

I wanted to say the bracelet might not be a permanent bridge to peace for Chenlei. Her troubles might be far from over if not addressed thoroughly through counseling. Dr. Chambers was still seeing her, and that was probably going to be the real cure, but instead I changed the subject.

"Quinn, I know who Alana's father is."

"Without a doubt?" Quinn looked surprised.

"Without much of a doubt. I suppose the only real way to know for sure is to have a DNA test done, and Grayson may well decide to do that."

Quinn took his little round glasses off and rubbed his eyes. "So, Grayson is the father then."

"It makes perfect sense. Journey's information in the letter lines up with what Shalana knows."

"I see." Quinn nodded.

I stood up and walked to the window, observing the manicured grounds rustling in the strong wind. If I didn't know the afternoon gusts would die down as quickly as they had formed, I would think a storm was brewing.

"I haven't decided what to tell Chase yet."

"Doesn't he return tonight?"

"Yes."

"So you've decided to tell Grayson he's the father?"

"I guess. What right do I have not to?" I turned and looked at Quinn, forgetting about the wind whipping through the palms. I wanted his permission to lie.

Quinn gazed at the disarray of books and papers on his desk. All the texts before him were about history, how people had tried to manipulate it, and how fate had often destroyed even the best-laid plans of men.

"I don't have an inkling of how I will get the words out, without choking on them," I confessed.

Quinn didn't look up as he gave his response. "Maybe you have every reason to believe there is a purpose to no one knowing but you."

"Are you serious?"

Quinn put his glasses back on, as if to hide behind them. "Quite."

I plopped down heavily in the leather chair. "Quinn, you're telling me I can keep this to myself? To the grave?"

"Only if you have the balls for it. Pardon the expression." He began to tidy his desk as he spoke, slowly closing books and stacking papers. It had been time to go home an hour ago. "It's really a matter of what you want to believe, and then what you can live with."

"What do I want to believe?" I asked.

"You want to believe that God has given you this child for a reason. He has intervened more than once on your behalf, and therefore Grayson will never know the truth, unless you tell it. The important thing to remember, in taking on this philosophical view of the situation, is that you must live it with conviction." Quinn stopped arranging his desk and folded his hands in the middle of it. "In a way, Journey set this up. Leaving only letters to reveal the truth, letters that fall behind chests-of-drawers and get rolled up in canvases."

"Are you suggesting she hesitated for the truth to be known?"

"I'm suggesting she didn't shout it from the mountain tops even knowing that her time here was in sudden jeopardy."

"So, perhaps a part of her wanted fate to sort it out?"

"Perhaps."

"How could I live with that, even if I wanted to?"

"That's just it. If you aren't convicted about how it's all meant to be, it will destroy you." Quinn broke a pencil in his hand that I wasn't aware he'd been holding. It made me wince. Somehow, I hit a nerve in him, and I couldn't begin to understand why that was.

I left, saying I would give some thought to what he said. And indeed I would. Especially the part where he didn't respond as I thought he might. Quinn had merely given me permission to continue playing God. And for one magical moment I imagined that it would all be so easy. Just hold my tongue and have Alana forever. Be convicted. Don't look back.

The only real question was which pain I could more easily live with, giving up my lost sister's child knowing I would never have a child of my own, or living with the untold truth of who her father was. I knew Chase to his very core. He would never intervene and tell Grayson. Nor would Quinn or Elise.

Despite having driven all the way home with no memory of a single traffic light or curve in the road, when I turned off the ignition and entered the dark house, I had not a single answer I could live with. Leaning against the closed door in the unlit room, this inability to decide whether to be noble and honest, or neither, scared me more than the fact that Chase was not home yet, and hadn't even called.

On the commuter plane to Maui, Chenlei read from her book, *Little Women*. It seemed to fascinate her as she quietly absorbed each sentence. I marveled at her ability to comprehend the print, let alone the concepts behind it. The setting of the novel had to be as foreign to Chenlei's life as it was advanced in text for her age. But she patiently reread each word, sentence, and paragraph until she understood it.

I admired this trait in my little friend. Always pushing herself beyond her limits. She was blossoming like some exotic flower that just gets more and more breathtaking every time you glance at it. No ordinary daisy, this girl. And I suspected her mother wasn't either. I wish I could have known Ling for even a brief time.

Watching her daughter sip orange juice and read an American classic, I considered the ways in which I did know Ling. I knew what drove her: books and knowledge. Probably hoping an education of any sort, no matter how limited, might allow a better life for herself and Chenlei. I knew that she was also driven to care for her child in the best way possible, considering her circumstances. Most importantly, I knew what carried on through this child at my side. Perhaps some day I would have the opportunity to speak with Ling face to face, in a place beyond earth, where her God and my God merged as one.

Chase, on the other hand, I knew intimately. Yet he was more foreign to me at this moment than Chenlei's mother, dead two years before I had the privilege of becoming acquainted with her. He had called to tell me that his job in Colorado was extended for another week. I explained to him that I had made a commitment to attend Alana's open house at school the day he would finally return, and would be bringing Chenlei with me. So as his plane was landing on the Big Island this Thursday morning, mine was landing in Maui. I clung to the hope that nothing had changed while he was away in Colorado, that Chase was still crazy about me despite my being here for Alana instead of being there for him.

Grayson and Alana met us on the tarmac and there were hugs all around, complete with squeals of delight from the girls. It felt strange to hug Grayson. I was surprised by how hard and muscular he felt. I had read his poetry book cover to cover on the commuter flight, which established an intimacy between us he could not fathom existed. It seemed unfair to have studied the intricacies of his mind without his knowledge or consent, even though he had put his thoughts in public view for just that purpose.

"Alana thinks we should take Chenlei to the Hula Grill for old time's sake. That is, after all, where we met," Grayson said with one of his rare smiles.

I thought back to my dinner with Alex and how Grayson had shown up with this little spitting image of my sister, only with lighter features. I remembered thinking even then that her father, whether Grayson or not, was surely someone with coloring such as his. I recalled the disapproval in his eyes for someone who made no effort to locate Journey while she was living. Everything about Grayson since meeting him that night had caused me to question myself; my motives, my thoughts and feelings, my very ability to be honest about these basic things. But after examining his written words on the flight over I did not question having a connection to his poetry that was as comforting as the rest was disconcerting.

"Chenlei, you will love the Hula Grill," I said. They have yummy shrimp, pan fried, just the way you like it." She giggled as I said this, and I realized she rarely giggled unless in Alana's presence.

We all piled into Alex's jeep, which Grayson cared for while he was away at college. We wouldn't have fit in Grayson's little gray convertible, but I smiled at the memory of his escorting Alana and I from the airport in it on my last visit.

Dinner at the Hula Grill was very different from my first meal there. The only thing similar was Alana's snuggling up to Grayson, while perched on the edge of the booth across from me. Chenlei snuggled a little herself, up against my side, as I thought about how this was her first time away from The Big Island, and the family that brought her to America.

After the open house, where Alana's teacher raved about her multiple talents and endless abilities, we all lounged on the deck of Grayson's boat and sipped root beer floats through a straw. The girls chattered on and on about the kids in Alana's classroom that Chenlei had met during the evening. When they had finished their root beer floats, they put on their PJs and rummaged through the books on Alana's shelf above the bed. Then the girls positioned all the stuffed creatures around them to view illustrations as they took turns reading out-loud. Grayson and I left them there, entertaining the velvety dolphins and cushiony sea turtles.

We decided to watch the stars from the upper deck, where after several strong Mai Tais I managed to pull *Storms at Sea* from my leather bag.

"Where'd you get that?" Grayson asked, as if he'd forgotten all about it.

I stared at the cover, and then looked into those blue eyes. "I got it from your daughter."

Grayson sat down in the chair next to me. "Taylor?" he whispered.

"Yes." I cleared my throat, which felt thick from the rum. "It would seem that I am tutoring her. In English."

"How could that be? And why?"

"Taylor has fallen behind in her school work."

Grayson just stared at me.

"Aren't you the least bit curious as to why I even know your daughter, let alone that I'm tutoring her?"

"I'm assuming you're going to explain."

"Gwyneth has been hired through a university grant to help our students design a resort on the beach," I confessed, feeling lightheaded from the rum. "I met her shortly after my last visit here. It felt very odd, I might add, considering the impact your final parting with her had on me."

Grayson didn't say anything.

"Anyway, she approached me about tutoring Taylor."

"What got in the way of Taylor's learning?" Grayson sounded confused, as if he had envisioned her as a straight-A student. Now that fantasy was shattered.

"She seems to be rebelling against her mother's controlling nature. But more than that, she's confused about her father, who writes poetry and heals native children, but has buffered himself from her on a yacht in Lahaina Harbor."

Grayson furrowed his brow and looked as if I had sucker-punched him. "She could've come to see me, if it was such a pressing issue for her. Why in the hell didn't Gwyneth let me know about this?"

I cleared my throat again. All that courage I had gained from the rum was now making me weak in the knees. "When, exactly, is the last time you spoke to Gwyneth about *anything*?"

There of course was no response. We both knew conversations between them did not exist. I envisioned them signing their names in divorce court with no eye contact, and only nods of the head for legal notation.

Grayson poured himself a straight shot of rum from the open bottle on the deck table. I would have had one too, but thought better of it, not wanting to be carried to my bed.

"She wants to know you more than anything, Grayson. It's eating her up inside, believing you don't care, especially when she loves you so much."

"Michael has failed her then. I thought him a better man than that. I thought he'd be the father I would have been, given the chance, which he took from me."

"That's not fair. Michael, from all indications, has been a wonderful father to her . . . but he is after all, only a stepfather. Children never forget the difference. Blood is thicker than legal ink."

I felt the deck swaying, and not from the tide. It was time to excuse myself and let him sober up to the reality of this situation, alone.

*Oh the tangled webs we weave* kept running through my mind, and even full of rum I was aware that I had constructed a few *very tangled* webs of my own.

# CHAPTER SIXTEEN

*His eyes widened and jaw tightened, as if I had just confessed to a murder.*

Friday morning Alana wanted to take Chenlei to her favorite beach on the far side of Kaanapali. The older more established hotels were spread along the beachfront there, set further apart and farther from shore, allowing occupants more seclusion than in the newer section of Kaanapali. There was a sunken ship not far offshore and we planned to explore it while snorkeling. Lots of sea turtles hung out in this same area and Alana claimed it was where she first fell in love with the gentle giants.

Once we arrived Chenlei and I climbed into one of the two tandem kayaks we had rented at the edge of the shore. Grayson took Alana in the second one. The sunken ship was quite interesting, and the many turtles it attracted made the whole event very special. I could see why Alana had grown so attached to these sea creatures with their unique shells of armor and wise, gentle eyes. Afterwards Grayson and I helped the girls look for heart shaped coral that had washed up on shore along the secluded stretch of beach.

We returned to the yacht just before lunch, and I presented Alana with the photo album from Journey's chest. The girls and I spent some time going through it while Grayson busied himself in his den. After eating tuna sandwiches Grayson prepared for us, we left Alana and Chenlei to re-examine every picture while Grayson and I took a walk along the harbor front. We tossed off our flip-flops and dangled our feet in the sea at the end of a distant dock. It was the first opportunity we had to address the night before and my news about his long lost daughter.

"I'm sorry, Grayson, that as fate would have it, I've become involved with Taylor," I said, apologetically.

"I can't tell you how much I have missed her all these years." Grayson sighed. "I wake up with her on my mind and she is still there as my last thought at night. It has taken every ounce of my strength to stay the hell out of her life."

"But you're her father. Why stay the hell out of her life?" I asked.

Grayson shrugged. "At first I stayed out of the picture so she wouldn't be torn from pillar to post like in most typical divorce situations. Some time ago I regretted that decision, but then I thought reentering her life midstream might be worse than if I'd asked for partial custody from the start."

"You must wish things had turned out differently, for you and Gwyneth. Perhaps if you had forgiven her she'd still be your wife."

Grayson picked up a small stick beside him on the dock and hurled it into the Bay. "I don't think we were ever a match, Gwyneth and I. Our thoughts were often foreign to each other. The fantasy of loving someone completely, and forever, was what kept me going in our young marriage. It wasn't until I found her with Michael that I realized to love someone completely, you have to love them for who they really are, not for who you wish them to be."

"How did finding her with Michael tell you who she really was?"

"It told me that she didn't love me completely, or she wouldn't have turned to someone else. And truthfully, I wasn't that surprised. I don't think anyone is ever truly surprised when finding a partner has wandered. Because we all know deep inside whether our connection to that person is everything it should be. It's more a matter of finally admitting it isn't."

"Maybe she was just lonely, Grayson. You said yourself what a workaholic you were then."

"Yes, loneliness opened the door, but what she was seeking she could not have found in my presence. We didn't have the magic that defies all odds."

"Some marriages recover from infidelity."

"Michael loved Gwyneth more than I ever could have. He felt that connection with her that I didn't."

"How can you know that?"

"Because looking back, it was in their eyes, in the way they tried to avoid each other, and truthfully, neither of them are the kind of people that would do what they did if it weren't so big they couldn't fight it. I can honestly say I have forgiven them."

"Do you still write poetry?" I asked.

"Once a poet, always a poet they say." Grayson shrugged. "It's a great emotional release for me. The book was inspired by my new practice here, after I moved onto the boat. I threw myself into it, trying to forget the pain of losing my little family. My patients are mostly locals. Word of mouth sends them to me. Following their example of a simple life filled with small pleasures and quiet courage has helped me more than words could ever say."

"Well, your book is very moving. I hope you write another, but I wouldn't want to wish any more trauma on you for inspiration."

Grayson smiled, and that made me smile, too. It was as if I had penetrated some invisible armor he seldom let down.

"You were wonderful at Alana's open house. I can't thank you enough for coming. I know it meant a lot to her."

"I didn't do anything but admire her projects on display."

"No, you were splendid with everyone. Gracious and warm, just probing enough about her studies, her friends. And on the beach today . . ." Grayson grew quiet.

"What about on the beach?" I asked, almost defensively, thinking back to my playful mood with the girls. Did I make a fool of myself? Probably. "I can be as silly as any six- or seven-year-old," I admitted.

"You were charming. It must be hard for you to have no children of your own. I've never seen a more natural mother. Gwyneth was always a bit reserved with Taylor, almost awkward at times. But you, you have no inhibitions with them. They're like pure joy to you."

I was sure that Grayson's praise had left me blushing.

"We better get back and see what the girls are up to by now," I said, standing to put my flip-flops on. Our walk back was swift and silent. This was the pattern that seemed to shadow our growing friendship. We would be distant as if mere acquaintances and then without warning become connected on some subject. It would cause an immediate retreat into a neutral place, a silent space between our guarded thoughts.

When we returned the girls were ready to go swimming. Grayson and I lathered them up with sunscreen. I packed some snacks and drinks while he found beach towels and a book to read, then I sent them on their way, and stayed behind to get acclimated to the galley. I wanted to make their dinner while they were gone.

First, I steamed some sticky rice. Nothing really went better with the mild island fish of Mahi-Mahi, which they had all three promised to stop and buy from the fishing boat two docks down on the way back from swimming. Next, I made a pineapple upside down cake for dessert, since there seemed to be no end to Grayson's supply of pineapples, having done knee surgery on a plantation owner. I had an assortment of baby vegetables to sauté from someone's garden, someone who had also been a patient of Grayson's.

When I had done as much prep work as I could before they returned with the fresh fish, I wandered lazily about the yacht. It was quiet and peaceful in the late afternoon, there among the other vessels tied to their slips. A gentle trade wind cooled the muggy air while water lapped against the sides and made a slight rocking motion. It felt odd to be alone in someone else's home, running my fingers across Grayson's bookshelves, viewing his pictures of family and friends. I might not have entered his den, but the office space (which housed a small library as well) was the far open end of the main living area. There was a small TV attached to a wet bar and a black leather sofa with matching chair on the living room side.

I sat down at Grayson's oak desk, as solid as it was compact, and picked up a hard copy of his poetry book he had there, between other books that must have held some significance for him. Again I read my favorites and thought about what a gift he had for touching one's very soul with his words.

Somehow it felt too intimate to be there, sitting at his desk, reading his work. It felt wrong to be so touched by it. I closed the book and returned it beside the others, with glass dolphins at either end of the small collection. Then I returned to the upper deck where I lay in a lounge chair and dozed, trying very hard not to think about Grayson Conner, or his poetry.

Dinner turned out perfect. The girls helped clear the table and do the dishes in the small galley kitchen, which led to a lot of giggling as they tried not to run into each other while putting plates and cups away.

Once the little girls were tucked in for the night I returned to the upper deck, where Grayson was making drinks at the wet bar. Stars twinkled above us and somehow gave me the courage to share what was on my mind.

"Grayson, Taylor needs to spend time with you. I could bring her on my next visit," I said, dropping this statement like a bomb as he handed me a Mai Tai.

He froze there, leaning over me as I carefully reached for the drink from his hand and innocently took a sip. His eyes widened and jaw tightened, as if I had just confessed to a murder.

"Kylie, you're not like anyone I've ever met."

I wasn't sure if I wanted to be like anyone he'd ever known. Most of the people in his life, the ones that I knew anyway, had let him down. A shiver ran along my spine, for surely I was poised to let him down too if I didn't stop dabbling in deity matters. A game Quinn seemed to feel was a fair one to play, if only you were convicted enough to pull it off.

"I'm sorry, Grayson. But I see the hurt in Taylor's eyes, the feelings of rejection. And I see the hurt in your own eyes, every time you or I say her name."

"Why does my relationship with Taylor matter so much to you?"

"Taylor is my student, and I owe her the truth because she confides in me and will feel betrayed if I don't tell her that I know you, have known you since before meeting her, and I want to tell her that I have set up a meeting for the two of you."

"Then you haven't told her yet that you know me."

"I haven't. But I must. Soon."

Handing me a refill, Grayson sat beside me on a deck chair.

"I have been here, on this boat, since she was five years old. Why do you suppose she has made no attempt to come and see me? How can you be sure that meeting me is what she really wants? Maybe what she really wants is just a reason to hate me, because how could she not?"

"I can assure you that Taylor does not hate you. I have sensed nothing in her but a desire for you to reach out to her. I sense that same desire in you. It's a standoff, Grayson. Even though you want to approach her, and she wants to approach you. Let me make it easy for both of you. Let me tell her how and why I know you, and let me bring her to you."

"But what about Alana?"

"What about Alana?" I asked. "Alana will understand that you have a long lost daughter. What Alana wouldn't give to know who her own father is!" I said, and then chugged my Mai Tai in one gulp, hoping it would sooth my throbbing conscience.

"What would Taylor think of my having Alana here, raising someone else's child when I wouldn't bother to raise her?" Grayson stood and walked to the rail. For a moment I thought he might fling himself over, his tone being so sorrowful.

"I'll explain all that," I said, "how Journey was your patient and how I don't want to rip her from your yacht where all the memories of her mother are, at least not yet, not until I have won her love and trust."

Grayson laughed. "Admit it, Kylie. You haven't collected your niece and run off with her to the Big Island because you fear it will end your marriage. Your husband wants no part of your sister's child. We both know it is because of your husband that Journey ran away in the first place, and didn't return to you on her death bed, and didn't bequeath her child to you, either."

"Chase only wanted what was best for Journey," I said, defensively. "It was inevitable that they would be at odds. Journey and I had just lost our mother and how could she not resent Chase, when she had never had to share me in the past, and now she had no one *but* me?"

"You don't need to defend the oddities of fate to me, Kylie. I am all too aware of how little control we have sometimes over what matters most."

I didn't know how in the world this whole conversation had gotten so turned around. I did know that once again I was on Grayson's top deck, thick with twinkling stars and blurred by strong liquor. The same liquor that allowed Grayson to forget he had slept with Journey, which put him at a full disadvantage now where Alana's future was concerned. Perhaps that was fate, too. Perhaps Quinn was right, and if I had the missing pieces to the puzzle in my pocket, then who was to say that God above would disapprove of my keeping them there?

"Grayson, do you want a relationship with Taylor, or not?"

"Of course I do."

"The next time I see Taylor I will let her know you're receptive to meeting with her."

He didn't respond to that, at least not in the few seconds he had before I left the deck and went to bed, where I tried not think about how vulnerable he had looked standing there wondering if Taylor would forgive him. It was even harder not to think about what a wonderful poet he was, with muscles of steel and eyes as blue as the bottomless sea.

I was fuzzy from the rum and tired from the day as I lay there in the guest bed, moving gently with the swells. Nonetheless sleep wouldn't come for the longest time, during which it was difficult not to dwell on Grayson, who fascinated me beyond reason.

Before I boarded the plane the next day, and while Alana hugged Chenlei tightly, Grayson confirmed he would welcome a visit from Taylor, whenever I wished to return with her. I told him I would keep in touch on that subject. Chenlei slept throughout the entire flight and all I could think about was this charade with him about Alana, and how I should tell them both the truth, as soon as he and Taylor had reconnected. I should apologize for taking so long to confess, but I had to be sure, after all, before I legally turned Alana over to Grayson. And then I should walk out of his life forever, having my niece come to the Big Island for visits, rather than my going there.

This was a good plan and everything would be fine if I followed it. But the plan didn't make me happy, or relieve my stress, or bring me even an ounce of peace. All it did was sadden me, and make me restless. And I knew why, but I couldn't admit it, even to myself.

All I could do was hope that somehow I would be able to follow that plan, to the letter.

# CHAPTER SEVENTEEN

*An invisible wall was growing relentlessly thick and wide between us.*

Chenlei was excited to tell Quinn all about her adventure. Even her brothers were listening intently as she told them about the yacht where Alana lived, and all the things to do in the harbor. It was mid-day by now, and Elise was at the bookstore, as usual on a Saturday. I left with apologies in the middle of Chenlei's narrative of our two-day visit, but Chase was home waiting for me.

Pulling up in the driveway I felt more a sense of dread than an inclination to run into his arms the minute I exited the car. It was an odd feeling to associate with the man I loved, my husband of almost twelve years. But Chase and I had been through a lot lately. Some of it had to do with my sister, some with our inability to have children. And then there was the fact that Chase was gone too much. We never really talked about it, but it was there between us. I didn't wish to stifle his growing company. Chase had made an admirable commitment to his business and he had put his sweat into it for the last decade. C. Hudson Helicopters wasn't all sunset flights over the ocean. I respected everything he was doing to build his dream from the ground up, but now my concern was that the real cost might be our marriage.

I dragged my suitcase from the trunk and wheeled it to the porch steps, where Chase left the swing to carry it inside for me. We kissed briefly as he lifted it up, but neither of us said a word. I followed him inside and when he placed it on the bed, I sat beside it. He leaned over and kissed me again, both of us falling backwards on the bed for a

*Journey* 149

genuine make-out session. When finally coming up for air, Chase did all the talking.

"Kylie, I've been a fool to be gone so much."

He sat up with his back to me, and sighed.

"I need to have you with me. It isn't healthy for us to spend so much time apart." He stared out the window and I knew by heart what he was looking at: gentle hills rolling down to the sea. He seemed to need something that was not within his grasp, and I longed for it, too. If only we could define it, then perhaps we could pursue it. Once upon a time I thought it was a baby. Now I wasn't so sure.

"Kylie, I want to move to Colorado. Business is booming there. Besides fire season, there are all the thinning and seeding jobs. It takes a good pilot to maneuver the Rockies. Meagan and I are two of the best. It wouldn't be long and I'd have the funds to expand the business."

Chase began pacing the bedroom floor and I just watched him from the bed. I decided to let him speak his mind before responding. Truthfully, everything he said left me speechless.

"I miss us having any kind of family around, any roots for our children to feel a part of. I love my family, Kylie, and I didn't realize how much I missed them until I went back there this time, for this last job."

He stopped pacing for a minute and stared at me with scrunched brows, as if I might have an objection to living near his family. I had no animosity toward them. They all seemed nice enough when we had visited shortly after getting married. It was difficult for them to understand why Chase wasn't bringing me back to the mainland at that time. Perhaps they had finally convinced him that we belonged there, and not here.

I stood up and began unpacking my suitcase.

"What if I never get pregnant, Chase? Then what? I know you don't want a little girl from China, or my sister's child. Are we just going to get a Labrador retriever to complete our family?"

I was hanging clothes up in the closet and neither of us laughed at my suggestion. I hadn't thought we would.

He sat on the bed, watching me unpack. "My uncle Jake has a lawyer friend that can get us a baby."

I was standing in front of the suitcase when he said this and I just stared at him. He looked confident, with one brow slightly raised. Obviously, he had thought this through and liked the idea of buying a Caucasian baby we could pretend was our blood child. No one would ever know otherwise unless we said something. And maybe it would be a boy.

"Chase, unless I conceive it myself, I see no reason to start with a baby. There are plenty of older children out there that need a home."

I put my suitcase in the closet and sat beside Chase on the bed where we both stared into space. An invisible wall was growing relentlessly thick and wide between us. As in all good marriages, one of us needed to yield, to be the silent hero that abides by the other's wishes and desires out of a pure and selfless heart. We both knew that, but neither of us could let go of our personal dreams.

Chase leaned over and kissed my cheek, and then my neck. I ran my hands through his hair, and then he pulled me on top of him. We lay back as our passion surfaced like a pulsing thread that ran through all the otherwise impenetrable issues of our life together. It did everything except what it was supposed to do: make a baby. It eased the tension, soothed the wounds, and made us feel as one. It was why we didn't give up on each other, or our marriage.

We didn't leave the bed until mid evening, after having made love numerous times, but then we were suddenly starving and decided to take a picnic dinner down to the beach and watch the sunset. We hurriedly threw some leftover chicken and asparagus salad into a backpack and headed out the door, deliriously happy.

Sometimes an indefinable magic such as this would sweep us up like fairy dust and our feet wouldn't touch the ground for days. When we were first married, this feeling of amazing bliss could last for weeks. But life was wearing us down and reality was able to seep into our ecstasy much sooner. This particular time it snuck in and took our joy the minute we returned from watching God's brilliant colors bleed through the sky, while lying together on the warm sand. In fact, that loving feeling disappeared at precisely the moment Meagan called. I happened to answer the phone. Awkwardly she asked if Chase was there to which I replied of course, where else would he be?

I was pleasant enough, and inquired about her trip to Colorado with Chase. Her responses were short, and too sweet. Just like Meagan herself. Handing him the phone I busied myself with cleaning up the picnic dinner, while straining to listen for his every response. Nothing is more tedious than trying to guess what someone you wish did not exist is saying on the other end of a phone.

They stumbled through a conversation that had something to do with Meagan trying to pull Chase away and down to his office on this Saturday night for important business that couldn't wait until tomorrow. Chase did a lot of tourist runs on Sundays, and it was the icing on the cake for his monthly gross, but anyone that needed him on a Saturday night in reference to a Sunday flight was not respecting the hang-loose Hawaiian style of business.

Chase didn't end up going to the office. But our magical mood did not resurface. We watched an Indiana Jones movie with various limbs entangled on the sofa, neither of us wishing to discuss Meagan, C. Hudson Helicopters, moving to the mainland, buying babies from lawyers, adopting orphaned girls from China, or out-of-wedlock next-of-kin.

We slept in a spooning position, naked and exhausted. Intimacy was never more special than when being depleted of any energy to fight, or think, or make love. It was cozy and warm, two hearts beating in unison. It blurred frustration, disappointment, and fear, and left only an ache for harmony in the pit of your stomach.

Intimacy was the one thing that Chase and I shared perfectly, that and an inability to resolve our needs, aside from our need for each other.

Over breakfast Chase announced he was moving his office temporarily to Colorado and permanently, if he could convince me to move with him. He said the jobs he secured there over these past few weeks would make it impossible to spend any time in the Hawaii office for months. Maybe all winter, if he got even more jobs while there. I inquired as to what I was supposed to do in the middle of a semester at the university and he simply said *quit and come with me.*

He made it sound so simple. *Choose me and Colorado over Hawaii and your teaching. Choose living near my family and buying a baby, over your sister's bastard child or an orphan to raise here on an island where you have no family.* Seeing it all through his eyes, I didn't blame him. If my own roots weren't scattered to the four winds I might want to return to them, and have a tiny baby to mold and shape, and transfuse those roots into.

Why couldn't I bring myself to be a part of his dream? Why couldn't I just walk away from Chenlei, Taylor, my students at the university, and this house on the bluff where I still felt my mother's presence, still heard my sister's voice? Now would be the perfect time to tell Alana that Grayson was her father, to turn a page, begin a new chapter, redirect my focus, my heart, and my will.

I could write Elise and Chenlei letters, coaching and encouraging them toward better communication. Always the tutor was I. Always the teacher showing others the open door, the enlightening knowledge, the exciting ideas, the practical living, although I had no clue how to direct my own life or fulfill my own needs. I couldn't even live selflessly for someone else in lieu of achieving my seemingly impossible personal dreams.

"I can't, Chase."

Nearly choking on the toast in my hand I put it down and intertwined my fingers as if in pain, or perhaps defiance. "I can't walk out in the middle of a semester. My students are depending on me." As I said this I thought of Taylor and Chenlei, the only students who really were depending on me, and they were not in any of my university classes, they were both being tutored privately. My students at the university would be fine with another instructor, although it didn't settle well with me to walk out on a job before it was finished. It didn't seem fair of Chase to ask.

He sipped his coffee and gave me that *why not* look. It was a wicked mixture of accusation for improper priorities and being hurt because I wouldn't drop everything and rearrange my whole life out of complete love and devotion.

"Have you found an office yet? Where would you live?" I decided to take the pressure off of myself by interrogating him. The only thing I really wanted to know was whether or not Meagan was coming. There were plenty of good pilots. Having her transfer to Colorado with C. Hudson Helicopters would seem over the top for thoughtfulness on my husband's part, but I didn't have the courage to ask.

"Yeah, I found a small office to rent. And I could live with my brother until I found something appropriate for us. I could be doing that while you finish up the fall semester, and then you could move over the holidays, if I can't convince you to come now."

I just nodded and stared at my toast. "Chase, when did you and I ever discuss possibly moving back to the mainland, near your family?"

"When did we ever discuss living here on this island forever? You knew I was only here for graduate school, and that I wasn't from here. You aren't either. You mostly grew up on the mainland. The fact is, we never discussed where we'd spend our whole lives. I think we just thought it would all fall into place, and it did for a while, but now things are different."

"Why did I think when we bought this house we would stay?" I looked at him with disbelief, thinking he had shifted gears on our future rather suddenly.

"I only ever thought of it as an investment. We'll make a killing on it when it sells. And then we can buy something really nice in Colorado, to raise our kids in."

"The kids we buy from your family's lawyer friend?"

Chase stood up and threw his napkin on the table. "Kylie, there's nothing wrong with giving a home to a baby that the mother is too young to raise, or for whatever reason she's giving it up. Not any more so than taking a child from another country, or from their own father who doesn't even know it!"

"You started C. Hudson Helicopters here and it was doing fine. We bought this house, and we've been talking about adopting ever since we gave up on me getting pregnant. Then all of a sudden we're moving to Colorado where your company can do better, and we're buying a *better* house and a *better* child to raise than what we can get here." I was carelessly tossing dishes into the sink.

"That's not how it is, Kylie. You're not thinking clearly. All I want is what's best for you and me, for our future." Chase walked over to the door and looked at me before opening it. "I have some helicopter tours to do. We can discuss this more tonight."

With that he left. I finished the dishes while imagining Chase in a new office, living with his older brother Colin, who never married. I imagined eating Sunday dinner at his parents' house and perhaps Meagan being there, his right hand woman in all C. Hudson Helicopter endeavors. It made me want to lose the little bit of breakfast I had eaten. Maybe I was jealous, and not just of Meagan. Certainly nothing could be envied more than having a family such as his. They were all strong, educated individuals with barely a divorce in the entire tree. Close knit and always together for summer camping, fall football, winter skiing, or holiday celebrations.

I was beginning to hyperventilate. The stale kitchen air was suffocating me. I walked out onto the front porch and inhaled deeply. Then I just kept walking across the hill and down the cliff steps, onto the beach and along the tide line. Saltwater was splashing on my feet and tickling my ankles. I saw two little girls running ahead in my mind: Journey and I, holding hands, giggling. Sitting on a rock I remembered Mama's graceful gait, even with a swollen belly, walking this same tide line at dusk.

What ghosts were clinging to me, holding me here, where happiness was fleeting, but where contentment often crept in with the tide and pooled in my heart? The sea wasn't for everyone, but it was a vital part of who I was now. I could no longer say with conviction I was sorry Mama had dragged me here all those years ago in a whirlwind of confusion. I couldn't say I was sorry she had given birth to my baby sister out of wedlock, or that it had been my task to raise her on this barren beachfront.

This place was who I was, where I belonged, and it held all that I wanted to share with the child I would eventually call my own. I couldn't convince Chase to stay if he didn't want to. If he didn't need me more than his family in Colorado and the baby his family's attorney could purchase, then perhaps he would be better off without me. Indeed, perhaps the woman that he really needed would be the only one going, his copilot. They say if you set free something that you love and it returns to you, then it was meant to be a part of you forever.

Otherwise, it was never really yours to begin with.

It was a small K-12 school where Taylor attended, private, and on well kept grounds. The tennis courts were not far from the building that housed the middle grades. I had no trouble finding it. Taylor had just begun her second game and didn't notice my appearance until after winning a couple of hard-earned points. She smiled at me right after winning round two. During the last game of the set Michael walked up and spied me in the bleachers. He sat next to me and explained how he had trouble getting away from the office. "I don't usually miss her matches, but sometimes I'm late. More than I care to admit." He grinned, sheepishly.

"What about Gwyneth?" I asked.

"Gwyneth seldom makes it. Her schedule doesn't usually allow for being here at three in the afternoon."

"I see," was my response, but I didn't see at all. Gwyneth didn't have a regular office or standard working hours. She dealt independently with clients and did projects randomly, like the grant opportunity through the university. If Gwyneth had wanted to be there, she would have been. I was beginning to understand that Taylor's apathy about her grades went beyond a controlling mother and absent father. If one didn't make time to watch her play tennis and the other didn't make time to get to know her, why should she make time to earn grades that would please them both?

After a strong start and solid 6-0 win for her first set, Taylor ended up with two powerhouse opponents on her last couple of sets and lost both. Her weak backhand failed her each time. Just as she had mentioned that first day we met. I decided a two-handed backhand was the solution. It had certainly strengthened my own game. Chase and I used to play all the time in graduate school, and he was always impressed with my backhand.

While Taylor changed in the locker room, I told Michael there was something important I needed to speak with him about. He was watching the match after Taylor's, but turned to look at me.

"I know Grayson," I blurted out. "In fact, my niece lives on his boat with him. I was just in Maui this past week for a few days, to attend my niece's open house at her school."

"You know Grayson?" Michael sounded confused more than surprised.

"He befriended my little sister, who died recently of cancer. Grayson was her doctor. She wasn't married, and had nowhere to turn for help, since she wouldn't come home to me. It's a long story."

"Kylie, I don't know what to say. I'm sorry about your sister. Why didn't you tell us you knew Grayson when Gwyneth first approached you about tutoring?"

"It was awkward. I really had just met Grayson myself. My sister passed away recently, and the story Grayson told me about his marriage isn't one for idle conversation."

Michael looked wounded, as if he hadn't healed from his own self inflicted wound.

"I understand. And I can see what a dilemma this is for you, tutoring Taylor and all."

"Michael, Grayson wants to get to know Taylor as much as she *needs* to know him. I want to help. But I need your cooperation, and Gwyneth's."

*Journey* **157**

"Whatever you want to do is okay by me. I know you genuinely care about Taylor and have her best interest at heart. And she's crazy about you. A rare thing for Taylor these days—bonding with a teacher."

"I want to tell her the truth about knowing her father, and offer to take her to Maui for a visit."

Michael didn't have time to answer as Taylor walked up and joined us. She had a large grin on her face, despite having lost two of the three sets. But then, having two fans in the audience was evidently a rare experience for her. And I remembered from our earlier conversation that she really never expected to win.

My father had exited my life a few years before Grayson would be reentering Taylor's. I had longed to know him as an adolescent and young adult. Even now there was a hollow place inside of me that nothing else could fill. I often heard the sound of his voice when speaking to me as a young child. *Put your bike away, Kylie! Pick your skates up! Do you want to come to town with me and get some ice cream?* Taylor deserved a genuine relationship with her father. And I would see to it that she got one.

That, and a better backhand.

# CHAPTER EIGHTEEN

*I could only believe, by watching them interact, that some people share an unexplainable connection.*

When I returned from getting milkshakes with Michael and Taylor, Chase was waiting for me on the porch. After nearly a week of the same arguments with the same outcomes, and no more lovemaking to sooth our ruffled feelings or squelch our pride, Chase had had enough. I could tell by the dulled expression in his eyes.

He pretended not to hear me when I told him why I couldn't leave the island. Perhaps I hadn't listened either when he explained why he must. But now the time had come for us to be apart, until either he or I caved and became the noble, self-sacrificing peacemaker. Could our love endure separation? Would it make us miserable or show us that our parting was for the best?

He packed more than the usual amount of bags and spoke the whole time about how he would call every night and make arrangements for me to spend Thanksgiving there, rather than him coming here, because I was due to see his family and he wanted to show me the new office. Even better, perhaps I would help him find a house for us to live in, hinting that we could put this one on the market. I didn't argue. I just nodded and sat on the bed, watching him pack.

We slept restlessly, and barely touched until we hugged and kissed at the door the next morning. Both of us found it arousing and almost went back to bed, not having pursued our physical desires since last weekend when Meagan called. Neither of us had mentioned Chase's copilot all week, and I couldn't help but wonder if she would be on the flight to Colorado with him. I never got up the nerve to ask if he had included her in the C. Hudson Helicopters relocation to Colorado. Part of me, the strong-willed stubborn part, didn't want Meagan to appear important enough to fight about. I didn't believe for a second that Chase had eyes for anyone but me, not even perfect little perky Meagan, but still, a lonely man is a vulnerable man.

Chase had no sooner exited the long gravel driveway in a cloud of dust than Gwyneth's Z3 convertible emerged from his powdery white trail. I didn't have time to gather my wits about me, or swallow the emotional lump in my throat before she marched up the walkway to the front porch. What a vision of perfection she was, from her smooth soft curls to her pressed white shorts. I had barely run a comb through my hair this morning, and had thrown on my favorite faded running shorts with a wrinkled white tank top. I hadn't bothered with even the small amount of makeup I normally wore, but instead had poured myself a cup of strong coffee to watch Chase pack his pickup with every last piece of his personal gear.

"Was that Chase flying out of here?" she asked innocently enough.

"Yes."

"Is he going to be gone on one of those long jobs again?"

"Yes."

I could feel her staring at me while I focused straight ahead, where I had last seen my husband's truck disappear around the bend. Finally I looked at her. Gwyneth shifted her weight onto one hip and relaxed a little. Something about my mood had taken the wind out of her sails. Stammering in the awkward silence she finally managed to say something. "Kylie, why didn't you tell me you knew Grayson?"

"It never seemed like an appropriate time to mention it."

"Do you really think it's wise for Taylor to meet with her father? I mean after all this time? Wouldn't that be rather strange for both of them? What good could possibly come of it?" She smoothed her hair back in nervous frustration and folded her arms across her cherry-red blouse. I thought about how it matched her cherry-red car and decided she must really like red. It was becoming on her. As a blonde, red should have brought out my better features, but I never thought it did. I'd always preferred blue tones.

I suddenly realized what a bad hostess I was being and invited Grayson's ex in for a cup of coffee. It was still early I reminded myself, regardless of having had more activity before ten a.m. than on most days. Gwyneth followed me into the house and sat down at the kitchen table. I placed a mug in front of her and emptied the last of the coffee into it.

"Gwyneth, what kind of relationship did you have with your father?" I asked.

"I didn't. My father died in a hushed-up military accident when I was just a baby. He was a Marine. The whole time I was growing up, Mother had a string of long-term boyfriends. None of them ever committed to the point of paying me much attention. I think Mother never got over Father's death. She kept pictures of him all over her dresser like it was some kind of a shrine. I used to stare at them and wonder what he was like. I figured he had to be pretty easy going to put up with my mother." Gwyneth sipped her coffee. "I guess I'm just like her. It's always our worst nightmare, isn't it? To grow up and be just like our mothers, but most of us do, don't we?"

Gulping down the rest of my cold coffee I shuddered as if it were scorching. Was I turning out like my mother? Only instead of being the one running away, letting my husband do the running for me?

"Wouldn't you like your daughter to have the opportunity you never had to know her father?"

Gwyneth studied the view past me, outside my kitchen window. I knew that view by heart. It was a sloping field sprinkled generously with wild blooms of every color, but mostly white. Beyond the hill was blue sky, with a darker patch of blue below it. That darker patch of blue was the Pacific.

"My mother taught me that a girl needs to look out for herself," Gwyneth confessed. "Don't rely on a man. It's why she got me a good education and always encouraged me to pursue a career that would pay well. And that's what I want for Taylor," she added with conviction. "Besides, she has Michael. He's been a wonderful father to her. Grayson, well, Grayson may just give her ideas an adolescent doesn't need to hear, including the idea that she can pursue whatever pipe dream she may have instead of choosing a solid career path."

"But Grayson didn't do that himself. He's a surgeon," I said, in his defense.

"He has the hands of a surgeon, but the mind of a poet," Gwyneth replied.

"What's wrong with that?" I asked.

"Nothing. It's just, I fell in love with the surgeon, but the poet was there all along, between us. I can see that now. I read his poetry book about the sea, and love and loss. It made me wonder why he never wrote when we were married, or even mentioned that he wanted to."

I knew what she meant. There was a part of Grayson that hadn't let her in, and so she turned to Michael out of loneliness. Michael was so obviously over the moon for her even now, after all this time. Whenever they were in the same vicinity of one another his eyes betrayed his devotion to her.

"Why not let Taylor make her own decision about whether or not to spend time with her dad? Just knowing that you care about what *she* wants could make all the difference. I'm sure Grayson wants her to do well in school. He would only be an advocate for that. It's worth a try, isn't it?"

"Okay. That's a good point. If Taylor decides to see Grayson, I won't stand in her way, but I don't want anything to do with it. Will you help get them together, that is, if she decides to go through with it?"

"Yes, of course, I'd be happy to. Gwyneth, please don't say anything to Taylor yet about my knowing her father. The last thing she needs is to think her tutor has been keeping secrets from her all this time."

"Right. I won't say anything. She thinks the world of you, and I don't care what she thinks of me right now as long as she's willing to get her grades up." Gwyneth shook her head. "I thought having the stability of one father was best, even if that was her stepdad, and so did Grayson apparently, although we never spoke about it."

"I know," I said consolingly. "But children have minds of their own, and they rarely see things the same way we do."

I cleared the mugs away and Gwyneth rose to leave. She seemed much more relaxed than when she arrived, and as I walked her out, she thanked me, awkwardly, for helping Taylor. She didn't mention in what way I was helping her. I concluded that Gwyneth didn't wish to face reality any more than Grayson did. No wonder they hadn't spoken since the child was five years old.

The next day I picked up Chenlei after school and we headed to Taylor's junior high. I wanted to help Taylor with her backhand, and the school had a ball machine for introducing Chenlei to the game of tennis. Elise had loved the idea when I told her about it. At first the balls flew gently by Chenlei and she would giggle at her late swing. Even on the lowest setting she was hesitant to connect her racket with the ball. By the time we left the tennis court, however, Chenlei was hitting every one with a graceful forehand, sending them back over the net in a perfect arch. The child never ceased to amaze. She had the focus and determination to achieve whatever she set out to do.

Taylor had her own challenges with adapting to a two-handed backhand, but after several sets against me she was beginning to hold her own. We left the tennis courts hungry and exhilarated from all we had accomplished. The girls decided on their favorite Asian carryout, which we brought back to the house and ate on the front porch. About the time we finished, Quinn appeared from over the hill. Chenlei literally bounced off the porch and ran to greet him. It was a beautiful sight, watching him scoop his little girl up into his arms. The adoration between father and daughter seemed to be more instinct than effort. I could only believe, by watching them interact, that some people share an unexplainable connection.

"Taylor," I began, once Quinn and Chenlei had said their goodbyes and were headed back over the hill, "I have a confession to make."

"Really? What?" Taylor glanced up at me from the porch swing where she was opening her fortune cookie from dinner. "Wow, listen to this. *Nothing can keep you from reaching your goals*. Does that mean I'll win the rest of my tennis matches and make the playoffs?"

"Maybe," I replied cautiously. "Or maybe it means you'll get to visit your dad."

Taylor shrugged, not unlike Grayson did when at a loss for words. "I can't imagine discussing it with my mom, let alone her cooperating."

"I was just talking to your mom about that. I needed permission from her to discuss something with you."

"You needed permission? You can tell me whatever you want. You don't need my mom's permission," Taylor answered emphatically.

"It's a matter of respect, Taylor. Because she is your mother and I am only your tutor. I need to discuss with her anything important that might affect you. Does that make sense?"

Taylor shrugged again and then slowly nodded her head.

I sat down next to her on the porch swing.

"I know your dad, Taylor."

"You're kidding." Taylor scrunched her blonde brows together and stared at me.

"Your father is the one who sent Journey's chest. He was her doctor, and friend. She lived on his boat with him towards the end of her illness. And I have been to see him several times since then to visit my niece, Alana, who still lives with your dad for now, at least."

"Why didn't you ever tell me this?" Taylor asked, still staring at me, although her expression had softened.

"It never seemed like the right time to mention it. And since I hadn't said anything to your mom, I didn't feel I should say anything to you."

"So you know my father? Have you told him about me? What did you say?"

Taylor seemed fine with my secret and I sighed with relief. "I said that you would like to get to know him, and there is no question that he wants to know you."

"If there's no question about that, why has he stayed clear of me all these years?"

"Only he can tell you why, Taylor. But I can tell you that he loves you very much, and thinks about you all the time."

"Whatever." Taylor grabbed my fortune cookie. "May I?" she asked, and waited for a response before breaking it open. I nodded, and watched her slip out the tiny piece of paper. *Life is a journey, not a destination.*

"What does that mean?" Taylor asked, looking puzzled.

"It means life is more about what we do every day than where we ultimately end up. Someone with lots of money and a big office may be a complete failure as a person in all of the most meaningful ways when defining success."

Taylor thought about that for a few seconds while staring at the tiny sliver of paper. Then she looked at me with her eyes bright and twinkling. "It's sort of saying to stop and smell the roses along the way, right?"

"Yes. It's more than that, though. You need to water those roses and tend to them. Roses take a lot of effort if you want them to thrive and bloom. Hard work goes into reaping something beautiful and lasting."

"When can I see my father?" she asked, with her piercing blue eyes focused on me, the fortune cookie all but forgotten.

"I'll let him know you want to come for a visit."

"Okay. Will you call him tonight?"

"I will."

"And let me know what he says?"

"I'll let you know at our next tutoring session."

"I have to wait that long?"

"Longer, if you haven't edited your essay."

Taylor rolled her eyes at me.

"Can we walk on the beach before I have to go home?"

"Of course we can," I said, giving her a motherly hug.

I was sure that Taylor didn't received many hugs from her mom, who needed to tend to her garden before she lost her most special rose, blooming more each day.

Taylor won all her tennis matches for the next two weeks. The playoffs were becoming a very real possibility. I didn't miss a single game of any set and always brought Chenlei with me. Michael would sit in the stands with us, cheering, but never Gwyneth. That was soon to change now that there was a chance her daughter might shine at something again. Michael had shared how Gwyneth was rearranging her schedule so she could attend the next few matches.

Elise came at the end of Taylor's last set, to take Chenlei and Taylor shopping. Chenlei had been excited about spending an evening with Taylor looking for tennis gear, since she was suddenly a big enthusiast of the sport. Taylor had invited our little Asian friend to attend practices with her and the other middle school girls on the tennis team were growing quite fond of Chenlei, who always cheered them on enthusiastically.

Gwyneth was away on a business trip, so Michael and I decided to grab a bite to eat before parting ways. We stopped at a local seafood place and ordered the Mahi-Mahi special with sticky rice. It reminded me of the meal I had cooked on Grayson's yacht.

"Next weekend is when I take Taylor with me to Maui, to see Grayson," I reminded Michael.

"I know. She doesn't talk about it, but there's an uncharacteristic giddiness about her these days. I think it probably has more to do with her upcoming visit to see Grayson than her winning streak in tennis."

"Michael, what kind of relationship did you have with *your* father?" I asked, while squeezing lemon into my water.

"My father was a real estate tycoon. We lived in a string of mansions, one more elaborate than the next."

"My Daddy was a contractor," I shared. "He built homes, but they weren't mansions and we weren't wealthy, although looking back, I felt rich."

"Well, you were lucky then," Michael said.

"I miss my father," I admitted. "I remember him as being honest, and kind. Whenever I would tell a fib, he would lecture me about the importance of being truthful. But I never really felt scolded. It wasn't his lectures that made me want to please my daddy. It was how loved I felt by him, and the kindness always there in his eyes."

"I don't miss my old man, and so that would be the difference between our fathers." Michael shook his head. "My father was not honest, or kind," he added before finishing his microbrew.

"I'm sorry, Michael. I remember you telling me how most mansions shut out happiness rather than confining it."

"Did I say that?" Michael laughed. "I must have been having a moment of philosophical self pity."

Michael folded his arms on the table as the waitress cleared our plates away and brought us two more microbrews.

"My father built his empire by taking advantage of others when they were down on their luck, or their backs were turned. He was always being sued because of the loopholes in the property laws that he lived by. His attorneys would get him out of one sticky situation after another. I refused to take over his business. I've always wanted to be a doctor, for as long as I can remember. My goal was to be nothing like him, but I guess the apple doesn't fall far from the tree."

"What do you mean? You *are* a doctor." I swallowed hard, because I *did* know what he meant. A picture of Grayson walking in on Michael and Gwyneth flashed through my mind. "You help people every day," I said, truthfully.

Michael leaned in a little and looked me in the eye. "I've failed as a person, Kylie. Despite becoming a doctor to help others, I've managed to be just like my old man: selfish and thoughtless, taking what I want even when it belongs to someone else and not giving a thought to the consequences."

He took a large swig of his foamy beer and set it down carefully before continuing.

"I fell in love with my partner's wife," he admitted, more to the mug of beer he was staring at than to me. "And to top it off, rather than be a man and confront him about the whole situation, I let it reach the point where he caught us in bed together."

Michael looked up at me.

"Every day when I look at Taylor I am reminded of what I did and how it has affected her and Grayson, living on that boat all these years, never remarrying. My God, I altered the course of his entire life, both their lives, and yet I love Gwyneth. I will probably rot in hell for it, but I have loved her every minute of every day just as I have hated myself for it."

"Michael, you're beating yourself up over something that wasn't entirely your fault. Grayson would be the first to admit he was gone too much, and didn't quite know what to do with Gwyneth. She was a mystery to him from the moment they met. They didn't have that special bond the two of you share. He told me if she hadn't gotten pregnant, they never would have married. And truthfully, she played as much a part in what happened as you did."

I paused, hoping that would all sink in.

"Grayson chose not to handle it in a conventional manner," I pointed out. "It isn't as if he's not capable. He's intelligent and attractive. If he has decided to become an eccentric recluse on a yacht in Maui, it's no fault of yours. As far as Taylor is concerned, well, all human error is prone to consequence. She doesn't look like she's suffering all that severely to me. You have to keep it in perspective. Being raised in an unhappy marriage by Grayson and Gwyneth might have been the real tragedy you've all avoided."

"Thanks for the pep talk, but they had a fine marriage, if I'd kept my distance."

"Maybe. But since there's no going back, Michael, perhaps it's time you forgave yourself."

"What about your marriage? Why is Chase never around? And now I hear from Taylor that he's gone to Colorado, perhaps indefinitely."

"That's true. But I need to stay here for now."

"You need to?"

"I have a commitment to the university."

"Don't you love him?"

"Yes, very much. But . . ."

"There are no buts about it. If you love him, go with him now."

"I can't." I thought about his crazy over-the-top love for Gwyneth and what he had allowed to happen because of it. I wasn't convinced hindsight would cause him to do anything differently despite his philosophical agony. I realized he could never understand where I was coming from, being torn between my marriage and this island. I wasn't sure *I* understood where I was coming from, so how could I explain it?

"Of course you can. You either love him or you don't. Living in Colorado isn't a death sentence. I hear it's a beautiful place."

"There's more to it than that."

"Like what?"

"Chase's family is there and they are somewhat overwhelming. All my memories of my mother and my sister are here, in that house on the bluff Chase wants me to sell. I need time to think about it, get used to the idea."

"How much time?"

"I'm not sure. At least until the fall semester is over."

I changed the subject, giving Michael the details of my flight with Taylor to Maui next weekend, as we finished our microbrews and paid. I told him Grayson was looking forward to it. What I didn't tell him was how much *I* was looking forward to it, maybe because I didn't want to admit to myself how much I wanted to escape to Maui next weekend.

I arrived home just in the nick of time to answer Chase's nightly call. I thought it was appropriate to mention where I'd be next weekend, and why. Chase reminded me once again that I needed to tell Grayson he was Alana's father.

I explained to Chase that after Grayson became reacquainted with Taylor, I would tell him about Alana. I defended my need to have absolute proof of paternity before saying anything. I didn't mention my personal disappoint that Alana would not be coming to live with us, in the house her mother grew up in, on the bluff above the sea. I didn't voice my growing resentment over him wanting me to sell it and move to Colorado with him.

But I think he got the message anyway, loud and clear.

# CHAPTER NINETEEN

*The rebellious teenager putting up a brave front had been transformed into a vulnerable and exposed little girl.*

The initial face to face for father and daughter was not nearly as awkward as one might have anticipated. They smiled at each other, hugged briefly, and then Grayson said, "Welcome to Maui, Taylor." Her classic teenage response was to smile shyly and toss her head of silky blonde tresses. It translated to *I am delighted to be here.*

Grayson hugged me next, briefly, the full appreciation of my having orchestrated this event glowing in his eyes. Then he stooped down to say hello to Chenlei while I hugged Alana. The little girls giggled in unison. Together they stuffed books and snacks from the plane ride into side pockets of Chenlei's luggage.

"How was your flight?" Grayson asked, looking at his long lost daughter.

"It was fine." Taylor shrugged.

Grayson hugged her to him again, gently but firmly. "I've missed you more than you can ever know," he whispered.

Taylor softly replied, "I've missed you, too."

"Let's catch up with the girls," I interjected, seeing Chenlei and Alana heading across the tarmac pulling Chenlei's wheeled luggage, chattering nonstop.

We caught up with them and conversation all the way to the yacht revolved around school. Chenlei, Alana, and Grayson did most of the talking and it made my heart soar to hear the English flow freely from my little prized pupil, who hadn't known a word of English six months ago. It reinforced for me how quickly things could change, sometimes for the better.

When we reached the yacht Alana and Chenlei went straight to Alana's room, probably to unpack Chenlei's things. If Alana was the least bit nervous about meeting Taylor, it was not apparent. I wondered what Grayson had said to prepare her for this event. I made a mental note to myself to be sure and ask him later. I did consider it a coup on my part to bring Chenlei as a diversion for Alana.

I put my things in the bedroom Taylor and I would be sharing while Grayson gave Taylor a tour of the yacht. Grayson and I had e-mailed each other about what might be good activities for this weekend with the girls. We seemed to have an energy that flowed better through the keyboard, rather than the phone line. I had thought about this each evening when Chase called, because although he used a computer for his business, he never e-mailed me.

Until now I hadn't given much thought to how some people are more expressive when speaking, and others when writing. Like father, like daughter, Taylor's thoughts on paper in her written essays were quite deep and fluid in comparison to the awkward and defensive tone of the young teenager I verbally communicated with. Chenlei, on the other hand, still found writing her biggest challenge. Despite her near perfect memory and already articulate English, forming written sentences was difficult, if not a roadblock for her, but one I felt confident the determined Chenlei would eventually overcome.

Neither Grayson nor I wanted this weekend to be awkward for anyone involved so we planned it carefully. As soon as the tour was over we changed into swimsuits. Grayson and the younger girls gathered snorkel gear while Taylor and I made sandwiches. We were headed to a special place not far from Molokini for a day of snorkeling and swimming with the turtles. It was Alana's favorite thing in the world to do. I felt confident that Taylor and Chenlei would be equally impressed.

All the way to Molokini Grayson had Taylor by his side, showing her how to steer the boat, and letting her try it herself. Alana and Chenlei took no notice of them as they sat on the starboard side and watched for fish jumping out of the water, hoping to see some dolphins and whales that often surfaced in the distance this time of year. Once we were there and anchored it was a mad scramble to be sure everyone's equipment was secure and comfortable before propelling with our flippers away from the yacht. I kept close to Chenlei, and was officially watching Alana, too, but she was as difficult to keep track of as the fish themselves, always diving beneath the surface and wiggling around from one school of tropical delights to another. Grayson and Taylor were not far behind us to the right, where they soon spied the turtles and waved us over.

There was no containing Alana among the gentle giants. She might as well have been one of them, snuggling near and following their every move, surfacing for air as smoothly as a dolphin. Watching her took me back to my own childhood, when Journey and I had done exactly the same.

I had to focus on not tearing up inside my mask as I watched my niece's acrobatic moves in the water, each one an exact replica of Journey beneath the surface of the sea. I could not indulge in watching Alana much longer as a small school of round yellow-fish with black stripes and puckered lips fascinated Chenlei. She began to follow them, paying no heed to where her friend Alana had gone, or anyone else for that matter.

I followed Chenlei away from the group and let her chase the fascinating school of fish until it no longer held her attention. When she finally turned her head she saw me motion to change direction and head back toward the yacht. We no sooner surfaced near the anchored boat than the rest of our party appeared, too. Taylor was the first to leave the warm, inviting sea. She grabbed a towel and headed for the stern of the yacht where she arranged it on the deck and lay down to dry out in the sun. Taylor hadn't said a word to anyone about her undersea adventure.

Grayson and I helped the younger girls up the ladder, fetched them towels and lemonade, and didn't bother Taylor at all until Alana and

Chenlei were settled on the port side with tuna sandwiches. Grayson was leaning against the back railing, observing Taylor, when I approached him with her lunch on a paper plate.

"Do you want to take this to her, or should I?"

"You do it," he said, looking perplexed.

"What's the matter? Did something happen snorkeling?" I asked.

Grayson shrugged. "I'm not sure. She was excited to see the turtles. I showed her how to swim so as not to frighten them away." He paused, as if reflecting on what *had* happened. "Then Alana joined us, and I saw you following Chenlei. Alana wanted to swim through the rock cave. We do it all the time, so I followed her and encouraged Taylor to come too, but Taylor doesn't spend near as much time in the water as Alana. She wasn't comfortable with swimming through a rock cave. We did it several times hoping she'd take a deep breath and give it a try, but she just watched. Then Alana took hold of a turtle and let it pull her through the water, and I stayed with them, to be sure she didn't get too carried away. When she finally let go and we came back, Taylor had surfaced and was ready to get out of the water. That's when you and Chenlei showed up."

"I see." And I really did see, but obviously Grayson didn't get it. Taylor was jealous of their relationship. That special bond that reminded Taylor of what she had missed, and what had consequently caused an open wound in her adolescent heart.

"Maybe she'll talk to me." I gave Grayson a sympathetic look and went to join Taylor.

"I bet you're hungry after all that snorkeling," I said cheerily. Taylor opened an eye and saw that I came bearing food. She sat up and looked at her sandwich, as if trying to decide whether or not to eat it.

"What's wrong, Taylor. Did you swallow too much saltwater?" I smiled.

She shrugged and nibbled at the sandwich.

"What'd you think of all those turtles?" I asked.

"They were pretty cool, I guess." Taylor smoothed her wet hair back, and glanced out at the open sea.

"Are you having fun?" I hoped this question would open up the dam of her emotions.

Taylor looked right at me, her expression as bright as the sky on the horizon. "I don't know. This is like a dream come true, being on my dad's boat. I've spent so much time thinking about what it would *feel like* to be here. But . . ."

Taylor made no attempt to finish her thought. "But what?" I prompted.

"He's really great, and I kind of remember things, like his voice. It brings back memories of him reading to me. And his expressive blue eyes. His warm smile."

I grinned. "Look in the mirror, Taylor. You have the same eyes and the same smile."

Taylor's smile was decidedly absent at the moment, and her blue eyes were tearing up.

"But I want to hate him. I don't know why. I just feel like, he wasn't there for me and he let me down, you know? I remember now how much I loved him. I had forgotten. Or didn't ever admit it to myself maybe." Taylor bunched her towel up and smashed her face against it to dry a flood of tears. Then she looked at me and I saw a glimpse into the five-year-old of long ago. The rebellious teenager putting up a brave front had been transformed into a vulnerable and exposed little girl.

"I think he regrets his absence as much as you do, Taylor. He clearly realizes what he has missed."

We both turned our heads at the sound of giggling and then heard a splash. The little girls were jumping off the front of the boat. Grayson was perched on the rail, watching them. I was thankful Taylor didn't know yet that Alana was his daughter, too.

Suddenly the giggles and splashing turned to screams. Taylor and I ran to the bow of the boat.

"What happened?" I asked, frantically.

"It's okay," Grayson answered. Lots of thrashing about had now become complete stillness as Alana and Chenlei treaded water, staring into it without a word as we watched from the deck. Suddenly Alana dove down as expertly as a sea lion after a fish and came up with a much more valuable find: Chenlei's bracelet from Journey's chest. Apparently it had come loose in the water and the minute she realized it was missing, Chenlei had panicked.

Grayson smiled. "Good job, Alana."

"I saw the little red stones shining under there as it was sinking!" Alana grinned up at us. She held the find tightly in her hand as we helped them climb off the ladder and gave them towels. While they sat in the deck chairs, out of breath, Grayson reminded Chenlei gently that he had suggested it was not a good idea to wear the jewelry in the water for that very reason. Chenlei looked remorseful, but something told me nothing could have convinced her to take it off no matter the practicality of it. Nor would she consider removing it if she were to swim again. Reason did not go hand in hand with the garnet bracelet.

Later that evening after all the girls were tucked in, Grayson handed me one of his Mai Tais, and asked why Chenlei had this paranoia about the silver band.

"I'm not sure. The first time Chenlei met Alana, it awakened something in her that had been dead a long time, maybe since her mother died. It's hard to define what that might have been. But when I gave Chenlei the bracelet that Journey had made, her eyes lit up in a way I'd never seen before, or since. The jewelry could not have been better suited to her if made to order. The red stones bring out her dark features, don't you think?"

"I think the fascination comes in having a comrade. Someone who battles the ghost of a mother lost. How unnatural is it to lose your primary nurturer, your only source of stability and strength. It must emasculate the bravest soul, and Chenlei recognized those battle scars in Alana. That endeared her to the mother behind the comrade, Journey." Grayson sipped on his Mai Tai and stared at the stars, close enough to reach out and touch.

"Maybe. Or perhaps Chenlei just saw the bracelet as a sign of love from her own mother, up above somewhere looking down at her, affectionately."

"Perhaps." Grayson smiled.

"What did you say to Alana?" I asked. "About my coming and bringing Taylor?"

"We discussed why she had bonded so quickly with Chenlei, and decided that it was partly because they had both lost their mothers. I told her that a young woman about twice her age had lost her father when she was only five, and that she was coming with you and Chenlei this weekend. Alana wanted to know who that little girl was and why she was coming. So I told her."

"Did she have any questions about why you had stopped being a dad to Taylor?"

Grayson handed me a refill on my Mai Tai.

"Yes. I told her I was wrong, but that I was hurt because her mother had left me for another man, and I thought at the time Taylor would be better off with one dad, not two, competing for her love and loyalty."

"What did she say? About all of it?"

"She crawled in my lap, gave me a big hug, and said she wished I were *her* father. Then she told me Taylor would forgive me, just like she would forgive *her* daddy, if she ever got to meet him."

I sipped on my Mai Tai in silence and stared at the stars. This was my perfect opportunity to tell Grayson the truth. *You are her father, Grayson. Journey told me in a letter. I just had to be sure before I could pass on that information, and after visiting Shalana in Honolulu, I am sure. But I thought I should wait until you and Taylor were squared away.*

The words stuck in my throat and that's where they stayed. Silence fell between us punctuated by the water lapping against the hull. It was an uncomfortable silence. I walked over to the rail where I could stare at the moon reflecting off the ocean. Grayson followed and I could feel his warmth beside me. Telling him about his second daughter was less urgent to me than wondering about him and Journey. *How could you sleep with my sister and have no recollection of it?*

I wanted to believe he was so inebriated as to not recall what happened, but any man that drunk has no hope of making love except in his dreams, and dreams did not create the living breathing Alana. If he was not being honest about it because he wasn't proud of having slept with a vulnerable eighteen-year-old full of rum, I could understand that, but with Alana's paternity on the line I had to believe he would speak up if he knew he might be the father.

"What are you so deep in thought about?" Grayson asked.

"Chase," I lied. "He has left the Big Island and opened a new office in Colorado."

"That's surprising news. I guess you'll be moving soon then won't you?"

"I don't know."

"You don't know?"

"I guess you might say there is trouble in paradise," I answered.

"Because raising your niece is hard for Chase to accept?"

"Yes. But there's more to it than that."

"You aren't able to get pregnant. And he doesn't want to adopt."

"Yes," I answered.

"That's always hard on a marriage. Infertility. So is having an orphaned niece you disagree about whether or not to adopt. But two people who really love each other can survive all that."

"What about the anger, the constant fighting, the resentment that builds up and the blame you place at each others feet? Can people in love survive all that, too?"

Grayson shrugged. "I can't answer that for you, Kylie."

"Chase wants to adopt a baby from an unwed mother, through his family's attorney."

Grayson didn't say anything. He took the empty drink from my hand and refilled it from the bar. When he was standing beside me again I asked him if I was crazy not to pack up and move to Colorado with my husband.

"I think it's Chase who is crazy to leave you behind, even temporarily."

"You don't think I'm being incredibly selfish to stay and finish my fall semester at the university?"

"I think staying to finish the semester is incredibly admirable."

"Michael has an entirely different take on it." I was instantly sorry I had mentioned Michael, but there was no taking it back.

"I don't doubt that he would," Grayson responded without skipping a beat.

"He thinks if I truly love Chase, nothing would keep me from following him, right now."

"It's not that simple. You have things to sort out here, and obligations to fulfill. Not everyone is able to be as impulsive as Michael."

"After all this time, how do you feel about Michael, Grayson?"

"I respect him for being a top notch doctor and how he has devoted his life to helping others, despite his parents not approving of his wandering from the family business. I respect that he has made an honest woman of Gwyneth and has been a good father to Taylor."

"You no longer hold a grudge for what he did?"

Grayson shrugged. "It was a long time ago. In a way, I let it happen. I'm not saying I wouldn't have been an equally devoted, loving husband, who would eventually have had more time for my family. I'm just saying that affairs cannot get a foothold without something being amiss in the relationship. Obviously, we were not as solid as we should have been. Maybe there was no hope for us regardless of what happened."

"You can't know that. And some affairs make marriages stronger, I mean after all the painfully honest communicating and complete forgiveness."

"Well, that wasn't true in my case, was it?"

"No. The question is, do you wish you'd made an effort to fix your marriage?"

"I have never wished Gwyneth were by my side since she left. Whatever feelings I had for her died that day. Does that answer your question?"

"Completely," I answered.

Grayson took a long drink of his Mai Tai, and watched the ice in the glass as he gently swirled what was left. "I am, however, tired of being alone on this boat. I know that temporarily I have Alana, and I care about her more deeply than I thought possible. I love her as much as I love my own daughter."

*Journey* **179**

He paused there and glanced at me. It was painful to look him in the eye, knowing I'd been stealing his mail and withholding the truth.

"I am grateful to you, Kylie, for reacquainting me with Taylor. It will make losing Alana a little easier. I only hope you will allow me to stay in touch with both of you. Selfishly, I'd rather you didn't move."

"Grayson, are you close to your parents?" I asked, wondering who had been instrumental in the making of this exceptional man.

"I loved both my parents very much."

"Loved?"

"They're dead. My parents were both doctors, missionaries. I was their only child. I don't think I was planned. But they didn't seem to ever regret having me around. I grew up in places like Nicaragua, Nigeria, and Somalia."

He paused there and downed the last of his drink.

"They died in Somalia when I was fifteen. Shot down by warlords in a civil squabble."

More silence. I leaned my back against the rail so I could see him clearly in the moonlight, watch his eyes follow the dancing light rays across the calm water.

"My parents were my whole life. I took it very hard. After their funeral I was shipped to my grandfather in the States. He was also a doctor, but one that relished the finer comforts rather than shunning them to serve the poor. All I knew at the time was that I never wanted to hurt again the way I hurt when my parents died. We were very close and happy, despite living in third world countries. We had all the amenities necessary to stay physically, mentally, and emotionally strong in order to help those in abject poverty.

"Of course, by my grandfather's standards the comforts of our humble home were meager indeed. But I loved the old man despite his weakness for luxury. He always gave a lot back to the community, and the patients he saw could easily afford his services." Grayson smiled. "The rich need doctors, too."

Walking over to the bar he retrieved the bottle of rum, brought it back with him, and gave us both a straight shot while continuing to tell me about his grandfather.

"He was a good man, as good in his own way as my father had been. What I learned from both of them was to use the gift of my intellect to help make the world a better place. What I learned from Grandfather alone was how to build a wall around my emotions, so as not to be susceptible to the kind of pain I felt when my parents were killed. He built his wall after my grandmother died from cancer at a young age, our age actually. Grandfather lived to be ninety. He never remarried. I don't know how he could be happy living alone for fifty years."

Grayson sat in a deck chair and set the bottle on the table. I grabbed another chair and moved it beside him, pulling my legs up around me, against the night chill creeping in. Straight shots of rum, I discovered, warmed you from the inside out. We stared at the stars for a while, and then Grayson continued where he had left off.

"It's why I never let Gwyneth in, not past a certain point. It's why she needed to look elsewhere for that emotional connection she couldn't get from me. I had built my wall, and I only exposed a small part of who I was to her. But I was wrong to think I could protect myself from ever being hurt again. Once Gwyneth and Taylor were gone I realized that for all my emotional aloofness in letting them go, it didn't stop the pain from settling in and nearly destroying me. I couldn't have hurt more if I had openly embraced them every day, and fought for them in the end, only to lose anyway."

He looked so lost sitting there, living in the most miserable part of his past since the death of his parents. I wanted to crawl in his lap and comfort him, tell him he would love again one day. Tell him that he had two beautiful daughters, not just one. It was hard to not follow my instincts, with the rum seducing my sense of decency. I kept envisioning myself that close to Grayson, although somehow I stayed rooted where I was, and then I discovered this longing in me for more than friendship. I wanted to be intimate with this man, and even full of rum, this realization shocked the hell out of me. Everything about him was too appealing.

*Journey*

Somehow I managed to say goodnight and went to bed, nearly passing out when I got there. I awoke in the morning with a headache, and it was suddenly clear to me how Grayson might not have known for sure whether or not he slept with my sister. My dreams had been so filled with images of Grayson that for a few seconds, I wondered if perhaps he had joined me for a time.

The sober light of day had never been an expression with clearer meaning to me than at this moment. I had let myself fall in love with Grayson. It never occurred to me until this minute that one could love two men, entirely, and without reservation. How awkward and impractical is that? Regardless of this harsh reality, I was committed to one. My mission now was simply to be true to him.

Perhaps moving to Colorado mid-semester was exactly what I needed to do afterall.

# CHAPTER TWENTY

*Unfortunately it appeared as if Chase and I had left our desire for one another on a line in the sand somewhere, along with our pride and our principles.*

I freshened up in the bathroom down the hall from the girls, and was dismayed at my red eyes reflected in the mirror. It was from the rum. I was grateful Taylor had slept on the floor in Alana's room, where the three girls had decided to have a slumber party.

When as presentable as I could make myself in fresh khaki shorts and a black sleeveless pullover, I made my way to the galley for some much-needed coffee. I was surprised to see Makana seated at the window table, watching Grayson fry bacon for the girls. All three of them were out on the main deck throwing bread to the seagulls.

I had seen Makana on several occasions at the Hula Grill, but was taken aback by how different she appeared in the morning light. She was wearing a blue tank top instead of the white button down shirt, worn by everyone who worked at the Hula Grill.

"I bet you're looking for coffee," Grayson stated cheerfully as he handed me a strong cup of his special Kona blend. I sipped on it gratefully, sliding into the bench seat across from Makana. We smiled at one another and made official introductions with Grayson taking the edge off any awkwardness. He explained to Makana what it was I did on the Big Island while frying potatoes and cracking eggs in a bowl.

I admired Makana's large brown eyes while he spoke, wondering how it was that I hadn't noticed them in the Hula Grill. She looked younger and prettier then I had originally thought from seeing her at work.

"Makana was raised on the Big Island. Her parents moved over there from California right before she was born. They have a dive shop," Grayson offered up.

"My parents couldn't resist giving me a Hawaiian name, to seal their new adventure." Her eyes twinkled as she said this. I was already endeared to her, having seen first hand the special care she gave her customers.

"I moved here and bought the Hula Grill after my divorce several years ago," Makana added with a flash of sadness in her eyes.

"Alana has told me that she rides the bus with your son, Jay." I smiled, thinking about how comfortable she looked sitting here in Grayson's little galley kitchen. I couldn't help but wonder if Makana and Grayson found solace in one another's arms on especially dark, starless nights.

Grayson called the girls and we all feasted on his expertly prepared breakfast while he reminded us that this was the only meal he cooked. Without the Hula Grill, he swore that he would starve. He added that Alana didn't notice because she lived on Honey Nut Cheerios, by choice.

"It appears to me that Alana also likes the one meal you cook, Grayson," I said while watching her put away the last of her fried potatoes oozing in ketchup.

Grayson laughed while refilling my coffee.

Makana left after offering to help with the dishes, which we had assured her wasn't necessary. The girls cleared the table and then hurried off to get ready for the day, leaving Grayson and me alone to discuss Taylor. While we did the dishes it was decided that Grayson would take her out in the yacht alone. He'd feel more comfortable with her while in his element, fishing and sailing. He could teach her some of both. I would take the younger girls to Lahaina shopping, and maybe drive down to Kaanapali. We agreed to meet up at the yacht after dinner. Grayson and Taylor would be back in the harbor by then.

"Next time I come let's put the sails up," I suggested.

"The winds have to be just right, but I think we can arrange that," Grayson agreed, taking a long careful look at me.

"What? Do I look hung over?" I asked, remembering my red eyes.

"No. That's just it. You look as beautiful as ever."

"Grayson, are you flirting with me?"

"I'm just being honest. If you weren't married I would kiss you. I've wanted to for a long time. Is that too honest for you?"

His blue eyes didn't waver as he said that. It made me wonder if Grayson's dreams had been similar to mine. And then I knew I was blushing. I put the rest of the cups in the cabinet as if his words were no more significant than a *thank you* for helping with the dishes. After the last cup was set on the shelf, I took a deep breath and turned to face him.

"Grayson, I'm feeling way too vulnerable for you to be so frank. My husband has moved to the mainland and we aren't seeing eye-to-eye right now on how to become a family. Lately I'm beginning to wonder why we would even want to become parents together."

I stopped there as emotions froze my voice and tears pooled up, blurring my vision. Grayson pulled me close and hugged me like a caring friend, with no overtures of inappropriateness. Nonetheless his strong body and the scent of his aftershave aroused desires I shouldn't have for anyone but Chase. Unfortunately it appeared as if Chase and I had left our desire for one another on a line in the sand somewhere, along with our pride and our principles.

Alana came bouncing into the kitchen and we tore ourselves apart quickly, but not quickly enough to escape her notice. Alana didn't say anything and Grayson got her a glass of juice.

I left without a word to tell Taylor and Chenlei of our plans for the day.

While browsing with the girls in the art shops and clothing stores along the main street of Lahaina all I could think about was Grayson. Later we went to Kaanapali for dinner at the open hut Barefoot Grill, with its swept sand floor and panoramic view of the Pacific. The sun was setting all rosy and soft while an island guitarist played melancholy tunes. I kept thinking of Taylor and Grayson out there sailing in the steady offshore breeze. I wondered if the day had gone well, if Taylor had caught a few fish and learned how to be a sailor. I wished I were sharing in the excitement of both, although listening to the little girls chatter away about their treasures we had bought while shopping reminded me of how delightful they were. I wouldn't want to trade the memories of our time together, even to learn how to sail.

When we returned to Lahaina the yacht was safely back in its furthermost slip, and Grayson was still tying the ropes to the dock. Taylor waved to us and ran to greet the girls, who gave her the package of keepsakes we had bought with Taylor in mind. They disappeared to the deck below after Taylor gave me a synopsis of her day. She shared with me that fishing had been more fun than she ever imagined and showed me her catch. Sailing was harder, but her dad made it fun and once they were really sailing it was *so amazing*. The sparkle in her eyes confirmed it, and I knew that all was well in the world of Grayson and Taylor, father and daughter, for the first time in many years.

"Congratulations," I said, when finally alone with Grayson. "You've won back Taylor's heart and her forgiveness, too."

"It never would have happened without you," Grayson answered, while mixing us a pitcher of his famous Mai Tais.

"I can't drink like I did last night," I said in earnest.

"I promise when this pitcher's gone, we're done. No rum shots." Grayson smiled.

"There's something I need to tell you, Grayson. It's about Alana."

"She spent her whole allowance, didn't she? I told her not to, that she should always save a little for a rainy day." He laughed. "Next week we'll open a bank account and I'll take her there the first of every month to deposit ten percent of her earnings. She does chores for the money, you know. That's why this deck is so shiny and the cabins are dust-free. I gave her all the jobs I don't like," he confessed, as he handed me a drink.

"I wish it were that simple," I admitted.

Grayson lit up all the little white lights lining the upper deck and sat down in the chair beside me. It was hard to tell where the strands of lights let off and the stars on the horizon began. He hadn't lit them before because of the full moon, but there was no moon tonight. Either it was hiding somewhere or just hadn't made an appearance yet.

"Have you decided it's time to face your husband about adopting her? And if he says no, then what will you do?"

"It's not that." I stood up and walked to the rail, wondering where to begin. *Grayson, I should have told you this a long time ago, but at first I wasn't sure, and then I met Taylor and things got complicated. Now that you're on solid ground with her, and I believe that everything Journey has confessed in her letter to be true . . .*

How would I explain the letter I had found? Keeping it from him? *Opening* it when it had his name on it for *god's sake*? Indeed, *only God* could help me now. I believed in God. I had grown up with Christianity. My mother was a strong believer despite her complexities that led us off His tried and true path on more than one occasion. First to the Big Island because of a divorce orchestrated by her, and then there was Journey. How different my life would have been had my mother stuck to the straight and narrow. But then, who was to say it would have been for the better?

"While I'm thinking about it," Grayson interjected, "I need to tell you that Makana has offered to take the girls snorkeling tomorrow morning with her son, Jay, down the beach by their house, which isn't far from here. It would give me a chance to take you sailing. Your plane doesn't leave until mid-afternoon. We'd have plenty of time."

I stared at him, at those large eyes so happy and carefree at the moment, more so than they had been since I met him. I thought about how angry he would be, at the very least disturbed, by my spilling the whole sordid story of Alana's paternity. I didn't have the heart to spoil this weekend for him, to add another blow when he had just healed from the last one. It could wait. It had waited all this time. It could wait a little longer.

I would plan how and when to tell him on the plane ride home, and that would ease my guilt for not having done it this weekend. Then I would never see him again, because that was the way it should be, in fact, the way it had to be. Grayson and I were beyond friendship in our feelings, past every red flag we had ignored along the way. We were fast approaching a danger zone, in which more than just the two of us might get hurt.

We turned in early, after just the one pitcher of Mai Tais, true to Grayson's words. The morning breeze was perfect for sailing and I would never forget the thrill of it. I believed I was as smitten with Grandfather Conner's yacht as I was with his grandson. The morning sea was bright and the foamy breakers dazzling. Sunlight reflected off of both. The shoreline slowly became a buzz of activity as we moved along beside it at a steady clip, all the way to Kaanapali, and then back again by motor.

When Taylor, Chenlei, and I hugged Grayson and Alana goodbye at the airport we were obviously more bonded than when we'd first arrived, so much so that each of us fought back tears, except maybe for Grayson. We held our newly made memories in reverence, and each browsed quietly through magazines during the entire commuter flight.

After dropping first Taylor and then Chenlei off at their homes I sat in front of my house on the bluff and stared at it for a while before I grabbed my bag from the trunk and unlocked the front door. As I entered I wished with all my heart that Chase were there to greet me. To sweep me up into his arms and take me to bed with him. I couldn't be sure my desire for Chase wasn't sparked by my inappropriate feelings for Grayson. That led to a Pandora's Box of guilt and confusion.

No matter how hard I tried, it was impossible to push away the image of Grayson on the dimly lit deck last night, there beside me at the rail. His bold eyes had twinkled like stars and his strong body repeatedly brushed against my side. I recalled the brisk morning with his arms around me, and his hands guiding mine as I learned to position the sails. And it was clear these new feelings were not mine alone. I could see the desire in Grayson's eyes, and it had only escalated mine.

I didn't want to plan my final trip to inform him of Alana's paternity and my feelings that could not allow us to continue our friendship. But plan it I must. I plopped down on the sofa and stared out the window at the hill rolling down to the sea. I tried not to think about my growing anger toward Chase for not being here, for deserting me, for allowing my heart to become fickle with so much time away from him. I knew it was irrational to blame Chase. He had wanted me to follow him to Colorado. He had also wanted me to be sensible about the situation with Alana. I'd been anything but sensible about her, or Grayson, since the day we met.

Had I listened to Chase, Grayson and Alana would already know they belonged to each other. Neither of them would need to wonder who Alana's father was.

There was another reason I sat on the sofa and stared out the window. It was the same reason I had stared at the house for so long before entering. I recalled the last time I had returned from Maui, and how Chase and I had made love all afternoon, and ate a picnic dinner on the beach at sunset. *I had not had my period since that day.*

Not able to hold off the *what ifs* any longer, I was soon rummaging under the bathroom sink for the pregnancy test I always kept just in case.

I held the box in my hand for the longest time, thinking about all the other tests I'd taken, foolishly, when only a few days late. That became its own kind of agony, as if I needed proof that I would never conceive. I vowed to let more time pass before taking a test, but then, more time never passed.

Until now.

I slowly opened the box as if it were a precious gift and studied the applicator. Why was this so hard for me to do? Was it because I'd had just about all the disappointment I could handle in one lifetime from a plastic stick not turning the right color?

Or maybe it was because Chase was about as far away from that day of lovemaking as he could get, all the way to Colorado with another woman, although that assessment wasn't fair on my part. Meagan was a good pilot. An employee. I really had no reason to suspect anything else, other than my over active imagination and insecurity from not being able to produce little Hudson juniors.

I took a deep breath and did the test. Staring at it in disbelief I decided that it wasn't blue. I was just willing it to be. I held it under the window and examined it again, as if a precious jewel.

*It was definitely blue.*

There was no doubt whatsoever.

*I was going to have a baby.*

One hour and ten tissues later I had finally calmed myself enough to call Chase. As soon as the phone began to ring I became overwhelmed with excitement. I suddenly had no uncertainty about what, and whom, I wanted. In the seconds that I waited for Chase to pick up the phone I could feel every shred of anger, hurt, and resentment toward him dissolve. All I could think about was having our baby and raising it together. It didn't matter where. *Our baby.* No two words in any language could be more beautiful.

"Hello?"

I froze when I heard her voice.

"Hello? Is anyone there?"

"Meagan. It's Kylie," I replied, my voice unrecognizable to me. It was cold and hard, as if I were holding a gun to her head, and for a minute, I wished that I were.

While I waited for a reply I glanced again at the address and phone number Chase had given me. He had found a furnished apartment and was no longer at his brother's. It was inconvenient, he had said, to never have his own space, and when I came at Thanksgiving we would be alone together.

"Umm . . . Chase isn't here right now. Can I take a message?" Meagan cleared her voice uncomfortably.

I wanted to scream into the phone *what are you doing there?* But instead I said nothing, and there was silence between us, a very loud silence.

"Kylie . . . um . . . do you want me to give him a message?"

"No thanks," I said as I hung up.

This time my tears were not of joy. I didn't know what to think. I hadn't called his cell phone because I knew he liked to keep it freed up for work-related communication. Now I wished I had called it anyway, and then I would never know Meagan was at his apartment, or why. Like an ostrich with my head in the sand I could simply pretend that everything was fine, if you don't count disagreeing about where to live or how to become a family. Ironically, that problem about how to become a family was finally solved, at least in part, but now there was a bigger problem.

I had always been Chase's whole world, and he had been mine. But he was so unhappy with me of late because of my poor judgment in withholding information from Grayson, and then there was my obsession with Alana, and my hesitating to come to Colorado with him just yet, just as Michael felt I should have, as he would have for Gwyneth. And because of all that poor judgment on my part, now everything between us might just fall apart.

I couldn't imagine having this pregnancy, this baby, without him. We had dreamed about it for years. Everything we would do from conception through college for our child. *Our child.* I was afraid if I became any more distraught I might actually lose this tiny fetus inside me, this fetus that I already cherished. So I unpacked, showered, and washed my hair while playing soft piano CDs.

Finally, I fell into bed exhausted and prayed for my baby to be healthy and strong, and survive this emotional mess I had made of myself.

# CHAPTER TWENTY-ONE

*I looked down into her near black eyes, and found them sparkling with joy.*

For the next few days I tried not to think about Chase and our baby. Instead I kept my mind busy critiquing mid-term papers. When I couldn't stand the suspense any longer I called Chase's brother. He told me that Chase was in Alaska on a job too lucrative to give up, even though his new Colorado office desperately needed him. Meagan, however, was holding down the fort.

I could only wonder why he hadn't called to tell me himself. I wasn't surprised however that he hadn't given up the biggest job he'd ever landed a contract for. It was with the Tongass National Forest, helping them airlift equipment to build a dam. And Colin made it clear to me why he hadn't called since arriving there. Most of the daylight hours were spent flying in and out of the endless forested valleys deep in the heart of Alaska. Cell service was iffy at best in the small outback inns that offered no conventional phone service. And generally the pilots were sleeping when they weren't flying.

Maybe he had tried to call while I was in Maui. Someone had hung up several times on the answering machine. Or maybe he didn't think about calling because Meagan had moved in with him, and he was moving on, without me. In total frustration I threw the cordless phone against the wall, where it knocked down the calendar. After they both went crashing to the floor, I sat at the table and stared blankly out the window.

What was the matter with me? The last thing I needed was an emotional breakdown that might cause me to lose this baby I had waited

*Journey* 193

well over a decade for. Why did I feel so insecure about Chase's love? Was it because I thought he might have succumbed to his human weaknesses just as I had been tempted to do? Even now my thoughts were partially of someone else. I could not get Grayson off my mind, despite being pregnant and afraid that I may have lost my one true love. Or was he? Surely these taunting thoughts were my punishment, and richly deserved, after all the manipulating half-truths I had told of late to everyone I cared about.

No longer able to contain the great news of my having conceived, I walked over the hill to see my best friend, Elise. Quinn and the boys were at soccer practice and Chenlei at dance class. Elise was glad to see me. She had just baked oatmeal cookies for school lunches and happily made a pot of herbal tea for us.

It was uncanny how Elise was always there for me when the walls of my world started closing in. Most recently when Journey's tragic death became known, and now with my wanting to raise Alana, against Chase's wishes. Elise knew the ongoing ache I had for a pregnancy to finally occur. She understood all my secret longings and crosses to bear, with the exception of Grayson's firm hold on my fickle heart. That troubling truth I would take to my grave, ashamed for what I couldn't seem to control.

"How does Chenlei like her dance class?" I asked, thinking she must love it. Chenlei didn't enjoy contact sports, but she excelled at individual athletic endeavors such as tennis or swimming, and now probably dancing.

"It's going well. She's the youngest and smallest in the class, but Chenlei's holding her own." Elise stopped pouring tea in my cup and looked at me seriously. "Chenlei's quit having the nightmares, or at least, she doesn't cry out anymore when she has them. I think that might be the case. But the bracelet is another thing altogether. She still refuses to take it off, ever."

"It's probably just a stage she's going through, Elise. Another phase of her grieving. It will pass. Something eventually will cause her to want to take it off."

"I hope so. It's just another reminder to me that she hasn't put the past behind her yet."

"Someone with a past as traumatic as Chenlei's can't be expected to forget and move on without a lot of transitional behavior."

"You sound just like Dr. Chambers." Elise smiled.

"So Chenlei is still seeing him?"

"Yes, but she hasn't really opened up to Brandon. She won't talk about her mother, or say *how* and *where* she died, which we all know is what has traumatized Chenlei. Maybe her time with the street vendor and in the orphanage contributed, too. But she won't talk about any of it, not since that one time she shared her nightmare with Quinn. She just rakes the little therapeutic Zen garden smooth and places the pretty stones equally apart, according to Brandon, while he does most of the talking."

We sipped our tea in silence for a minute. I reflected on Chenlei and the tragic way in which Ling had died. How inconceivable to awaken with your mother cold beside you, her warm blood trickling over your legs, still interwoven with hers.

"Elise, I'm pregnant." The words spilled out as their meaning sank in. *I was going to have a baby.*

"Are you sure?" Elise asked cautiously, as if afraid to believe it.

"Yes."

"Oh my goodness, Kylie. That's amazing news!" She grabbed my hand from across the table and squeezed tightly, her eyes tearing up. "Does Chase know?"

"Chase is in the wilds of Alaska."

"That's terrible timing, isn't it?"

"Terrible timing seems to be my fate these days."

"Kylie, I'm so happy for you." Elise began to cry and grabbed the tissues off the counter. She handed me one, seeing that I, too, had begun to cry.

"Will you still adopt Alana? I mean one has nothing to do with the other really, except for Chase and how he feels about it. Maybe knowing he's going to have a child of his own will make him more accepting of Alana."

"I doubt that, Elise, and anyway, Alana has a home. Grayson is her father," I said, these words spilling out and sinking in, finally, too. It made my tears begin to flow more out of sorrow than joy.

Elise's eyes had widened in disbelief. "How do you know?"

I cupped my mug of tea tightly and looked out the window beside my friend because I could not look her in the eye, suddenly ashamed of what I was about to confess.

"Journey said Grayson was the father in her letter to me, in the chest. I didn't believe it. Journey always had a way fabricating the best-case scenario for any given situation. But then I found a letter from Journey, meant for Grayson, in Alana's room. I stole it, Elise," I said boldly, looking her right in the eye now, as if confessing was healing for my conscience. "In the letter to Grayson she told him he was the father. Of course, I still didn't want to believe it, so I tracked down Shalana, who confirmed that Journey's ex-boyfriend was probably not the father."

Elise nodded, speechless. She began to pat my hand and absorb all of this. It had to be disappointing to know Alana and Chenlei would never be neighbors on the hill where we lived.

"Have you told Grayson?"

"No. The longer I wait, the harder it gets. Mainly because I have no explanation for what I have put him through, put both of them through. It was wrong of me to take a letter meant for Grayson, and then keep that information from him. And even if I was justified in visiting Shalana to be sure Grayson was the father, why have I waited all this time since?"

All of my news had barely sunk in when Quinn returned with Chenlei and the boys. We had just finished off the last of the tea. I whispered for Elise not to say anything, especially since Chase didn't know yet, and she understood completely. Then she asked me to stay for dinner. I was eager to, since my seemingly endless lonely nights without Chase were beginning to depress me.

Chenlei and I set the table and cut up vegetables for the salad while Elise stir-fried one of her famous Asian dishes—sweet and sour chicken with orange sauce. The boys had finished their homework, with Quinn's help, while we prepared the meal. It felt wonderful to sit at the Damask table and listen to Quinn and Elise interact with the boys about their day at school, their soccer team, and their chores still not done. Even Chenlei spoke when they all encouraged her to share about school, and her new dance class. The boys were respectful when Chenlei answered questions about her day. They looked at her when she talked, and said something encouraging when she finished. They had obviously grown to love their little sister, who had no doubt won their affection with her tough as nails determination to excel at any task she took on.

Quinn announced after dinner that if chores were done quickly, there would be time for swimming and snorkeling. Everyone moved as if set on fire and soon they were all putting on their swimsuits. Elise was packing a book to read as I headed out across the hill to change my clothes and join them. I agreed to meet up with everyone at the beach.

When I arrived Quinn was throwing a football to the boys while Chenlei splashed in the shallow surf. Elise was reading her book in the cave not far from the cliff steps, just down the beach from us. I swam out a couple hundred yards from shore, and then turned back toward the beach, thinking how good it felt to stretch my stiff muscles, tight from fretting about Chase and Meagan, and the amazing news I couldn't share yet with a living soul, except of course, with Elise.

As the sun fell lower on the horizon Quinn told the boys they would need to snorkel soon or it would be too dark. Elise said she would watch them, leaving Quinn and I free to walk along the shoreline. I knew that Quinn walked the beach every night, sometimes after dark. It was his way of unwinding and processing the day.

"Have you heard from Chase recently?" Quinn asked, after we had walked for a while. He leaned against his landmark rock for turning around and heading back. I crawled up on it to watch the sun go down.

"No," I admitted, "but he's on a job in Alaska right now and phones aren't very accessible where he is, even if he had a free minute to call me."

Quinn nodded in understanding. I wasn't sure why I said what I shared next. Perhaps it was just so heavy on my heart I needed to lift the weight off of me. "When I returned from Maui I called him at his new apartment and Meagan answered."

I looked carefully at Quinn for a reaction, but there was none as he studied the colors forming in the sky, preparing for the sun to set.

"Meagan works in the Colorado office?"

"Yes."

"The perky little blonde?"

"Yes." Quinn had made her acquaintance at Chase's annual picnic for his pilots. We always included enough friends for a serious football game on the beach, before cooking up a pot of crab.

"Don't you think it's odd that she would be at his apartment when he isn't there? Or even if he were for that matter," I added, annoyed.

"You didn't ask her why she was answering his phone?"

"No. I didn't want to seem concerned. Was that silly?"

"Maybe there's a reasonable explanation, Kylie."

"And maybe there isn't."

Quinn turned and looked at me, studied my face. I could tell by the look on his that he could not convince me otherwise.

"Kylie, I don't know what to say. Chase loves you very much. I know that for a fact. But things happen sometimes, things you never could have predicted, things you feel you have no control over. Your feelings consume you sometimes in a situation like Chase is in, where suddenly the woman you love is not there but someone else is, someone who needs you and wants you."

Now I was the one studying Quinn, his eyes especially, for they were jumping about in a nervous way. Either he knew something about Chase and Meagan that I didn't, or he had something else on his mind. I didn't want to pursue it. There was nothing positive to say about the situation I was in, and Quinn would never dream of giving me false hope. We headed back in silence, neither of us eager to discuss any of it further.

The kids were wrapped in towels when we met up with Elise, who happily shared that Chenlei had gone snorkeling, too. And then the turtles had come, Chenlei and the boys chimed in excitedly, telling us how they had swum and dove with them for the longest time. Elise looked elated that Chenlei was chattering away about the turtle adventure with Wyatt and Austin. The three of them talked nonstop about swimming among the huge tortoises all the way back to the cliff steps. It warmed my heart to have the usually somber Chenlei be as enthusiastic as her brothers. She had been an active participant in something, finally, rather than a silent observer.

We said our goodbyes at the top of the rough-cut steps, where Chenlei hugged me tightly. I looked down into her near black eyes, and found them sparkling with joy.

"I love you, Auntie Kylie. Thanks for taking me to Maui."

"You're very welcome, Chenlei. I love you, too." I winked at her and she winked back. It made me laugh. I was so happy for this little orphan, finally coming out of her shell, finally believing that she *belonged.*

After the last goodbye I headed across the hill in the dim light of dusk to my empty house, exhausted from the day both physically and emotionally. I took a long, hot shower and read Wuthering Heights for a while. It was one of my favorite go-to books when wishing to escape reality. Sleep finally overcame me and I dreamed of Heathcliff and Catherine roaming their rugged moors forever, sharing a love that never abated nor was reconciled for all eternity. I had other dreams of Chenlei's dazzling smile and bright eyes when looking up at me on the hill above the cliff steps. My unusually vivid dreams made my heart both race and soar all through the lonely, restless night.

At six forty-five a.m. Taylor knocked gently on my door. I had agreed to help her edit a class assignment before she turned it in this morning. I waved goodbye to Michael, having already told him I would drop Taylor off at school on my way to the university. We had barely begun to look at her essay, me holding a cup of fresh coffee, and Taylor eating toast with jam I had just made for her, when we heard screams outside the window. Instantly alarmed we both pulled back the curtain and saw Wyatt there, his face red from running, his hair not yet combed, and wearing only his baggy shorts with all the pockets everywhere, usually stuffed with things.

Taylor and I ran out to the porch and listened as Wyatt told us, between labored breaths, that Chenlei was missing.

"Missing?" I asked, perplexed, her smiling face of the night before flashing through my mind.

"Mom went to wake her up for school, and she wasn't in her bed." Wyatt stopped there to catch his breath. "We looked everywhere for her, all over the house and the yard. Dad sent me here, and if you have her, please call his cell phone."

"She's not here, Wyatt. At least not that I know of." With that said Taylor and I began to look frantically, calling her name. I went through the house checking in closets and behind doors. Perhaps something had frightened her and she had come here and hid somewhere. Taylor was combing the grounds between the house and the cliff above the sea. I could hear her shouts of *Chenlei* from that direction. Wyatt was standing on the porch, stiff and still. I glanced through the screen door and could see him staring at Taylor on the hill. He no longer appeared to be panicked, but paralyzed with fear instead.

I stood before the chest under the window and studied it, listening to Taylor's strained shouts, wondering if it would be silly to open it and look for her there. But I did, in desperation, and of course Chenlei wasn't in the chest but the wooden jewelry box caught my eye. Everything inside of me froze, as if even my blood stopped pumping through my veins in that instant. Somehow I managed to move my body to the porch, aware that I was shaking, as if a blast of ice had blown in off the Pacific.

"Wyatt, listen to me," I said, as I knelt beside him and gently turned his face to look into his eyes. "Did Chenlei wear her bracelet snorkeling? Did she have it on when she went to bed?" I asked, hoarsely.

Wyatt looked at me blankly for a second and then responded slowly.

"No, Mom made her take it off. She said it might come loose in the water, and she would lose it forever. They put it in the cave, on a little round rock."

"Think carefully, honey. Did she put it back on when you were done? Did she have it when she got back to the house?"

Wyatt shook his head. "I don't know."

"Where is your mama?" I asked, thinking if I knew Elise she was calling every emergency service on the island and making her house a contact place, where they could gather and organize.

"She's . . . she's making phone calls . . ." Wyatt looked like he might cry.

"Go home to your mama and stay there with her. Tell her I'm out looking for Chenlei and not to worry, we'll find her," I said, firmly.

Wyatt took off running without another word and I felt Taylor standing beside me, her breath short and shallow. Before she could speak I squeezed her hand and looked into her tear-filled eyes.

"Taylor, last night we all went to the beach, and Chenlei was swimming with the boys. I think she took her bracelet off and left it in the cave. She was having such a good time that she might have actually forgotten about it. Sometime during the night or early morning she must have remembered, and went to get it."

Taylor stared at me. "You mean she went to the beach cave and maybe fell asleep in there? Afraid to climb back up the steep steps by herself?"

"That's what I'm hoping," I answered, while tying my running shoes. Taylor followed me across the field and along the path to the cliff steps, neither of us shouting now, but making haste in silence while the morning birds cheered us on, and the sun began to climb over the hill. As we approached the steps I looked out across the sand below and fixed my eyes upon our beach cave, looking dark and cool, with the sun not having reached it yet at this hour.

The heavy breeze swept past my face and played with my hair. I could feel Taylor's warm, sweaty body close beside me. Bright sunbeams danced across the gentle surf in a dazzling view from atop the cliff. It imposed a false serenity amidst our sheer despair. Warily I began to descend the steep steps, shaking so hard it made me clumsy. I stumbled several times in my haste. Taylor followed close behind, her sandaled feet slipping often in her agitated state. Seconds later we stood on the ground and I held Taylor back.

"What is it?" she asked, but I didn't answer. I kneeled in the sand and pointed to a long irregular line, or indentation. It led to the familiar arched rock, open wide on the seaside of our beach cave. Could Chenlei have fallen and hurt herself? Perhaps dragged her little body along the sand? And why hadn't Quinn looked there? He must not have thought about the cave, where Elise had read her book. Or about the bracelet that might be the reason for her coming here alone in the dark, and maneuvering the dangerous steps we had warned her not to ever attempt on her own.

Quinn must have believed that Chenlei had wandered down to the beach to swim with the turtles, perhaps because it had brought her so much pleasure the night before and had been a milestone in her adjustment with the Damask family. She had been so fascinated by the gentle creatures. Did he think she was eager to see them again by the light of early day? I wondered this because Quinn was out there, offshore, where the children had swam. He was diving down and then up again. Taylor also saw him and ran to the water's edge, distracted by the sight of Quinn.

I went alone to the cave. My eyes followed the line in the sand all the way to the entrance, and beyond. But I stood at the arch and didn't enter, waiting for my vision to adjust to the dim light. Slowly her little body came into focus. Chenlei's hand was stretched out, cupping the bracelet. Her legs were twisted in a way that told me one had to be broken. Her eyes were open . . . staring, looking past me to the sea, as she lay there on her side—stiff, and still.

# CHAPTER TWENTY-TWO

*Silence fell between us like a curtain, the events of his life and mine in the last few days barricading communication.*

Before I had recovered from this vision of my fragile Chenlei, lying there twisted and broken on the sandy floor of the cave, Taylor began screaming from somewhere behind me: hysterical, piercing screams. I turned and grabbed her to me, burying her head in my chest, and then her screams turned to sobs. Quinn walked quickly past us and over to his little girl. He took her pulse, and closed her eyes. Then he sat down in the sand and picked Chenlei up, gently, laying her in his lap. He looked at me calmly and said, "Kylie, please go to the house. Tell Elise. Call the paramedics. Tell them they'll have to airlift her out."

Quinn's voice broke there. When he recovered a bit he added in a whisper, "Stay with Elise, okay?" He gently stroked Chenlei's shiny dark hair. I left him holding his little girl, her limbs falling at unnatural angles, her face ghastly white and somber. Quinn's silent tears were falling on her cheeks.

I brought Taylor back with me. She had been stunned into silence and was stumbling at my side as we crossed the sand to the cliff steps. Michael was at the top of the rough cut stairs when we arrived. He was out of breath from running across the hill.

"It's all over the news," he said as he approached us, "that Chenlei's missing. I thought you might be part of the search team," he added, catching his breath. Taylor buried herself in his side and began to sob.

"Chenlei fell from the cliff steps, Michael. She dragged herself into the beach cave, and now she is with Ling." I paused there, not sure that I could maintain my composure.

Michael looked confused.

"Quinn is with her," I added. "I need to tell Elise and the paramedics."

"Should I go down there to be with Quinn?"

"No. Quinn's fine," I said, knowing full well that he wasn't but also knowing that he needed this time to say goodbye to Chenlei. "Give him his last moments alone with her." I nodded at the physically limp and emotionally numb teenager he had his arms around. "Taylor needs you right now more than Quinn does."

He glanced down and smoothed her hair back, nodding in agreement.

"Call Grayson, Michael. He needs to know, so that he can tell Alana before she hears it on the news."

Michael knit his brows. "Call Grayson?" he said, as if hoping he had heard me wrong.

"Please call him as soon as you get home. Promise that you will?"

"Yes, of course," Michael answered with certainty.

He took Taylor and left, while I headed in the opposite direction to tell Elise. When I reached the Damask home just over the hill, there was a police officer on the front step. He was talking into a cell phone. It sounded as if he was checking in with a ground crew somewhere. I told him that Chenlei had been found and he squinted his eyes up at me.

"What?" he said in disbelief, and then, "Wait a minute, John, just a sec. What did you say?" he asked again.

"I said Chenlei has been found. She's in a small open cave on the beach, just below the cliff steps there. She is with her father, Quinn."

He stood up now, forgetting about the cell phone, even though someone spoke impatiently on the other end. "Is she okay? Should I send the paramedics?"

"Send a helicopter to airlift her out. Chenlei did not survive her fall from the cliff," I added, not wanting to believe what I was saying, not able to fully comprehend it.

Roy just stared at me. I assumed the officer's name was Roy, since that's what the person on the cell phone kept shouting. Finally he regained his composure and put the phone to his ear, beginning to relay my message as I climbed the few steps to the front door. I opened it slowly, thinking that Elise would be pacing the floor, phone in hand, calling anyone who might have an idea about where her daughter was. I pictured the boys in their room lying on their bunk beds, quiet and scared.

But that was not the case.

They were all three rummaging through photo albums on the coffee table in the living room. Austin told me excitedly that the TV news station wanted a picture of Chenlei, and Wyatt added how they were looking for the most recent one. I didn't say anything. I was barely holding on. *Somehow holding on* for Elise. She had always been there for me, and now I would be there for her. It wasn't a choice so much as a necessity. Like breathing in and out, I told myself. *Just keep breathing. Don't faint. Don't fall to the ground and pound on the earth in a miserable rage, hoping that it will open up and swallow you whole.*

She was like in a dream state, my Elise, sitting poised and calm, paging slowly through an album. The album had baby pictures in it of the boys. Chenlei was there too, at the end, when they had brought her home from China. I stood over her shoulder and stared in disbelief at the fragile little girl in the pictures. She was so pale and thin, her eyes reflecting panic, no, terror. It did not seem possible that this was the child who hugged me tightly just last night, her smile genuine, her cheeks rosy, her eyes twinkling. Nor was it the child I saw in the beach cave only minutes ago, or was it hours? It felt like such a long time ago, and far away. It seemed so surreal, the blank staring eyes, the bluish gray skin, the slender twisted limbs, and her little hand clutching that bracelet. *Journey's work of art and labor of love, just as Chenlei herself had been.*

I knelt beside Elise and looked into her face. She knew. *Somehow she knew.* I couldn't say the words. I just buried my head in her lap and wept. I could feel her hand stroke my hair. I could hear her wavering voice. "She's gone, isn't she? Gone to be with Ling."

I didn't answer.

"She went looking for the bracelet," Elise said slowly, in her dreamlike state. "I'm sure of it. I asked her to leave the bracelet with me before she went snorkeling. She didn't want to of course, but she knew she had to, because the latch was loose and it might come off in the water. Quinn was going to fix the latch. Someday soon, when he had the time. I told Chenlei it would be safe there on the little round stone in the cave, beside me. And it was safe, wasn't it? If only we hadn't forgotten about it."

I picked my head up and looked into Elise's face. "How did you know that I found her?"

Elise smiled down at me. "It's written all over your face, Kylie. She fell, didn't she? Fell down the cliff steps. I told her never to go near them without an adult. Never." Elise broke down there, and now it was I that held her, while watching it all sink in on Wyatt's and Austin's faces. They looked so lost, so unsure of what to do or what to feel about the death of their sister, and the breakdown of their mother. It was too much for them, too overwhelming to react with anger or tears, or questions. They just sat and stared into space, and I realized that I had never seen them so still, so very still. Almost as still as Chenlei lying on the floor of the beach cave, clutching her treasured bracelet for the last time.

She wouldn't need it anymore.

She was with her mother.

"Hello, Kylie?"

I sat stunned, holding the phone to my ear, staring at the ocean beyond the hill. Was that Chase? Saying anything at all seemed like a chore, but I forced myself to respond.

"Hi Chase."

I heard a sigh at the other end. "It's good to hear your voice."

Silence fell between us like a curtain, the events of his life and mine in the last few days barricading communication.

"I'm sorry I haven't had a chance to call. I've been in Alaska all this time. You weren't home when I left and I didn't want to leave a message. I thought I'd have a chance to get in touch before now, but things have been crazy here. Building this dam is a bigger project than anyone anticipated."

I nodded, but of course Chase couldn't hear that. Then I stood at the window and studied the sun reflecting off the sea.

"Kylie? Are you okay? I'm really sorry, honey, that I couldn't call sooner."

"Chase. It's Chenlei." I didn't have the energy to continue, so I fell silent again, staring at the surf beyond the hill.

"What about her? Has something happened?"

"She's gone, Chase. She fell. We found her in the beach cave."

"She's gone?"

"Her injuries were fatal."

"Kylie, I'm so sorry. When did this happen?"

I thought for a moment. When *did* it happen?

"Yesterday. It happened yesterday," I said, although my mind was fuzzy from not sleeping or eating. But I remembered Quinn had come by this morning to check on me. He wanted me to walk over later and just be with them. I could still hear his words in my head. *You have to eat, Kylie. Keep your strength up. Get some rest. I can see you haven't slept.* Then he made coffee and toast before he left. I glanced at the table, and it was still there, untouched.

"This is terrible news, Kyl. I am so sorry." Chase sounded sad, shocked. His voice was strained and every word was spoken slowly, as if he couldn't fathom, really, what it was I had said.

"When will you come home, Chase? The funeral is tomorrow." My eyes began to tear up and I was surprised I had any tears left. I wanted him beside me, more than anything or anyone. I *needed* him more than I ever had. I thought about our baby. I had to tell him, but not now. It would have to wait, just as it had waited for years and years to happen. Now the joy of it would have to wait, too. There was no joy in me right now, not at this moment.

"Oh honey, I would love to come home and be there for you, and for Quinn and Elise, but I can't. There's no way I can leave here right now. Everyone's depending on me. I can't let them down."

I wondered why it was okay to let me down, and to let his best friends down, to not be there for them, or me, or his unborn child. I wondered if Meagan was standing beside the phone, pretending to be sad for him, but I had too much pride to ask if he'd flown her in to Alaska.

"No, work must come first," I whispered, hoarsely.

"That's not fair, Kylie."

"I'm sorry. I'm just not thinking fairly today. I'm not thinking at all, except about that sweet little girl being lowered into the earth tomorrow. I have to go, Chase. Elise is waiting for me."

"Kylie, I'm so sorry. There's nowhere I'd rather be than there with you, especially now. Believe me, honey. Please forgive me for not being able to come. Tell Elise and Quinn how sorry I am."

"Goodbye, Chase," I whispered, tears flooding my face. It felt like such a final goodbye. Maybe in my heart it was exactly that. Or maybe my heart was just too numb to know what it felt.

I nibbled on the hard toast and sipped the cold coffee before walking over the hill to the Damask house. It wouldn't do to be an additional concern for them. They had enough to deal with. I couldn't believe that Quinn had had the presence of mind to check on me. I should have been checking on him. He seemed to carry such a burden for what Chase and I were going through. Quinn was a mystery to me, and yet he was as true a friend as I could ever hope to have.

When I arrived Elise was sleeping, thanks to some heavy sedatives. The boys were at a friend's house, and Quinn was walking on the beach. All of this information came from Quinn's mother. She was a frail little woman, with silver hair and a gentle voice. Mrs. Damask was a widow, and had flown in from back east. She had Quinn's smile and displayed the kind of optimism I had thought was unique to her son, by mentioning what a glorious sunny day it was. She had patted my hand and told me that despite the darkness of the moment, there was always something to be thankful for, and today it was the warmth of the sun despite the sad occasion.

I graciously excused myself and headed to the beach. I needed to face the cave where my precious Chenlei had breathed her last breath, and taken a piece of my heart with her to wherever that sweet little spirit had gone. Standing at the entrance of the arched rock I stared at the sand floor where her tiny body had lain, contorted and untouched until Quinn scooped her up and cradled her in his arms. A strange peace overcame me, only for a moment, as I stood there and remembered the love on Quinn's face. Surely love never dies. Wasn't this the symbolic reasoning behind Heathcliff and Catherine's eternal quest for a way to appease it?

"I still cannot believe she's really gone," Quinn said softly, as he walked up beside me. I jumped slightly, having been so lost in my thoughts of what lived on and what did not.

"I think it will be awhile before any of us can truly accept it," I said, sounding more together than I felt. I wanted to scream out in anger at God and at fate rather than rationalize any of it.

Quinn sat down against a wall of the cave and stared out at the surf. "This is my punishment," he admitted, in a voice I almost didn't recognize, it was so high and strained.

"I doubt God ever uses death as a punishment, unless it's your own eternal death," I said, perplexed by his obvious self-inflicted guilt.

"You don't understand," he said, and then put his head in his hands.

I sat down beside him. "Then why don't you explain?"

Quinn looked out at the surf again, his eyes moist. "Chenlei *was mine*, Kylie. *I am her father.*"

His voice broke there, and his body began to shake. Watching him, examining his words, and then reflecting upon conversations of the past that seemed odd to me, made it all so clear.

"You met Ling at the college, and one thing led to another. Before you knew it, you'd fallen in love." As I summed this up for him, I realized that my empathy came from knowing how very easily such a thing could happen. Grayson and I were no different in our need and our vulnerability than Quinn and Ling had been. Something crossed over in Quinn when I said this. He looked at me surprised, perhaps unable to believe that anyone could understand. It opened a floodgate in his soul and his story spilled out.

"I met her that first summer at the college there," he began. We e-mailed every day after I returned home. Ling had access to the Internet through her job at the college, where she did filing and audited classes. I was hopelessly in love with her, and yet, I never stopped loving Elise. I loved them both, but so differently. Ling made no demands of me. We shared our thoughts and our dreams. It was more of a fantasy than anything. But eventually I knew I had to let her go. Ling needed to find someone to spend her life with, in her own country. I couldn't leave Elise and the boys. They were my destiny. My responsibility. My *reality*."

"How is it that you adopted Chenlei?" I asked, my own eyes tearing up at the thought of her never knowing Quinn had been her real father.

"I didn't know about Chenlei. Several months after returning home that last summer I received a letter from Ling. I sat at my desk and held it for the longest time in my hands, staring at her handwriting. But I couldn't open it. I reasoned that there was nothing she could say I wished to hear. I was feeling weak, needy for her, guilty. Always there was the guilt, for cheating on Elise, for leaving and hurting Ling. It would destroy me, I believed, to read her letter. I wouldn't be able to resist finding a way to be with her if she pleaded. I chose to believe that she would find someone and be happy."

Quinn paused there, and looked at me for the first time. "It sounds incredibly selfish, doesn't it? My love for Ling. And it was selfish and wrong. It was destructive for both of us. But still, even knowing that, I loved her so much and I always will. Even now after her death. I believe she is out there somewhere, and I pray with all my heart she can forgive me."

"I don't think love can ever be wrong, Quinn. Or selfish. It's just an emotion we have little control over. But our behavior can certainly be both, and there are consequences for wrong and selfish behavior, I believe. God only grieves for us, that we have been led astray. I'm just glad he is a forgiving God, even when we can't seem to forgive ourselves."

Quinn nodded, staring at the sand floor of the cave. "I should have opened the letter. Ling had probably written to say that Chenlei would be better off in this country with me, because no one would marry an unwed mother, or provide for the child."

"Someone at the college must have told you that Chenlei was yours, after Ling died," I reasoned.

"Yes. Laura Jennings. I had worked with her during those summer terms at the college. She knew about Ling and me, and about Chenlei being born after I had left, but didn't feel it was her place to tell me, especially since Ling was with someone else: a businessman from the community. But when she heard of Ling's death, she called me. I couldn't believe that Ling had died, or that we had a daughter. I was so angry with myself, and what I had done. I nearly destroyed my office after she called: throwing and smashing things. I felt ashamed for what I had done to her. I had to find Chenlei. And Edward was my only hope. I knew that he went to China often and worked with the orphanages there. I told him the whole story and how we must protect Elise from it, and Edward was more than happy to find Chenlei and keep my secret."

"I think Elise knows," I said, recalling her emotional difficulty with accepting Chenlei, and her odd behavior when telling me what Edward's associate had found out.

"How could she possibly know?" Quinn whispered hoarsely, a puzzled look on his ashen face. "She doesn't treat me any differently. If anything, we have become closer than ever through Chenlei and her nightmares, her difficult adjustment to our home and our country. All because of her mother's tragic death so fresh in her mind, never fading with time, never allowing her any peace, until now. Maybe now Chenlei is with Ling again."

"I hope so," I said. It was the only thing that comforted me in all of this, the thought of Chenlei being with Ling again. I could almost see Chenlei's broad smile and dark, sparkling eyes at the sight of her mother, just before running into her arms for eternity.

"Will you tell Elise?" I asked.

"I don't know. I don't think she wants to hear it, or she would have asked before now. I do know one thing. I love Elise more than I ever thought possible. And I feel her love for me. I pray that this will not break us, that it will only make us closer, that somehow God will bless our family despite it nearly being destroyed through my weak and selfish ways."

I hugged Quinn then, and tried to console him, telling him how everything would be okay, that God would forgive him and he must forgive himself. Once he had control of his emotions, Quinn returned home.

I took a long walk down the shore, his recent words echoing inside my head over and over again until I couldn't walk any further. I was feeling sick to my stomach as I sat in the sand and buried my face in my hands. There was a suffocating, stabbing pain in my heart for the loss of Chenlei, whom I had loved as if she were my own daughter. What an endearing child she had been, championing every challenge presented her. *Why God?* I cried, looking up to heaven. *Why would you take this beautiful little spirit from us so soon? Chenlei would have accomplished so much in her lifetime and been such an inspiration to so many. Why did you take her from us?*

My grief was inconsolable as I sat crumpled in the sand, fearing I would lose my baby from the trauma of it all. I wished Grayson were there to console me, and not Chase, who at the moment seemed to have his priorities mixed up, and even if he didn't, it sure felt like it. Tomorrow Chenlei would be lowered into the earth, and part of me would be buried with her. Something inside had hardened from my grief; had crossed over a threshold from which there was no going back. Hope did not abound in me anymore, and joy would never come easy again.

I was sure of nothing else at this moment, except for that.

# CHAPTER TWENTY-THREE

*I longed for the scent of her, and how I would constantly delight in her fragileness, and yet I was so moved by her remarkable stoicism.*

The hill overlooking the ocean where the Damasks had chosen to bury Chenlei was not far from our own hill, as the crow flies. It was several miles on a narrow winding road by car. I drove it alone, behind the Damasks. Their vehicle was full with Quinn's mother visiting. None of Elise's family had made it from France, not that any of them were expected. However, the Damask home was filled with flowers and cards, and the phone never stopped ringing whenever I was present.

I hadn't been there often or stayed long since delivering the tragic news to Elise and the boys. Whenever I did stop in, Elise was drugged and sleeping, and the boys were not there. Friends from school and church had kept them ever since this tragedy unfolded. And Quinn, well Quinn spent most of his time on the beach, where only he and God could find a middle ground for him to live in, what with all the burdens of his heart.

Chenlei had not been displayed after her death, but otherwise it would be a normal burial. Her tiny body in a white pearl casket would be lowered into the earth, and the pastor from Elise and Quinn's church would speak. The Damasks couldn't bear to view her in the satin-lined box, but needed the reassurance of seeing Chenlei put lovingly into her eternal resting place.

I felt adrift from my body, as if floating somewhere above it watching myself throughout the entire day. It began when I left the car and walked across the gentle slope, passing tombstones of others who rested there. A seemingly endless string of slow moving vehicles entered the cemetery beneath a brilliant robin's-egg blue sky. It was unusually warm and muggy, and the heavy air fit the occasion perfectly. Doves cooed in the short thick palms, and leaves rustled gently from an occasional breeze. Soon the lawn became dense with people, standing as still as little Chenlei must have been, lying in her pearl white bed.

My eyes looked out across the crowd as the pastor began to speak. I was standing beside Quinn and Elise, and the boys. Quinn's mother stood bent over with one arm around each grandson, and was not much taller than either. Austin had buried his head in her side, but Wyatt studied the grass beneath his feet.

The Damasks had insisted that I was family, that Chenlei loved me as much as any of them. I think it was not having Chase there that prompted Quinn and Elise to keep me near and with a watchful eye at that. Both of them glanced at me occasionally, their expressions concerned, despite their own numbing pain. I knew the hollow face staring at me in the mirror that morning was what concerned them. I truly looked as if I might lose my ability to stand upright at any moment. But I had convinced myself, and them, that I must be there for Chenlei.

The pastor's words sounded distant and muffled, but the rustling palms and cooing doves were sharp and clear. The flowers surrounding Chenlei's little casket only yards from where I stood were bleeding together; their colors blending like a sunrise, yet certain faces in the crowd stood out, no matter how distant or partially hidden.

One of those faces was Taylor's, standing between Gwyneth and Michael. Not far behind them to the left was Grayson, with Alana at his side. I worried about the effect another death, so soon, would have on Alana. She looked stoic and attentive. Grayson looked serious and alert, unlike Michael and Gwyneth who looked dazed. Taylor appeared to be positively numb. I remembered suddenly that her tennis playoffs began this afternoon, and wondered if she would play. Probably, I decided. If I knew her parents, all three of them would encourage her to get on with life, and to dedicate her wins to Chenlei.

I wondered if Michael and Grayson would finally speak to one another, and if Gwyneth would acknowledge Grayson's presence, or his new relationship with Taylor.

My eyes swelled with tears over the large crowd of people there. So much love for this little girl, this family. All of Chenlei's schoolmates were present. They stood together with her teacher. Wyatt's and Austin's teachers were there, too. The whole school, I decided, had attended. Of course the Damask's church congregation was present, and the regular customers from Elise's store, along with other businessmen and women from the strip where Elise had her shop. Colleagues of Quinn's and mine were among the crowd, all of Quinn's soccer team he coached, and the adult team he played on. The tribute to the Damasks was impressive, the love for Chenlei touching.

Even the rescue crews that had come that morning Chenlei went missing were present. I recognized Roy and John from the cell phone conversation, and the paramedics who airlifted her out.

Ashes-to-ashes and dust-to-dust was the extent of what I heard the pastor say. The rest escaped me, floating away like salt in the sea breeze. My mind was wandering to the Pacific below us, to times when Chenlei and I had played on the shore with Alana and Taylor or her brothers, Wyatt and Austin. Images and memories came and went from me, and when finally they lowered her tiny casket into the earth, I was not prepared for it.

Elise cried out and the boys sobbed openly. Quinn hugged his wife to him tightly and I fell to my knees. I noticed there was a rose in my hand, a baby red rose not quite in bloom, just as Chenlei herself had not been fully formed yet. I didn't know who put it there, in my hand, but I was grateful to have it. I tossed it gently on her casket. And after that I couldn't say what happened. I woke up on the leather couch in my living room with Grayson seated at my feet. He was reading a book, and music was playing softly in the distance. It was piano music. Light streamed in from the window, and for a minute I truly believed that I was dreaming. So I just lay there without moving and stared at Grayson. He must have sensed that I was awake because he turned and looked at me.

"Welcome back," he said, and then he smiled. "I hope you don't mind that I'm here. Taylor took Alana with her to the tennis playoffs. Michael, Gwyneth, and I had an actual conversation believe it or not, and it was decided that Alana would spend the night with Taylor so that I could care for you. I told them I'd pick her up at noon tomorrow for our flight back to Maui." Grayson paused, but I had no response. "I'll check into a local motel later this evening, as soon as I know it's safe to leave you here alone." He paused again, hesitated really, as if not sure of what to say. "I offered to keep an eye on you. Elise and Quinn were more than happy to let me do it. They're very concerned about your health."

I slowly sat up and then held my very heavy head in my hands. "I should be at Taylor's match."

"I think she'll understand why you're not there. I would love to have gone, too. I told her to win this round for Chenlei, and we'd both be at the finals next weekend. Alana and I will fly back up for the event."

I nodded.

"Would you like some tea?"

"Yes."

When Grayson returned with the tea I asked him about what had happened, there at the cemetery, and he said when I passed out beside the casket he came forward, being a doctor and all, and then carried me to the car. Elise was sure I hadn't eaten or slept and just needed rest, so he brought me here, after turning Alana over to Gwyneth and Michael. He added that he and Alana had taken a taxi from the airport and so he brought me home in my jeep.

"Quinn and Elise will be by later with dinner," Grayson added, as he handed me the cup of tea. "People have brought them so much food they're eager to share it."

I didn't respond right away. Instead I thought about everything he had said. The one thing that stood out in my mind was that he was leaving. I didn't want to be alone. Not tonight. "Please stay here. We have a guest room. It's quite comfortable," I pleaded.

Grayson studied me, his intelligent eyes uncertain. "I'm not sure that's a good idea, Kylie. What would Elise and Quinn think?"

"My friends wouldn't think anything. They aren't judgmental and they trust that I know what's best for me."

"Okay, if you're sure that's what you want."

I sat cross-legged and held the tea in my lap. It was such a relief to know he would be staying. I wasn't feeling courageous enough to be alone. My heart grieved for my little shadow, Chenlei. I missed her solemn eyes peering up at me, her tiny hands forming letters on notebook paper or cracking eggs into a bowl for baking cookies. I recalled how her shiny hair would toss about as she scampered from one room to the next, fetching me this or that for her lessons. I longed for the scent of her, and how I would constantly delight in her fragileness, and yet I was so moved by her remarkable stoicism. How I ached to see her again. Oh how I loved her! She had become a part of me, and now that part was missing.

Tears began to cascade down my face like a dam had burst. And then I realized I hadn't really cried on this sad, sad day. Only a single tear had trickled here and there that I immediately would shore up, to be strong again, to get through this day of putting Chenlei to rest. I couldn't accept that I would never see her again, never touch, hold, or teach her while sitting quietly by my side.

Grayson took the tea from my lap and set it on the coffee table. Then he held me as I sobbed into his strong arms, wishing I had but a tenth of his strength to live another day without Chenlei. I couldn't imagine it, life without her. It would never be the same. Perhaps nothing would ever be the same. Perhaps it was too late to fix all that had been broken, as broken as Chenlei's tiny body at the base of the cliff. My marriage for one was either already broken or poised to fall irreparably apart, along with Grayson and Alana's trust in me, once they knew what I had been withholding from them.

I pulled away from Grayson then, feeling as guilty as I should. Without looking into his face I grabbed a wad of tissue from the box on the table, and walked to the window, where I stared into the late afternoon sun. It should have been black, the sun, and all the flowers weeping. It wasn't fair that the world outside my window was not affected by Chenlei's death: her tragic, senseless, and irreversible death.

Grayson joined me and I wanted to turn toward him, kiss his cheek, his forehead, his mouth. I wanted to get lost in Grayson, so lost I would never find myself again. But instead I questioned him some more about the funeral. Did the crowd disperse quickly or linger while speaking in hushed tones? Was it difficult to talk to Michael and Gwyneth or not nearly as awkward as they had anticipated?

Yes, the crowd lingered, and no, it was not awkward to speak to Gwyneth and Michael. Grayson added that his ex-wife was distant and sparse with her words, while his ex-partner spoke warmly and to the point, just as he had expected. No surprises.

I thought about how being brief and polite came easy to Grayson, and so he managed somehow to get through it all, the tragic and unbelievable death of Chenlei, the incredibly sad burial, the long overdue civilities between him and his ex-wife, and ex-medical partner. And then there was Alana, no doubt sad for her personal loss of a best friend, and yet happy that Chenlei was with her mama at last. We both agreed it would be years before anyone knew how all this grief might affect Alana.

Soon our conversation became personal. I had to take all the credit for that, or blame, if there was to be any. Because I told Grayson how some of his poems about love and loss were stuck in my head now, on rewind, and they were a comfort to me, although it was sad to finally understand them so well.

"I'm glad they could be of comfort to you, Kylie," Grayson replied.

I looked at him, into those seemingly bottomless pools of ocean blue eyes. I should not have been as affected by him or his poetry as I was.

Fortunately for both of us, the doorbell rang.

Grayson went to answer it and helped Quinn carry the food in. I assured Elise that I was fine and we insisted they stay to eat with us. It was a mournfully quiet meal. We all felt the crushing numbness of having recently lost Chenlei, but there was comfort in each other's company. We spoke of the funeral; the people present, the things said.

When they left I shared with Grayson how much I hurt for them, losing Chenlei when she had just begun to take a foothold in their lives. I didn't share what I knew about Quinn and Ling, the shock of it still fresh in my mind. Did Elise Know? Had she known all along? Had Quinn confessed it all to her, as he had to me since Chenlei's passing?

Grayson and I went for a walk on the beach at sunset. I needed the fresh air to clear my head. The brisk walk released endorphins into my system, which partially lifted my spirits. Grayson seemed refreshed, too. We both showered, he in the guest bath.

I let the warm water wash over me for a very long time, until the room was filled with thick steam, like the fog my mind was in. I hoped that it would help me sleep rather than to toss and turn as I had of late, which only exhausted me more.

Afterwards I purposely kept my distance from Grayson, cuddling up in the chair by the front window where I could peer out into the inky blackness, lit up festively by twinkling stars. I had put on a conservative t-shirt, baggy and long, and some running shorts, rather than my regular skimpy PJs. Grayson wore running shorts and a t-shirt, too, making me wonder if that's what he normally slept in.

He put on a soft jazz CD and sat at the table keyboarding something on his laptop. I decided that must be what it was like to live with a writer, always listening to the sound of the keyboard late at night. I rather liked it, finding the rhythm of tapping keys soothing.

Finally my eyes were heavy and I told Grayson I was going to bed. I glanced his way politely and said goodnight as I softly shut my door. I thought of Chase and how much I ached for him to hold me and calm my fears, tell me everything would be fine. I needed his strong arms wrapped around me. I tried to shut Grayson out of my head, but it was hard to do as I listened to the tapping keys for what seemed like a long time, and then it was quiet. The lamplight slipping under my door was gone, causing the room to blacken with a heavy silence. I fell asleep, for a while at least, but then I heard screaming and sat straight up in the bed. The screaming continued until I realized that it was *me. I was the one screaming.* I held my breath as the door flew open and Grayson stood there, hesitating for only a second, perhaps until his eyes adjusted to the moonlight.

He sat gently beside me and whispered something I didn't quite hear. I realized when he touched my arm that I was shaking.

"What is it, Kylie? Did you have a bad dream?"

I nodded, but I couldn't speak. I tried to remember what made me scream, and then I recalled my dream.

*I was standing in the beach cave, but the little body twisted and broken on the sand floor was not Chenlei. It was a baby. She was tiny and frail, and wore a little white gown. Her hair was dark brown and her cheeks were rosy; but she was dead. And then Taylor was screaming at my side but it wasn't Taylor screaming . . . it was me.*

I began shaking harder, overwhelmed by this nightmare. Grayson pulled me to him, and just held me.

"I'm glad you're here." It was all I could manage to say.

"I'll be here all night, Kylie, just a few feet away in the other room. If you need anything, just call for me." With that he stood up, but I grabbed his hand.

"No! Don't go. Please don't go," I pleaded.

Grayson sat on the bed again, his hand still in mine.

"Lie down with me. Just hold me," I asked.

Grayson was so gentle as he held me that I barely knew he was there, except for the warmth from his body. We lay together breathing in unison for some length of time that I could not determine, but try as I may I could not block out the demons haunting me: images of Chenlei's little broken body, and my baby, so stiff and still on the beach cave floor. I saw images of Chase with Meagan, images of shocked anger on Grayson and Alana's faces because I'd told them of my deceit about the letter.

I turned to look at Grayson in the moonlight. His eyes were open, watching me.

"I'm so sorry. You're not getting any rest, are you?" I whispered.

"Don't be sorry. There is nowhere I'd rather be than here, comforting you," he replied, and just that quickly he had chased the demons away with his low, husky voice that sent a different kind of shiver down my spine.

"What were you writing all evening?" I asked.

"Another poem."

"What was it about?"

"It was about how after a tragedy, survivors somehow manage to live on."

I pondered that for a minute. How *do* they live on? How would *I* live on? After Mama's death, I'd had Journey and we helped each other through it. Chase was there to hold us both up, although he'd never met Mama. Journey's death had brought a rush of guilt along with the stinging pain, a guilt that caused me to resent Chase, and to blindly seek possession of her child for recompense. It had drawn me to Grayson, my grief for Journey, as I coveted the child I discovered to be his. I thought of the teak wood chest and how I would never have met Alana if it hadn't been delivered to my door. Then I remembered how I had stood before it, with Wyatt scared to death on the porch and Taylor calling out across the grounds for Chenlei. I remembered seeing the jewelry box the instant I opened the lid and then I knew. I knew where we would find Chenlei. I only hoped that she would be sleeping, just sleeping there in the cave.

For a few seconds, lost in these thoughts as I lay there, I must have dozed. When I woke up I believed it was Chase beside me where he belonged. And then I remembered Chase had not come in my hour of need, either because I had so completely driven him away, or because Meagan had reined him in. It was Grayson lying beside me, and he felt different. He was different. He was different in every way I needed, in ways I hadn't even known I needed. Maybe because I was different, of

*Journey* **221**

that I could be sure. I would never be the same again. A page of my life had turned forever with the passing of sweet little Chenlei, with the sound of Meagan's voice on Chase's phone, with the little baby growing inside of me, and no one to share the joy with.

I wasn't sure what happened next. I don't know who kissed whom. But if I didn't initiate it, I was not sorry it happened. It was wrong, but it was wonderful nonetheless. It was everything that grief and pain wasn't. The oppression suffocating me had lifted, and in its place grew a raging passion. Hurt and despair melted beneath my pleasure, became lost in my consumption of Grayson, for surely if we could have consumed each other we would have, our feelings were so intense.

My t-shirt and running shorts were soon lying in a heap on the floor next to his. Our bodies became intertwined for whatever hours were left in the long night. When morning came, we just held each other and dozed.

Grayson left then, silently. There was nothing to say. There was no going back, no undoing it.

Lying there alone I could still feel his touch, taste his lips. But I could not allow myself to think about him, about how much I loved him. Instead my thoughts were of Quinn and Ling, and how I feared knowing the pain they had endured, the suffering they had caused one another because of their love. *I don't think love can ever be selfish or wrong, Quinn. It's just an emotion we have little control over. But our behavior can certainly be both, and there are consequences for wrong and selfish behavior, I believe.*

And I did believe that with all my heart. But my strength had somehow slipped away, and I thought maybe my sanity had as well, from grieving for Chenlei and worrying about my unborn child, from fretting about Chase and Meagan, and my hiding the truth of Alana's paternity. Grayson, I knew, had as much to reckon with as I did. He was now no different than Michael had been. Or Gwyneth. He had morally become his own worst nightmare.

As I had become mine.

# CHAPTER TWENTY-FOUR

*Playing this tennis match for her little friend fresh in the ground was the only thing keeping Taylor in the game.*

Elise stopped by at noon, the same time Alana and Grayson's flight took off. I thought about that as I glanced at the clock, still in a t-shirt and running shorts, the same ones that had lain in a heap on the bedroom floor all night. It kept alive the image of Grayson removing them, and allowed the warmth of his love to linger even now, in the stark light of day. The remaining warmth of Grayson's love also caused me agonizing guilt, because Chase still mattered to me despite everything. Despite the hurt and the anger and the miscommunication between us of late. Despite his not being here for Chenlei's death, and having made his career a priority over us. Despite the possibility that he might have found someone else, someone less complicated, someone he probably hoped would be more fertile. I knew that deep within me somewhere I still loved him, but the love was hiding beneath all that had happened, and confusion had taken its place.

Elise had been busy in the kitchen all this time, while I sat in a chair by the window, absentmindedly twirling a piece of hair around my finger. Finally my best friend entered the front room, placing a tray of food on the coffee table.

"You shouldn't have bothered, Elise. I don't know where my mind has been, sitting here lost in thought while you're fussing over my lunch in the kitchen."

"It's noon, Kylie. You're not even dressed. I bet you haven't slept.

None of this is good for your baby, you know." Elise sank into the leather sofa and sighed heavily. "You have to get on with life, Kyl. Chenlei isn't coming back."

I studied my meticulous friend, who had chosen not to be defeated by recent overwhelming realities, which is surely how I appeared: defeated. Her gallant effort was admirable, although her normally perfect hair was slightly askew, and her shimmering cat green eyes swollen. But my Elise was a fighter. I knew that she would be okay, that she would get through this. I wasn't so sure about Quinn. I suddenly wondered if she would hate me, were I to share that Grayson and I had slept together. Of course, I would never admit that to a living soul, but what would she think if I did? I truly didn't want to know. I hated myself enough at the moment for both of us.

"Elise, I have to tell Grayson about Alana, this weekend when he comes back here for Taylor's tennis finals."

"Did Taylor win?"

"Yes. Taylor left a message on my answering machine. She's doing this for Chenlei, you know. She couldn't possibly play, except for wanting to win the trophy in honor of Chenlei."

Elise smiled. "Chenlei loved tennis. I think she would have been a good player one day. The child was so agile, and coordinated."

I sat down on the floor by the coffee table and nibbled on a sandwich. "How do I tell Grayson that Alana is his? Do I just hand over the letter meant for him? Tell him that when I found it I didn't trust him yet, and I wanted to be sure he really was Alan's father before I said anything?"

Elise sipped on the iced tea she had made for us and searched my eyes. "Why is this so hard for you? Why do you care how he reacts? You don't need to defend yourself. I think it was wise to wait and be sure that he really was Alana's father. Journey didn't always see reality clearly. She may have wanted him to be the father so badly that she convinced herself he was."

"Elise, there really isn't a good reason for keeping and reading that letter." I stood up and walked over to the window, staring down at the beach, where Grayson and I had just walked last night. *What was I thinking, opening mail that wasn't mine?* I had obviously been more than a little obsessed with the idea of raising Journey's child. Chase had been right. My husband had been the sane one all along. It was wrong of me to selfishly pursue raising Alana when Journey made it clear that Grayson was her father, just as it was wrong of me to blame Chase for Journey's running away.

"Don't tell him about the letter," Elise suggested. "I found a letter once, meant for Quinn," Elise confessed. Her voice wavered somewhat, but she continued. "I did exactly what you did, and opened it. I've never told him, but the letter changed everything."

I came and sat next to her. "What did the letter say, Elise? And how did you end up with it?"

Elise cleared her throat and looked hesitant to continue. Her eyes welled up with tears and I handed her a tissue as her story spilled out.

"I took Quinn's dinner to him one night and it caught my eye there in the trash. It was an unopened piece of mail lying right on top, but it didn't look like junk mail. The address was written in unusual cursive, with wide strokes carefully penned. As if the person wasn't overly familiar with English. Anyway, I put it in my purse out of curiosity. I thought I would ask Quinn about it later. Why he'd thrown it away. He wasn't there when I found it. Someone told me he was in the library looking for a particular history book."

"Why didn't you ask Quinn about it?"

Elise shrugged. "I don't know. I looked at it for a long time when I got home, and then I just decided to open it. He had, after all, thrown it away. It couldn't have fallen into the trash, which was too far from his desk. He had to walk over and put it there."

"Who was it from?" I asked, thinking that perhaps I already knew.

"It was from Ling." Elise looked right into my eyes, perhaps expecting to see shock or dismay, but instead she saw acknowledgement that I knew, just as she had known about Chenlei in the beach cave before I came to tell her. Her admission opened a floodgate in her, just as it had

*Journey* 225

in Quinn. How hard it must have been for both of them to keep all this pent up inside.

"She was pregnant with his baby," Elise confessed. "She wanted Quinn to come and take the child when it was born. Raise it here in America where it would have a chance at life. She must have been heartbroken. There was such sadness to her words that it made me hate myself rather than Quinn, for not being what he had needed. If I had been, he wouldn't have fallen in love with her. And Quinn of course, was choosing to do what was right by his family. I'm sure he didn't read the letter for fear of wavering in his resolve to end the affair."

"I'm so sorry, Elise," I said, squeezing her hand.

"When we made the trip to China to bring Chenlei home, there was a reference to her mother having worked at that same college where Quinn had been teaching during the summer. For an instant I wondered if Chenlei might possibly be Ling's child, but then I decided I was just being paranoid, until Quinn and Chenlei bonded almost instantly. After a while there was really no doubt. It was the little things that gave them away, traits and mannerisms most wouldn't notice, but I did. And then when Edward's associate told me Chenlei's mother's name was Ling, it just confirmed what I already suspected."

My best friend looked at me with no anger or resentment, but an unspeakable sadness in her eyes.

"Kylie, I caused Ling's death as much as Quinn did. I could have saved her, but my anger and pride prevented me from showing Quinn that letter. It makes me as selfish and wrong as both of them had been."

"You just have to forgive yourself, Elise. Your reaction was very human. You're not to blame for situations others have created. And anyway, you don't know how Quinn might have reacted, had you shown him the letter. You don't know that anything would have turned out differently," I said. "Fate has it own agenda, and hindsight is futile. The most we can hope for is to learn from the past, and move on."

I hugged Elise and prayed for my own forgiveness at the same time. Then we ate our lunch with heavy hearts, finding camaraderie in our misery. Elise added that she had forgiven Quinn, and loved him completely despite everything. I reassured Elise of Quinn's love for her in return, and how he had told me recently that he loved her more with each passing day. She asked when I would see Chase to share my news about the baby, and I said I wouldn't see him until Thanksgiving in three weeks.

When Elise left I showered and dressed, and sat in the den to organize my lesson plans for tomorrow's classes. But my mind kept wandering to last night. Grayson would be back this weekend for the final round of Taylor's tennis playoffs. I couldn't begin to think about that. Once I told Grayson the truth about Alana being his own flesh and blood, and how I had kept that truth from him, he would probably never speak to me again.

Perhaps that would be a blessing, now that I had my own baby to think about, and my baby's daddy, whom I still loved, despite everything.

Taylor won her first set of the last match easily. I had arrived midway through it and spied Grayson in the stands. I sat between him and Alana, at their insistence. Gwyneth and Michael were several rows away and had smiled politely while waving their hands in the air. I was relieved to observe that Alana seemed fine. As if experiencing the death of loved ones was a normal way of life for her by now. Grayson was pensive, concentrating fully on the tennis.

Taylor's expression, I noticed, was quite serious and without a hint of joy for her first playoffs. It had to be the hardest thing Taylor had ever done, focusing on her game with the whole school cheering for her, and right on the heels of Chenlei's funeral. Taylor hadn't known loss before, not of someone close to her. Of course, even if she had, losing someone you care about never gets any easier. And then there was her father, right there in the stands where she had only dreamed he might ever be.

Winning the regional playoffs would mean having a large trophy for the school display case, but in my heart I knew the trophy was the last thing on Taylor's mind. She needed to win this for Chenlei, whose enthusiasm for the sport had been so inspiring to the whole team. Playing this tennis match for her little friend fresh in the ground was the only thing keeping Taylor in the game.

Her opponent was a girl named Jessica. She looked hungry for the win, especially since a teammate had won last year, and keeping the trophy at their school was a huge incentive for her. Taylor's school had never won the regional playoffs. I was worried for Taylor. She looked tired and stressed, having been through a lot in the last few days, whereas her opponent looked steady and calm. And sure enough, Jessica won the first set.

Taylor glanced up into the stands, as if needing to pull some strength from an outside source before beginning her next set. She saw Alana, Grayson, and me instantly, and then her mother sitting with Michael not far away. It caused her solemn expression to melt into a warm smile. We waved and cheered her on, and this must have been energizing, for the next set was all hers. A second wind had found our Taylor all over the court, returning every ball Jessica slammed at her.

The last set would prove to be tedious. Taylor was flushed and breathing heavily. She didn't stand a chance if having to rely on her speed to reach every ball precariously placed at the outer corners by Jessica, who had been doing it so well. Tired but focused, Taylor stood her ground and put Jessica on the defensive by using her new and powerful two-handed backhand to switch the game up. For most of the last set it was Jessica running back and forth to return the balls that Taylor powerfully lobbed to the outer corners. After a very close score that had all of us holding our breath, Taylor drove it home with a perfect ace for a serve, and won the match for Chenlei, and her school.

Everyone stood and cheered, with Taylor squinting to see our reaction up in the stands. Her eyes zeroed in on me and we both began to cry at the same time, tears of triumph and joy. I could barely believe that was Taylor down there on the court receiving the shiny silver trophy from her coach. He talked about how she had never been in the playoffs before, but then had discovered a mean two-handed backhand that put her in the game to stay. Her coach asked if she had anything to say and Taylor took that opportunity to dedicate their school's first regional win to Chenlei Damask, whose love of the game had inspired the whole team, Taylor said, and who had especially motivated her personally to persevere and do her best. Taylor ended by saying how she hoped that Chenlei was watching from above, and then Taylor held the trophy sky-ward, as the whole team cheered and applauded.

There wasn't a dry eye in the stadium after that. Even the ever-brave Grayson's eyes were moist. Once the ceremony was over Taylor came bouncing up through the bleachers and straight to me. We hugged tightly and she whispered *thank you* in my ear. Then she hugged Grayson and turned to find Michael and Gwyneth, who gave congratulatory hugs and decided to take Taylor out for a celebration meal at her favorite restaurant. They encouraged all of us to come along. Alana looked longingly at Grayson for permission, which he gave, graciously declining to come himself. He asked Taylor if he could take her to breakfast in the morning before he and Alana returned to Maui. Her eyes lit up at the invitation, and all traces of disappointment for his declining dinner disappeared.

Taylor insisted Alana spend the night again, and there were no objections. I told Taylor how much I wanted to come, but I needed to speak with Grayson before he left. She understood. I wondered if everyone understood exactly how complicated everything was right now between Grayson and myself, and if I was the only one unsure and unclear about how all of this would be resolved. I hoped not and that my life was not quite the open book it felt like at the moment, vulnerable and poised for change in irreversible ways I would soon regret.

When they had left Grayson turned to me and asked where we might go for dinner. He looked a bit sullen, as if Alana and Chase, and other important matters were very much on his mind, too. I would have loved the privacy of my house on the bluff for this conversation, but thought better of being there alone with Grayson.

I let him drive my Jeep to a favorite secluded place for good food and a relaxed, unhurried setting. It was a private inn that overlooked the Pacific, and had a little known restaurant. Locals knew of it, but not many outsiders ventured near.

We were seated at a corner table out on the generous deck, with the ever-present Pacific looming below us, crashing relentlessly upon the black lava rocks. We ordered the house specialty, a stir-fried Asian dish with local fish and seasonal vegetables. Neither of us knew where to begin our conversation, or which conversation to have first. There were several subjects we needed to address and none of them were simple or easy.

Our moods were too tense for small talk, our emotions too close to the surface for discussing what had happened last weekend. The eye contact between us was igniting sparks of longing we could neither one deny. It was an unfortunate complication to our task of settling once and for all where Alana belonged.

And to whom.

# CHAPTER TWENTY-FIVE

*Chenlei's death and Alana's conception each happened
on fateful nights that belied, in a way,
any control we may have thought we had over our own destinies.*

Grayson and I talked about the surf on the rocks below. How beautiful the transparent sapphire blue sea was crashing against the rough, hardened lava. We chose not to order wine, both of us wanting to be completely alert for what we had to say, and I of course, didn't wish to drink in my condition. When dinner came we enjoyed the exquisite food, listening to the soft Hawaiian music being piped onto the deck. Once dessert had been ordered, I took the plunge and asked Grayson straight out what I had needed to know ever since meeting him.

"Grayson, did you ever sleep with my sister?"

He stared at me, or more correctly, he stared through me as if his mind was somewhere else, somewhere not beyond where I sat but deep inside of him.

"I did spend one night with your sister, a very long time ago."

Grayson studied his water glass.

"But I don't actually remember it, not really. In fact, I had completely dismissed the possibility that next morning and would have never revisited the issue, except for . . ." He didn't finish his sentence, as if the words would just not come.

"Except for what?" I prompted him.

Grayson took a drink of water and then looked at me again, only this time he was looking into my soul, not his.

*Journey* **231**

"Except for the fact that Alana had brought me a document she found in her picture album. The one you gave her from Journey's things out of the chest. It had fallen, she said, from a back fold of the slipcover."

"What document?" I asked.

He folded his hands together on the table.

"It was her certificate of birth, with my name written in as the father, and Alana's whole name written in as Alana Luvay Conner."

"Grayson, why haven't you ever mentioned this? How long have you known that Alana is your daughter?" I asked, my stomach nearly cramping from the shock of it, from the unbelievable knowledge that he had known for some time now, if not always.

Grayson shrugged. "Alana only had the album a week or so when she brought me the certificate. It had occurred to me that she might be my daughter but I didn't dare to dream, especially since Journey never mentioned it, even in all that time she lived on my boat, knowing that her days were numbered."

Grayson paused there, and shifted his gaze to the Pacific. "I assumed that the surfer boy who had broken her heart was the father, and that she hadn't told him, nor did she want him to know. When I sent you Journey's things I knew there was a chance you'd come for Alana, but that was a risk I had to take. I'd promised Journey I would deliver the chest to you."

"Grayson, she didn't tell you perhaps, but she left a letter for me in the teak wood chest. In it she said that you were the father. Obviously, my sister had wanted fate to play its own hand. She wanted you and I to decide who should raise Alana, so as not to force her on either of us."

We were both quiet as the waiter served our desert of chocolate truffle cake, and then leaning forward I added, "Can you understand how my first instinct, under the circumstances, wouldn't be to just come running to you with her information in the letter?"

Grayson nodded, not so much in agreement as in consideration of being in agreement, his intense eyes looking slightly stunned by my confession.

"Journey revealing you to be the father didn't necessarily make it true in my estimation, because my sister didn't always lean to reality in her thinking. So I went to Waikiki where she had lived all that time and did a little investigating on my own, only to discover that everything Shalana said lined up with what Journey wrote in her letter."

I stopped there not sure where to go next, and nibbled on the rich cake.

"Kylie, you went to Waikiki a long time ago," Grayson pointed out.

"Yes, that's true. But a part of me never wanted to believe it, that you had slept with Journey, or that you were Alana's father, because you know how desperately I want a child of my own, and how much Alana means to me."

I reached into my handbag and pulled out the letter I had taken from behind Alana's dresser. With a steady hand I set it in front of him.

"Journey left this in Alana's room for you. It fell behind the dresser and I took it. I still had to investigate for myself and be sure you really were Alana's father before I could give it to you." I didn't apologize, and I felt stronger than I had in days. It was so obvious to me now that everything had played out just as my sister had hoped. Grayson would know without a doubt he was the father, and could decide whether or not he wished to raise Alana, and if he didn't, Journey knew that I would.

Grayson opened and read the letter, and then carefully tucked it back into the envelope. He stuck it inside the pocket of his jacket, draped across the chair beside him.

We stared at one another in silence, while Hawaiian music played softly in the background and a waiter casually refilled our water glasses. The stare between us softened from disbelief to understanding, to desire. And then Grayson broke the silence.

"Let me explain what happened, Kylie, all those years ago, with your sister."

He hesitated, collecting his thoughts.

"There is a reason I haven't said anything before now. At first I knew that I had no proof I might be the father, and you were so determined to take Alana from me. If Journey had just once suggested I might be

*Journey* 233

Alana's dad, I would have fought for her. But she never did, and so I had to assume I wasn't the father."

He paused there, perhaps not sure if he wanted to continue.

"Once I began to fall in love with you, confessing what had happened all those years ago became harder and harder."

I still didn't say anything. It was hard to accept what I had known all along, that I wouldn't be adopting Alana, and it was somewhat of a shock to find out Grayson had secrets of his own he'd been keeping.

"I had a party on my boat," Grayson began in earnest, "a celebration for the local surfers, some of which I had sewn together more than once from surfboard injuries. No one on the beach cares what your specialty is when you're bleeding. The young men became my friends, and it wasn't the first time I'd invited them onto the yacht for a party, but it would be the last. I was drinking lots of rum then, trying to drown my troubles in it, having only left my family months earlier, but that was the only time a woman ended up in my bed, two women to be exact. It was Makana I awoke with the next morning."

"Makana?" I asked. I would have smiled if I'd been capable of smiling at the moment.

"We had been friends almost from the day I moved onto the boat and first ate at the Hula Grill. But we'd never slept together until that night. I remember waking up with a throbbing headache, and Makana cuddled beside me. Journey flashed through my mind and I could have sworn she'd been lying on my bed when I stumbled to my cabin in the middle of the night. I remembered talking to her about surfers and men in general. I had only just met her that evening on the boat, looking sad and alone, not really in a party mood. She told me she had hoped to see her ex-boyfriend, perhaps to patch things up with him. As it turned out, he was with someone else."

Grayson looked perplexed, as if even now he found it hard to believe that night ever happened.

"I recall us falling asleep together, and then I thought I remembered us waking up a while later, but when I awoke with Makana beside me

I dismissed those thoughts immediately, and wanted to believe it had only been my imagination, until of course, I fell in love with Alana."

Grayson's confession made me feel all the more as if Journey were orchestrating these events from her grave. First there had been the bracelet that brought Chenlei home to her mother, and now the certificate that laid bare the truth of Alana's paternity. Chenlei's death and Alana's conception each happened on fateful nights that belied, in a way, any control we may have thought we had over our own destinies.

Grayson looked at me somberly.

"I never had another party. The possibility of having slept with two women in one night, the first of which was someone I barely knew, prompted me to practice sobriety. I don't sleep around. I want you to know that. I haven't been with anyone after my wife except for Makana, who occasionally shares my bed. But I am not in love with her, and since falling in love with you, I have not been with her."

"Does she know you don't love her? Because she is obviously in love with you."

"If Makana is in love with me, she's never said anything. I might have called what I feel for her love once upon a time. But since I've met you, love has taken on a whole new meaning."

"So, you do love her then?"

Grayson shrugged. "Do you love Chase?"

We were silent again, staring, searching, as if our eyes could help us understand what we were to each other, and what we shouldn't be.

I answered him, taking care to be fully honest.

"Part of me will always love Chase, but I'm not sure we want the same things out of life anymore. I've resented him for moving his office to Colorado near his family and I resent Chase for not being here now, for making me grieve alone when I can barely stand any more sadness and pain. I've had to reach deep inside myself for a reason to get up in the morning and carry on with the details of life, because it all seems so pointless."

I hesitated before addressing what else was on my mind. Grayson didn't say anything as I took a drink of water.

"And then there is you. What I feel for you is something I've not experienced before. It does give new meaning to the word love, but maybe that's because it isn't meant to be and we know it. Maybe what draws us to each other is what draws the moth to the flame. In the end it is destructive."

Grayson had no response. What could he say? So I continued.

"Chase and I had a wonderful relationship, although we put a lot of pressure on ourselves to start a family," I admitted. We both wanted a child desperately, and he couldn't wrap his head around adopting, while I on the other hand, was ready to give up on becoming pregnant after so many years of trying."

Grayson listened attentively, his desert not touched, while I spilled out everything weighing down my heart.

"When the teak wood chest arrived, everything began to fall apart," I continued. All those feelings about Journey running away began to resurface, only this time I blamed Chase instead of Journey, or myself. I couldn't understand why he didn't want to adopt Alana, when it seemed the perfect solution for our childless dilemma, not to mention how much I had loved Journey, and now my little niece. It was wrong of me to think this way. I wasn't being fair to Chase, or to you. "

"Don't be too hard on yourself, Kylie," Grayson interjected. "It's only natural that Journey's death would cause you to revisit that difficult time in your life, when someone else became a priority over your little sister. You couldn't help growing up and falling in love with a man," he said gently, even lovingly, with his voice husky and low, the way it was last weekend when I'd had my nightmare and he was comforting me. It sent shivers of desire along my spine.

Grayson shrugged, as if to say *life happens*. "Then your mother died," he added, "and Journey became a very real burden to you, because now you were her sole guardian, and she was a rebellious teenager not able to cope with you having someone else in your life. When she left you were glad, despite missing her and feeling guilty. It was a very confusing time for all of you."

I felt relieved to have someone understand, and I felt a strong desire to show him my gratitude all night long.

"Grayson, what I blame myself for now has nothing to do with Journey, or Alana. It has to do with you. I care too deeply about you. I've broken my marriage vows because of you, because I *wanted* to, and I still do. But the bottom line is, I am a married woman, and I am pregnant with Chase's child."

Grayson's eyes widened.

"You're pregnant?"

I nodded.

We were silent as the waiter brought our bill, and after Grayson paid the check we walked along the path to the beach. He had made arrangements to spend the night at the inn where we had dinner, and I couldn't stop thinking about how easy it would be to stay with him. The sun was setting in all its usual glory and after a short walk we leaned against a large rock and watched the bright yellow ball sink into the sea. It officially became dusk, somewhere between the absence of light and a starlit night. I felt our love was very much the same. It was as magical as stardust, and yet it was oppressive, stolen from shadows, not meant to walk in the light of the sun.

"Grayson, I will see Chase in three weeks, at Thanksgiving. I wouldn't be able to live with myself if I didn't try to make my marriage work, if I didn't make every effort to rediscover whatever it was between us that we have lost. Not just because our baby deserves both parents present and accounted for, but because I took vows with this man, and I believe in what those vows stand for."

I could see by Grayson's expression in the fading light that he understood why I had to do the right thing. He had nothing at all to say in his defense. The lines etched in his handsome face were suddenly deeper, and showed how he struggled with our weak and selfish behavior as much as I did. Honor and dignity were on the line for both of us. Where would we find happiness without them?

I began walking back up the path and Grayson fell in beside me until we reached the jeep. Leaning against it I looked at him, wiping away tears that wouldn't seem to quit.

"This is goodbye, Grayson. I meant to tell you this evening that Alana was yours but of course you already knew that, and to say I cannot be a part of your life because of how I feel about you. But I still want to see Alana. Perhaps going forward she can come to visit me alone on the commuter flight. The stewardesses will look out for her. I've watched them do it for other children."

Grayson nodded in agreement. Without a word he lifted my face and kissed me, just as I had wanted him to. It was a kiss to remember him by, arousing and sorrowful all mixed together with the sweetest and purist love. I could have easily forgotten it was wrong. When he pulled away I managed to get into the car and start the engine, and with tears stinging my eyes I left him there, standing alongside a row of palm trees in front of the inn.

Why did honor matter? There was often little pleasure in honor, which made me question why I had chosen it. I wiped away the last of my tears and instinctively began to rub my abdomen.

It somehow strengthened my resolve.

I spent the next couple of weeks in a vacuum, between home and the university. Chase called once in all that time to see how I was holding up, and to say he was exhausted from having been one pilot short all this time. It meant his shift was longer and came more often, aside from running the operation. I told him briefly about the burial. I didn't wish to tell him of our child growing in my womb, not on the phone, not any more than I wanted to hear how instrumental Meagan was or wasn't in his newly transplanted business, or his personal life.

I couldn't help but think about Grayson, and how our kiss in the near dark might have been our last touch. I might never see those blue eyes again, or hear his deep, raspy voice. I mourned the loss of him as deeply as I grieved for my little Chenlei, who had spent so much time being tutored at my kitchen table, watching movies and reading books sprawled upon my living room floor, or baking cookies beside me. Often we would walk along the shore at low tide to find washed up treasures, but never again.

Quinn and Elise were a fortress of strength in the weeks after Chenlei's passing. I saw Quinn at the university and noted that he continued coaching and playing soccer. Elise busied herself in the bookstore while the boys became absorbed in their sports. Our hugs were tighter and longer when we met, our words weighted with encouragement. We were just hoping to survive the weeks and months it would take until our pain faded and transformed into shared memories of happier times.

I would never forget when the Damasks first arrived home with Chenlei. It warmed me inside to think back to that day, to when I first met her. Everything had been so right, so joyful. The small party I had planned to welcome her to our island could not have been more perfect. Only the Damasks were there, and Chase and I. Chenlei had been shy and overwhelmed, of course, by all that had transpired in such a short time. But nonetheless she was tenacious, determined to absorb her new environment with grace and wonder. Chenlei boldly accepted her new circumstances and made the best of them. She was an inspiration to all of us, every single minute of every day that we were fortunate enough to have known her. Chenlei was a gift from God, regardless of any wrong-doings or succumbing to weaknesses and human needs that had gone into the conception of this little girl and the demise of her mother.

And God had to have been smiling at that welcome party.

# CHAPTER TWENTY-SIX

*I thought about the agony of never asking for forgiveness, never truly feeling forgiven, never knowing whether or not I would have been.*

"Kylie?"

"Hi Chase."

"Are you packing?" he asked.

"How did you know that?" I replied.

"Because you always pack early in the morning, and I know your plane leaves this afternoon."

I sat down on the bed next to my suitcase, thinking it was good to hear his voice and I couldn't wait to see him.

"Kylie, I have some bad news."

Chase paused there but I didn't say anything. My mind raced through all the possibilities.

"I'm still in Alaska, Kyl. This job has taken longer than anyone expected."

"We're not going to spend Thanksgiving together in Colorado?"

"No. I'm so sorry. Believe me, there's nowhere I'd rather be than anywhere with you right now, but I'm stuck here through the weekend."

I started to cry, silently. My emotions had been on edge ever since Chase had left and I discovered that I was pregnant, and Chenlei had died, and I'd said goodbye to Grayson and now, well now it was all threatening to consume me.

"Kylie? Are you there? I'm so sorry, honey. I've already checked and your ticket is refundable. I promise I will come as soon as I can, to the Big Island, to see you. Next week, okay?"

"Okay." Somehow I managed to say that without a sniffle. I didn't want Chase to know I was crying. I still had some pride left.

"Will you go to Quinn and Elise's tomorrow? I don't want to think of you being all alone."

"Don't worry about me. I'll be fine. What will you do?"

"I don't know. I'll be flying as usual. Maybe the inn here will have a special dinner. I don't much care. I'm just ready to finish this job and get out of here."

There was silence on the airwaves, and it rested heavily on my heart.

"I'll call you tomorrow, okay? If you're not home I'll call over at the Damasks."

"Chase . . ." I stopped myself. I wanted to tell him so badly that I was pregnant with our child. I wanted him to get emotional and take the next flight to Hawaii and we would live happily ever after. What was I thinking? My hormones must have been affecting my sense of reason.

"What is it, Kylie? What did you want to say?"

"Is Meagan there?"

The silence at the other end of the phone told me that she was.

"Kylie, I'm trying to do as much business from here as I can while I'm stuck on this job. I flew her in to set up a makeshift office last week."

"I see." Somehow it was no surprise to me that Meagan would spend Thanksgiving with Chase, but I was somewhat shocked nonetheless. "I'll miss you tomorrow. I'll look forward to your call," I said, managing to sound coherent.

"Goodbye, honey."

Those words echoed in my head as I unpacked. Were they a foreshadowing of what he would have to say to me in person when we finally met face to face again? I couldn't let the child that we had conceived influence his decision. If he wished to leave me for Meagan, then I would not tell him of the pregnancy until after we severed our ties to one another. How would we share a child with me here, and him on the mainland? How did we let this happen to us? Now that we might fulfill our dream to be a family, distance and bad decisions would likely destroy it all.

The doorbell rang as I put the suitcase back in the closet. Glancing in the mirror I decided it wasn't too obvious that I had been crying. Even if it was obvious I knew that Taylor, whom I was expecting for her last tutoring session, would understand. I was certain she had to still be on edge herself, so soon after losing Chenlei, and the trauma of finding her there in the beach cave. It was quite a lot for a thirteen-year-old to handle. I was so proud of her performance at the playoffs. It took conviction to channel her energy into the game, playing so precisely, focused fully on the win for her little friend.

This was her last tutoring session because Taylor's grades seemed to have soared recently, due to her new relationship with Grayson, and probably because her priorities had changed from all that had transpired since I met her. Taylor had also learned, I suspect as much from Chenlei as from anyone, never to settle for second best but to persevere instead by finding a way to beat your adversary, fairly, through hard work and determination. I could see in her smile during the tennis awards ceremony how winning felt better then giving in and giving up. She must have decided it would feel better in school, too, not just on the tennis court. The best part was that Taylor was succeeding for herself now, not failing for someone else.

I thought about all of this as I answered the door, surprised to see that it wasn't Taylor standing on the porch. It was Elise. She wanted to say goodbye and have a great trip. I explained to her that there would be no trip and she insisted I come to their home for Thanksgiving. Taylor and Michael pulled up as she was insisting, and I was happy to have a reason not to discuss it any further. I kissed her on the cheek and told her I would be there bright and early to help prepare the feast, thinking as I said it that truthfully, I would rather not get out of bed until the day was over and forgotten.

Taylor hugged me when she entered the kitchen and Michael waved from the car. I got out a plate of cookies and poured some milk, but Taylor was nowhere to be seen or heard. I peered into the living room and there she was, staring at the teak wood chest.

"Does it make you think of Chenlei?" I asked, setting the milk and cookies down on the coffee table.

"Not really. It makes me think of Alana, and my father."

Taylor turned to look at me. I was standing there staring at the chest just as she had been doing.

"Did my father love your sister?" she asked.

"Taylor, it's complicated."

"Tell me," she begged, and sat on the sofa.

I sat beside her, with no idea where to begin.

"Your father was hurting badly from having given you and your mother up to Michael, even though he understood that he had not been there for either of you. He had been too busy with his medical practice. But there was no going back. And so for a while he tried to drown his sorrows in a bottle of rum. When he realized he had slept with a young woman he barely knew, he sobered up. No more partying. It was time to get on with life and live with his pain the best he could. He wasn't even sure it had happened and didn't know that Alana was the result until a few months ago when he found her birth certificate in the photo album we gave her. Remember?"

Taylor nodded. "He called me, and told me about being Alana's father. He said he wanted me to know in case I should find out some other way before I saw him again. He didn't really explain. He just said that he loved Alana very much, and that he loved me very much, too. He hoped I would like having a little sister."

I leaned back into the cushion and studied her. "Do you? Like having a little sister?"

Taylor shrugged. "Alana is awesome. I hated being an only child." She looked at me, into my eyes, and I wondered what she was looking for there. "He's in love with you, isn't he?"

I didn't know what to say. No words would come. I studied the teak wood chest as if it had the right answer to that question and would respond for me.

"I can tell he loves you, and that you love him," Taylor added, not accepting my silence as a denial.

I sighed deeply, and then I looked at Taylor, into her eyes. She deserved the truth from me, and not the lie I wanted to give her.

"I do love your father, Taylor. But it's wrong for me to love him. I'm married. I love my husband, too, and that's why I can't ever see your father again." I wanted to break down at that point, and throw a raging fit at the injustices of life, but instead I controlled my emotions perfectly.

"Why isn't your husband here? I mean, I've never even met him." Taylor seemed frustrated, as if she liked the idea of her father and me being together.

"Sometimes things happen, and you can't always be with the people you love the most. Look at your father and you. I can see how much you love each other, and I know how much you both hurt when you were apart, but circumstances prevented you from being together."

We were both quiet then, gazing at the chest, which somehow demanded our attention.

"Have you looked through the things in it since that day, with Chenlei?" Taylor asked.

"No," I admitted. "Did you want to see inside it again?"

"Yes."

It was almost as if the chest held something that Taylor needed, closure maybe to her relationship with Chenlei, whom she had met for the first time when going through the chest. It was when we gave Chenlei the bracelet that led to her death.

I knelt in front of it and Taylor sat beside me on the floor. Carefully I lifted the lid and we both inhaled the strong, sweet scent of teak. I removed the jewelry box and opened it for us both to see. On top was the ring with the oval shaped turquoise stone I had intended to give to Taylor. I picked it up and placed it on her finger where it still fit perfectly.

"You may have this, Taylor, as a memento of our day with Chenlei, exploring the treasures in this chest."

Taylor grinned widely and held her hand up to examine the beautiful inlaid stone. "Thanks," she said while reaching out to hug me.

We picked every piece of jewelry up again and held them to the light. We tried them on and admired each one. Next we went through a box of pictures that we had only glanced at before. There were pictures there of Chase and I, taken at our wedding. I stared at them, a flood of memories coming back to me. It was a good time. Journey had laughed and teased us about being so in love. I had forgotten how much she had laughed with us and how many things the three of us had done together, like picnics on the beach, snorkeling all afternoon, or preparing Sunday dinners. It was good to recall that not all our time together had been spent fighting about whom she hung around with or what time she got home at night.

The pictures of us being so happy made me miss Chase all the more, and made me grieve for what I had done to us. If somehow we found our way back to one another I wondered if I would confess my infidelity, but then all I had to do was recall Elise's pain when thinking of Ling, or the pain that Grayson had never gotten past until recently, to know that confessing would be unkind. It was a burden I would carry alone to my grave, rather than cause Chase that pain. I thought about the agony of never asking for forgiveness, never truly feeling forgiven, never knowing whether or not I would have been. Such pain would only be worth enduring to spare his feelings.

It became clear to me how much I still loved Chase while viewing those pictures. Why did I also feel that it was over? That it was too late for us? If he hadn't moved his office to Colorado right after Alana came into our lives, things might have been different, but then life was all about what-ifs. And there was no going back. Only forward. If only I knew what forward was. I felt stuck somewhere between the past and the present, and this chest is what held me there.

I kept out the box of loose pictures and a handful of the jewelry. Everything else I left in the chest. I told Taylor I would have it shipped to Grayson, for Alana. She liked that idea. We worked on her last essay together and walked the beach, standing reverently in front of the beach cave for several minutes. When Michael came to pick her up we hugged tightly, tears forming in our eyes.

"Will I ever see you again?" she asked.

I stroked her silky blonde hair and kissed the top of her head. "Of course you will." And then she left. I cried knowing that my words were tentative at best.

But I was tired of goodbyes.

The next morning I forced myself out of bed and made some strong coffee before heading over the hill to help Elise prepare a feast. I thought about my greatest blessing on this day of thanks, and it was of course, the baby growing within me. I had little doubt that God had perfect timing in His planting of that seed, or that I had messed everything up with my selfishness.

Nonetheless this baby inside of me was the one thing pulling me back from the edge. Children, family, all those values and reasons to persevere that I had nearly forgotten when I slept with Grayson. Perhaps there would be no recompense for that. No forgiveness, no healing. Perhaps my child would be born into a broken home that I had caused. Perhaps I had become my mother, bringing a little victim of my bad decisions along with me, just as she had done.

Elise was in a mood to equal my own dreary state, but she held her pretty chin up and had her smile in place when she greeted me at the door. There was a look of deep sorrow in her eyes that frightened me, and I worried for my normally nurturing friend, that perhaps her spirit had become too oppressed to recover, even for the sake of her marriage, and her boys.

Quinn, she shared with me, was as usual taking his morning walk along the beach. He never did it now without bringing his Bible, Elise added, and probably spent a good amount of time reading from it on a rock somewhere, because he lingered much longer than he ever had in the past.

I began peeling potatoes and Elise quizzed me about Chase's call, and when did we plan to finally get together? I told her he intended to make a trip to the Big Island as soon as he could get away. I didn't say it with conviction, because I wasn't sure I believed at that moment that I would ever see my husband again, except perhaps in divorce court, with Meagan waiting in the car for him to flee once the legal documents had all been signed.

I could hear the boys in the bedroom playing computer games and I asked Elise how they were. She shrugged and said they were as good as could be expected under the circumstances. I wondered if that meant the circumstances of having recently buried their little sister or the circumstances of her unrelenting depression and Quinn's growing obsessive-compulsive need for forgiveness.

And then suddenly my friend and colleague stood at the door, looking like a lost sheep. I had not really looked at him for weeks. He had grown a beard and his dark course hair was long and unruly. His eyes were empty and wild all at the same time, and it was suddenly clear to me that until Quinn got a grip on himself, his family wouldn't either. I had no idea how to help. It would take a miracle, I concluded.

And that's exactly what we got.

# CHAPTER TWENTY-SEVEN

*It was what the truest kind of love is all about;
weathering disappointment and defeat, sharing hopes and dreams,
building a life together and raising a family.*

In the open doorway behind Quinn I could see a car coming up the gravel road to the Damasks' home. It was unmistakably Gwyneth's Z3 convertible. The boys must have noticed it out the bedroom window because they left their video games to join us. We were all staring out the front window wondering what Michael and Taylor wanted. We could see that they were alone. Perhaps Gwyneth was home stuffing a turkey.

Taylor was holding something that looked like the school newspaper when she and Michael walked up onto the front porch. There were greetings all around and then Taylor handed the paper to Elise and Quinn. Right there on the front page was an article about how Taylor had won the regional finals in tennis for Chenlei, and had dedicated the trophy in honor of her tenacious little friend. It would be displayed in the glass case near the gym.

After Michael and Taylor were invited in for some hot apple cider and cinnamon rolls (the traditional Thanksgiving breakfast at the Damask house) Michael read the article out loud. It spoke of Chenlei losing her mother and coming to America, and what an inspiration this had been for Taylor. It went on to say how Chenlei's brave spirit and determination to do her best despite such obstacles as learning a new language and understanding a new culture had caused Taylor to reexamine her own values and goals.

The article mentioned that a picture of Chenlei would be displayed in the case with the trophy. It added that Chenlei had become a familiar face to other tennis players during practice. One of the players was quoted as saying, "Chenlei often hung out at the ball machine when not in use. She would just hit one ball after another until her forehand improved so dramatically that everyone noticed. We were all so inspired by her focus and determination that it caused us to work harder, too." It ended by mentioning Chenlei had never missed a game since meeting Taylor through their mutual tutor, Professor Kylie Hudson.

Taylor politely asked if there was a picture she could have of Chenlei, for the trophy case. Quinn gladly offered up any of the photos in the hall display. I escorted Taylor there while Michael spoke to Elise and Quinn, and the boys, who beamed with pride over their little sister's sudden fame.

Reverently, Taylor and I studied the beautiful portrait series of Chenlei. There were six poses, one more endearing then the next. The photographer had somehow captured our little friend's strength of character. Perhaps it was how Chenlei held her head high, while her shy grin indicated a readiness to take on the world in due time. Those dark, expressive eyes boldly embraced the camera, showing both confidence and vulnerability. There was a grace and beauty to the way she tilted her head, or sat with her tiny hands folded carefully in her lap. The camera had caught her essence, even that tinge of sorrow that was always there in her eyes, despite the obvious joy Chenlei had for living, and how she marveled at each new thing she learned.

Taylor chose a smaller picture, sitting on the table below the wall display. It was her school picture with a happy, full smile, and a hopeful gleam in her eye. It was perhaps the only picture ever taken of Chenlei in which she looked like any other happy child, without a care in the world. Just the way we hoped she was now, with Ling.

Michael and Taylor lingered for nearly an hour, and when they finally left I hugged them tightly, thanking them for bringing a much-needed moment of celebration. Quinn and Elise were both bubbling afterwards, talking for the first time about their memories of Chenlei. They spoke of how she would hit tennis balls against the house with her junior racket for hours, and how it was the one thing that got her to leave the mountains of books in her room that seemed to possess her the rest of the time.

The boys began to share their own memories of Chenlei, and how when she first arrived they thought she might break if they touched her, so tiny and fragile was she. But it wasn't long until she could tease as well as they did. They laughed at how clever she was and how she had learned to get the upper hand easily when wanting to watch a particular movie or have Elise buy a certain snack. I didn't join in this intimate family recollection of Chenlei, but I enjoyed listening to it. Sipping on my hot tea with lemon I felt a weight being lifted from my chest. Hearing the Damask family laugh together again cheered me up more than I could say, that and seeing Taylor one more time.

I studied Quinn and Elise and the looks they exchanged. It took the visit from Michael and Taylor to put everything back into perspective. Their life together was so much more than tragedy and loss, or the mistakes they had made. They also shared strength and courage, and a love that wouldn't give up or give in. Their two boys reflected that tenacity and ability to triumph over defeat in everything they said or did, from excelling in sports, to standing up for one another in school.

Quinn and the boys spent the next several hours playing soccer on the hill, while Elise and I prepared a traditional Thanksgiving dinner. I was too busy chopping and sautéing to fret about my own problems, and was grateful I had not spent the day in bed with the covers over my head. I suddenly felt ashamed that I had considered such self-indulgent pity. This was a day to spend with friends and loved ones. And there was an undeniable blessing in that, even if certain loved ones were not present.

When every dish had finally been lovingly prepared and placed on the table, we all sat down, each of us ready to share one special blessing.

But just then the doorbell rang.

No one moved right away. It seemed odd that there would be any more unexpected visitors on this holiday. Finally I said that I would get the door, since I was seated closest to it.

I found it difficult to believe there could be two miracles in the same home on the same day, but my eyes could not deny that it was Chase standing there, smiling at me, as if he had been expected.

"Hi honey." Chase looked me right in the eye as if to add *I really am here*. At the same time he handed me a sturdy burlap sack filled with special Alaskan treats, as far as I could tell, from what was sticking out on top. There was smoked salmon and wild berry jam, and some type of chocolates.

He glanced behind me where everyone was seated at the table staring at him, while I just stood there speechless, holding the burlap bag of gifts for the Damasks.

"Do you think it would be okay if I invited myself to dinner? It sure smells good in here, and I haven't eaten since I got on the plane last night."

Our eyes locked, and we stared at one another for what seemed like an awkward eternity, the Damasks behind us not moving or making a single sound. I couldn't believe he really was here. I wanted to drop the burlap bag and embrace him, perhaps never letting go. At the same time I felt ashamed, as flashes of Grayson crossed my mind. I wondered if Meagan was outside in the car and he would eventually ask to bring her in. Of course I knew better, but not having her outside in the car didn't mean she was out of the picture. It would seem Grayson and Meagan had become walls between us, as if Alana and C. Hudson Helicopters weren't walls enough of late.

Chase had no additional words for me, either. Perhaps he didn't know where to begin, or was afraid of where it all might end.

Finally Quinn got up and escorted Chase to the table where the boys had already pulled up a chair. Elise was busy getting an extra place setting. I set the burlap bag down in the kitchen and just stood there for a minute, trying to compose myself. Before anyone might notice I'd been gone too long, I returned to my seat in the dining room and quietly watched as Chase interacted with the Damasks. He discussed soccer with the boys, and said how sorry he was about Chenlei. Chase spoke a little about Alaska and his project there. He would glance at me in-between his comments, but I couldn't look him in the eye.

When it was time for each of us to choose one thing we were thankful for, Quinn said his family and looked straight at Elise. Wyatt was thankful that he lived in Hawaii where he could snorkel every day, and Austin was thankful that he got a B in math. We all smiled at that because Austin struggled in math and had worked hard for that B. When it was Elise's turn she said she was thankful for having known Chenlei even for a short time, because she had enriched all our lives so much, and now Chenlei would always be a part of them, an inspiration when obstacles seemed insurmountable. Everyone nodded and agreed with that, while Quinn tried to maintain his composure, overwhelmed with emotion by Elise's tribute.

Chase cleared his throat, and said that he was thankful to have made it here in time to share this meal with his wife, and his good friends who were just like family to him. I wanted to say that I was thankful for this child growing inside of me, but instead I said I was thankful for the Damasks, who had opened their home and their hearts to me, and to Chase.

When no one could possibly eat another bite, we helped put food away and clean up the kitchen before Austin, Quinn, and I beat Chase, Elise, and Wyatt at a game of touch football. We all took a walk on the beach after that and then returned to the house for pumpkin pie. I watched my husband talking with Quinn and it almost seemed as if he had never been gone. His hair still fell across his forehead in an unruly manner and his eyes still shone with a boyish curiosity. Chase was just as appealing to me as ever, even after all that had happened since the teak wood chest arrived at our door.

The conversations over pie with whipped cream were about college football and local news. As we finished our desert it was obvious Chase and I were eager to be alone together and sort out all that had transpired since his parting. The looks between us had become tense, and more frequent. Quinn and Elise completely understood when we left abruptly after the desert dishes were cleared.

When hugs and goodbyes were over, it was just Chase and I, crossing the hill together back to our own house upon the bluff. He told me that I had looked more than a little surprised to see him standing at the Damask door, and I agreed that it was quite a shock. We stopped to view the sun setting over the Pacific and Chase put his arms around me, holding me tightly without speaking. Soon we began to kiss, each touch making it harder to let go, but I pulled away and leaned against one of the few trees on the hill. It was a scraggly palm with a sturdy trunk.

"Chase, what are you doing here? I thought you weren't going to make it to Colorado, or anywhere for Thanksgiving, that you were going to be stuck in Alaska."

"What I said at the Damasks' is true. Things were winding down and I told them they could manage without me. What I didn't tell them is how much I needed to see you."

"What about Meagan? Did you leave her there in Alaska, all alone on Thanksgiving?" I tried to sound sincere, but truthfully, I didn't care if she was all alone in Alaska, or anywhere else. I only hoped she wasn't here somewhere just waiting for Chase to tell me how he felt about her.

"Kylie, Meagan came back with me."

I swallowed hard. "I see."

"No, you don't see. I fired Meagan, and so there wasn't any reason for her to stay in Alaska."

"You fired her?" I wasn't sure I could believe what I was hearing. "Why?"

"Because you were right. She wanted a whole lot more than just a job from me."

I stared at Chase, wondering how much more she had gotten before he decided to end their relationship, and then I thought about how unfair it would be to question his behavior. In fact, my stomach began to churn and my mouth became dry at my own unspoken deceit.

"Kylie, I never should have left here. I was just angry that you would consider adopting Journey's child, even knowing that she was probably living with her real father. I've always felt like I let you down where Journey was concerned, that I made you choose between us, and that was never my intent. Then I did it all over again with Alana, when really, I was just afraid of what a constant reminder she would be about my having run your sister off. "

"I'm so sorry that I wasn't more rational about Journey, or Alana for that matter," I said sincerely, as Chase and I both sat down under the scraggly palm. The sky was on fire with colors as intense as my feelings at that moment, feelings of love and relief, and of guilt and loss. The sun had almost reached the water; barely sitting on it, ready to sink into the cool receptive sea as we watched, cuddled together.

"I always thought that Journey would come back one day, all grown up, and we'd get along great," Chase shared. "She wouldn't be a pain in the ass anymore and she'd forgive us for trying to rein her in. But when she never returned I began to regret how we didn't really look that hard for her. I started to feel guilty for my part in her leaving, and then when you came to me that day with the letter and told me she had died, I knew it was my fault that you had missed the last ten years of her life. I wasn't sure you could ever forgive me for that. I wasn't sure I could forgive myself."

"I know, Chase. I felt the same way. But now I believe there isn't anything we could have done differently. And Alana's with her father. The birth certificate was in the photo album I gave to her. So that mystery is solved," I said as I lay back to view the stars, which were just beginning to pop out.

Chase lay down on his side, watching me rather than the sky.

"Kylie," he whispered, "I've been such a fool. My life has been miserable without you. The other night after we talked I was more depressed than ever. I went back to my room and Meagan was there. She'd been trying to cheer me up ever since we left for Colorado. At least, I thought that's what she was doing, and even though it was annoying having her constantly doing things for me after work, like making my dinner or renting us a movie to watch, it helped kill time. After she came to the back woods of Alaska there was no way to make dinner, so we ate together at the inn every night. They had a limited selection of old movies available to watch for free. We did that a lot in my room, and it felt strange to have her there."

I didn't say anything, and was almost afraid to listen.

"But one night, a couple days ago, was different," Chase continued. "That night when I got to the room the lights were down low and Meagan said she hoped I didn't mind that she'd taken a shower and washed her hair because the heat was out in her room. All she had on was a short little robe that she didn't have closed very tightly. I have to tell you that I was damn tempted. It had been so long since you and I were together and I was feeling so low. I'm sorry, Kylie, but I have to confess that I kissed her, and then I realized my hormones and my head were not in the same place. It was you that I longed for, not her."

Chase became agitated as he finished his confession, but I could only feel ashamed by my own behavior rather than upset with him for his.

"I can't believe what I almost did. I told Meagan how much I loved you and that I was sorry I had brought her to Colorado, and then to Alaska. I asked her to pack her bags and be ready for the next flight to Hawaii because we were going to be on it. Can you ever forgive me for being such a fool and running out on you just when you needed me most, and then taking Meagan with me on top of it all?"

I looked at Chase, there in the dim light, with only the dusk and a few emerging stars to light his face. I didn't know what to say. The words wouldn't come. Not to confess anything or to reassure him. In my heart I wanted to do both, but in reality I did neither.

"I don't care where we live," Chase added, "and I don't care how many children you adopt. I don't care where they are from, or whether they are girls or boys. I just want to spend the rest of my life with you, anywhere, raising a family or not raising a family. Whatever makes you happy, because that's what makes me happy."

I was crying now, tears running down my face. I felt horrible and relieved all at the same time.

Chase kissed my cheek and then my forehead, and I suddenly wanted him more than I ever had. I wondered how I could have questioned my love for him.

"Chase, we're going to have a baby."

He stopped kissing me and stared into my eyes.

"You're pregnant?"

"Yes. Two months."

"We're going to have a baby?"

"Yes."

"I'm going to be a father?"

"Yes."

Chase began to cry too, now, and so we just held each other until we began to make-out beneath the palm tree and the stars, first tenderly and then with a passion that was all consuming. We raced home in the dark, where we showered together and spent the night becoming reacquainted.

God blessed us in the spring with a little girl and we named her Emma Lei Hudson for my mama, and for Chenlei. Chase and I had a love that persevered through the test of time. It was what the truest kind of love is all about; weathering disappointment and defeat, sharing hopes and dreams, building a life together and raising a family.

I would never forget Grayson, just as I would never forget Journey, or Chenlei. People who truly touch our lives become a part of who we are, and they live on through our memories. It was a heavy burden to never confess my night with Grayson. It seemed so deceitful not to tell the truth and plead forgiveness, yet the hurt and anguish it would surely cause could not be worth the cleansing of my soul.

My journey was not what it would have been had my mother never left my father and brought me to the Big Island of Hawaii, but like all journeys, we have no say in some of the detours we must take. Perhaps what ultimately defines us isn't the smooth sailing we are always searching for so much as the rough seas inevitably thrown our way.

Perhaps in the end, that is what the journey is really all about.

# ACKNOWLEDGMENTS

My daughter, Sasha Mattingly, has been a godsend with this novel. Her reader reaction as a well-read woman has been invaluable to me, not to mention her editing skills as a University of Oregon graduate, Magna Cum Laude, in English.

My good friend, Ladd Woodland, is a wonderful designer, and I can't thank him enough for his genius with my cover art. He has a way of capturing the essence of the story, and that is a gift.

Good friend and fellow writer Dr. Virginia Simpson, author of the memoir *A Space Between* (to be released spring 2016), has also given me wonderful input and valued feedback regarding this novel.

# ABOUT THE AUTHOR

Award winning author Kathryn Mattingly has always had a passion for writing. Her short fiction has appeared in various themed anthologies, and in *Dark Discoveries* magazine. Kathryn's debut novel, *Benjamin*, was a New Century Quarterly Finalist, and her short story collection, *Fractured Hearts*, includes her award-winning stories. Kathryn enjoys mentoring other writers. She teaches creative writing at a local college and critiques entries for the Pacific NW Writer's annual literary contest. Kathryn is inspired by real-life events and all the places she has lived or traveled.